THE
COLLIDING
WORLDS
OF MINA LEE

EDITED BY ELLEN OH

Flying Lessons and Other Stories

THE
COLLIDING
WORLDS
OF MINA LEE

ELLEN OH

CROWN
New York

All rights reserved. Published in the United States by Crown Books for Young Readers, an imprint of Random House Children's Books, a division of Penguin Random House LLC, New York.

Crown and the colophon are registered trademarks of Penguin Random House LLC.

Visit us on the Web! GetUnderlined.com

Educators and librarians, for a variety of teaching tools, visit us at RHTeachersLibrarians.com

Library of Congress Cataloging-in-Publication Data
Names: Oh, Ellen, author.
Title: The Colliding worlds of Mina Lee / Ellen Oh.
Description: First edition. | New York: Crown, 2024. | Audience: Ages 12 and up. | Audience: Grades 7–9. | Summary: Seventeen-year-old Korean American Mina Lee's life is disrupted when she finds herself sucked into the world of her own webcomic.
Identifiers: LCCN 2023025691 (print) | LCCN 2023025692 (ebook) | ISBN 978-0-593-12594-6 (hardcover) | ISBN 978-0-593-12595-3 (library binding) | ISBN 978-0-593-12596-0 (ebook)
Subjects: CYAC: Space and time—Fiction. | Cartoons and comics—Fiction. | Interpersonal relations—Fiction. | Korean Americans—Fiction.
Classification: LCC PZ7.O364 Co 2024 (print) | LCC PZ7.O364 (ebook) | DDC [Fic]—dc23

The text of this book is set in 11.5-point Sabon Next.
Interior design by Ken Crossland

Printed in the United States of America
10 9 8 7 6 5 4 3 2 1
First Edition

This book is dedicated to Diet Coke
because I can't make it a day without you,
you monster. And of course to my family,
whom I adore. But mostly to Diet Coke.

CHAPTER 1

First Day of Senior Year

Monday, August 29, Washington, DC

Mina stood under her umbrella in the pouring rain, staring with dread at the doors of Bellington High School, a big imposing redbrick building that loomed above her like every scary mansion in the horror movies she despised watching.

First day of senior year.

First day of hell.

"Mina Lee, get your butt inside before we drown to death!" Her best friend, Saachi, grabbed Mina by the arm and began pulling her up the stairs.

Mina heaved a great big sigh as they joined the mass of students filing into the school through the imposing entranceway. The girl in front of her whipped back curly wet hair, slapping Mina across her face.

Mina flinched and swatted the hair away, causing the girl to turn and glare at her.

"Do you mind?"

Mina narrowed her eyes, her nostrils flaring with displeasure. "Yes, I do mind. I don't like eating hair for breakfast."

The girl turned without another word.

"Did you say something?" Saachi asked.

Before Mina could respond, an elbow rammed into her lower spine.

She whimpered. "I am a sardine packed tight into a smelly tin can of death."

"What are you mumbling to yourself?" Saachi asked. At five foot ten, Saachi could use her height to maneuver deftly through the crowds without getting hurt.

"I am a bunny rabbit caught in the coils of a deadly python."

"I am a girl who doesn't want to be late to her first class," Saachi cut in. Apparently annoyed at the snail's pace, she barged ahead, scattering kids left and right as she shouted "Excuse me!" at the top of her lungs.

"I am a salmon swimming against the current into the gaping jaws of death," Mina intoned. They'd finally made it inside the expansive lobby that led to hallways spider-webbing into the depths of the building.

"Listen, can you save your existential crisis for exams?"

Mina stopped in her tracks, causing Saachi to nearly trip and fall. "What's the point, Saachi?"

"Mina," Saachi said threateningly.

Students yelled their frustration at Mina, some even shoving her. But Mina refused to budge. She might be only five three, but she was a mighty five three and could plant her feet like small sledgehammers.

"I mean why am I even here? What's the point when I don't know what the future entails? My dad thinks he has my life all figured out, but I don't want what he wants. Do I? I mean what am I supposed to do? What do I need to do? Do I just listen to my father like a good Asian daughter?"

"Girl, I will pick you up and haul you into first period. I am not playing," Saachi fumed.

Mina saw the murderous intent in her friend's eyes and released a heavy sigh. "All right." She shuffled her feet to move forward, letting Saachi drag her. "I am a pawn in someone else's chess game of life."

"Shut up, Mina! Where's your first class?"

Mina pulled out her schedule and peered down at it morosely.

> First period, Psychology, Salatto, Rm 246
> Second period, Honors Calculus, Khan, Rm 225
> Third period, AP Studio Art, Ellis, Rm G84
> Lunch
> Fourth period, AP Art History, Butler, Rm 108
> Fifth period, AP English Literature and
>   Composition, Steinberg, Rm G20
> Sixth period, Advanced Figure Drawing, Vasquez,
>   Rm G82
> Seventh period, Women's Studies, McGinnis, Rm 157

Mina groaned. "I am a daisy trapped in the killing field of war."

"MINA LEE!"

It was clear that Saachi had reached the end of her patience. Mina hastened toward the large staircase.

"I am a cog in the education machine of mediocrity," Mina grumbled as she stomped up the stairs.

"Keep walking, cog," Saachi replied sharply.

• • •

The third-period bell rang, and Mina sped down the stairs and through the hallways for the first time since she'd stepped foot in school. She loved all her art classes, but this semester AP Studio Art was taught by her favorite teacher. Ms. Ellis was young and hip and not that much older than the seniors she taught.

A smile lit up Mina's face as she crossed from the monotonous void of high school drudgery into the vibrant chaos of the art room. She could smell the mix of old and new paint, both musty and milky wet, along with the pleasant chemical scent of turpentine. The sun had finally chased the rain clouds away and filled the room with bright natural light.

"Mina! So good to see you! How was your summer?"

Ms. Ellis had long straight brown hair that she kept in a loose ponytail and stylish black eyeglasses. What was most striking about her was the innate grace she seemed to exude, even when wearing a dirty paint-covered smock.

As they chatted, Mina let herself relax in the familiarity of her favorite classroom. She waved to a few old friends who were drawing in their sketchbooks and then went to sit down as Ms. Ellis greeted other arriving students.

Mina straddled the art horse at her usual spot next to the windows, which now shimmered with cascading streams of raindrops. She took a moment to stretch her back as she settled into her seat. Art horses were benches with movable drawing boards. While they were very practical, they were not at all comfortable.

All the students sat facing a large round table in the middle of the room. It was covered with an array of eclectic boxes that displayed a variety of interesting objects. Skulls, vases, antiques, tea sets, plates and jars filled with a mishmash of colorful stones, old toys, and small weird knickknacks. Satin fabrics and silk flowers were strewn in deliberate disarray. It was a display Mina could get lost in, providing hours of artistic inspiration. And that was the whole point.

Ms. Ellis made her assignments challenging and reminded Mina to think of art as more than just beautiful creations, but as things of power and structure and space. It was this belief in the importance of art that reminded Mina of her mother.

"Never forget, Mina. Art is magic," her mother told her.

And Mina had believed her. How could she not when she'd seen her mother breathe life into all her paintings?

Mina's mother had been a highly talented artist. She created realistic paintings that looked like vibrant photographs. It was her mother who taught her all about art from a young age. Put pencils and brushes in her hand. Let her roll her whole body in paint and decorate the walls of her art studio with handprints. Mina could communicate through drawing before she even learned to talk. It was in her blood.

"Hey, Mina! You're here!"

Mina saw Christina Jackson sit down in front of her, looking immaculate as usual, her black hair smoothed into a tight ponytail.

"I didn't think your dad would let you take this class," Christina continued.

Mina's face darkened, her lips tightening. "Yeah, he's not happy about it."

Christina frowned in sympathy. "I'm sorry, Mina. What are you going to do about art school applications?"

This was something that had been worrying Mina all summer. "I don't know. Maybe apply to universities with good art programs instead of just art schools?"

"But what about RISD? We talked about applying together."

Mina sighed. "He's fixated on me going to a 'real' college."

"Why don't you apply to the Brown/RISD program like I am? He can't possibly be against that."

Rolling her eyes, Mina snorted. "You've clearly mistaken me for someone else. I'm the Asian that's bad at math, remember? Brown would be offended if I applied to them. Unlike you, Miss Genius Jackson, sure to be valedictorian, who also happens to be a brilliant sculptor. All the top schools are gonna be fighting over you in one big nasty catfight. Rawr."

A flush spread on Christina's cheeks, giving her dark brown skin a rosy glow and highlighting the few freckles she had. Mina thought how cute her friend looked when she got embarrassed.

"That's not true," Christina demurred.

Mina pretended to talk into a mic. "Ms. Jackson, you've

been accepted to all the Ivies and fifty top schools across the world—where do you think you'll go?"

"Cut it out, Mina!" Christina laughed.

"No, the answer is whoever gives you the most money, of course!"

"Well, I'm hoping we both get accepted to RISD," Christina remarked.

"You'll definitely get in, but I don't know if RISD will even take me." The thought was depressing. It had been her first choice for a long time.

"Stop being so hard on yourself, Mina," Christina said. "You're smart and wicked talented. You can go to whatever school you want."

"Not if my dad won't let me." Mina grimaced.

"You've got to convince him! We've been taking art together for three years. I'd love to continue that in college."

"Yeah, me too," Mina replied. She loved having art with Christina not only because her friend was so talented, but because they challenged each other to do better.

"Oh, and I read your webcomic," Christina said, with a smile. "Your art's amazing."

"Really?" Mina beamed. "You must be, like, my third actual reader. It hasn't done well on Toonwebz." She'd been uploading a webcomic all summer on the popular online comics platform, thinking that if it became successful it would help convince her father that art school was worth it. But so far, it hadn't garnered many views.

"Your line art is really clean. Every panel is like a portrait. It must take you ages to do an episode—your art is so detailed!"

It was Mina's turn to flush. "Aw, thanks, Christina. That means a lot coming from you."

They turned their attention to Ms. Ellis as she began her welcome speech, but Mina was still thinking about her dad. He hadn't always been against art. He'd been her mother's greatest supporter. Bragged about how talented his wife was. Said he was also proud of Mina's art. But everything changed when her mother died three years ago.

It had happened so quickly. Her mom had gone out to get groceries on a rainy Saturday morning, and that was the last time Mina saw her. Someone ran a red light and slammed into her mother's car.

In his grief, her father packed away all her mother's creations. Art was too painful for him. At first, Mina understood. The mere whiff of linseed oil and paint thinner would stab her heart with such intense longing for her mother that it almost paralyzed her. But as time passed, she missed the bold vibrant colors of her mother's paintings, and she slowly brought them into her room. Art was Mina's way of staying connected to her mother.

"Mina, are you okay?"

Mina was startled to find Ms. Ellis standing next to her, a concerned look on her pretty face. The room was quiet, as all the students were busy sketching. But Mina's paper was blank.

"Yes, I'm fine." Mina smiled weakly.

"Are you having a problem with the assignment?"

Staring at her paper, Mina realized she hadn't heard what she was supposed to do.

"Um, uh . . ."

"Expressive self-portrait?"

Mina nodded. "Was just thinking about how to approach it," she answered.

Ms. Ellis nodded before moving on to Christina's work.

Mina looked around and could see that some students had snatched up the few handheld mirrors in the room while the rest were using their phone cameras. Ah, the beauty of art class, the only place where cell phones were actively encouraged. Mina pulled hers out, took a couple of selfies, and set the phone on her easel.

The key to portraits was how well the artist could depict emotions. It was Mina's mother who taught her to study people's faces to understand what every wrinkle conveyed.

"Every face tells a story," her mother would say. "Find the story that you want to share with the world."

Art made Mina look at people in a different way. Instead of the whole, she would focus on interesting aspects of a person's physique. The curve of their eyebrow, the delicate bones of their wrist, the subtle way they shifted their body, or their elusive dimple. Mina felt like she was in a constant state of observing others, all in her quest to perfect her art and tell a story. It was why she enjoyed creating her webcomic. Today, she had to turn that ability onto herself. Something she usually avoided at all costs.

Looking at her photos, she critically assessed them and began to sketch. Heart-shaped face, high cheekbones, average-sized nothing-special nose, half-moon eyes with a double eyelid on the right and a monolid on the left, and little bulges under her eyes that her mother used to call "aegyo sal," which is Korean for cute eye fat. Although "cute eye fat" seemed a weird compliment. It was her uneven eyes that Mina found the most interesting about her face. Her right eye was distinctly bigger, making her eyelashes jut out and appear longer than the lashes of her left eye. She could be a model for one of those double eyelid plastic surgery centers in South Korea. The left eye was the before and the right one the after. In fact, her paternal grandmother had wanted her to get double eyelid surgery on her left eye so she could be "pretty." Mina refused. She liked her uneven eyes. They made her unique. And she thought her monolid was just as pretty as her double eyelid. But what kind of story could she tell about them?

"Sometimes a face has yet to develop its story; sometimes you have to capture the promise of one."

Her mother's comments were often cryptic, but still, somehow, Mina understood what she meant. Not that she could explain it to anyone. It was just a feeling of knowing. Mina studied her selfies and thought, *My story has not yet begun, but it has great potential.*

The end-of-class bell rang and Mina had managed only a rough sketch. But she liked how she'd emphasized her eyes. They looked as if they had a lot to say.

CHAPTER 2

Best Friends

Lunch period was always a mass exodus of students charging out of school to hit up various fast food restaurants and the local grocery store. Mina always found it a colossal waste of energy. By the time you got your food, the period was almost over and you'd have to wolf it down before racing to your next class. Packing lunch was faster and healthier.

Mina followed Saachi into the courtyard. The sun was bright and no one could guess it had been dumping rain just hours ago. A trio of ninth-grade boys were already sitting at the bench by Mina and Saachi's favorite tree, a big beautiful red maple. Saachi walked over and gave them a withering stare. Mina watched as the ninth graders shriveled into human Sour Patch Kids before skulking away. They were both afraid of and in awe of Saachi. Who could blame them? Saachi was tall and beautiful with wavy black hair down to her waist.

Plopping onto the bench, Saachi smiled at the retreating boys.

"Is it wrong that I enjoy doing that?"

"Is it wrong that I enjoy watching you do that?"

The friends elbow-bumped each other in perfect harmony.

"This semester is going to suck so bad." Saachi sighed. "Ms. Fong just assigned a shit ton of homework today and I regret everything."

"And whose fault is that?" Mina was completely unsympathetic. "Who takes five AP courses senior year? A masochist, that's who."

"You're one to talk," Saachi retorted. "You're taking at least three APs."

"Please, you're in the hardest physics and calculus courses as well as Environmental Science, Stat, and Lit," Mina replied. "You are going to die."

"It's first semester senior year—we're supposed to be absolutely miserable."

"Yes, but when you have a cavity that just needs a filling, you don't ask the dentist for a root canal without anesthesia instead. Sick, I tell you."

"Don't judge me, I live my life on the edge." Saachi opened her lunch bag and began to sort several small containers of fruits and vegetables on the bench next to her.

Mina shook her head and tsked. "How can you be so tall existing on nothing but rabbit food?"

"Because cheese, my lactose intolerant friend," Saachi said.

"Jealous," Mina grumbled. "You don't know what I'd

give to eat as much pizza or ice cream as I want without running to the bathroom."

"Don't want to know." Saachi methodically shoveled grapes, cheese, olives, and crackers into her mouth in that order.

"Well, I guess you don't want any of my gim either." Mina waved a small rectangular package of roasted seaweed in Saachi's face.

With a high keening sound, Saachi grabbed the package and fondled it against her cheek. "My mom hasn't gone to Costco in a few weeks and I've been out of my precious!"

Guffawing, Mina tossed several more packages into Saachi's lap. "You don't need Costco—you have me, your friendly neighborhood seaweed dealer."

Saachi accepted the little rectangular packages with a smile.

"Thank you, best friend!"

Mina paused with a serious look. "But I don't know how to feel about Costco selling gim. It feels both weird and good. Something from my culture has gone mainstream American! And now white children everywhere are eating roasted seaweed, but without rice. Like potato chips. That's kind of wrong."

She opened a small bento box filled with Korean purple rice with beans, tiny anchovies, soy sauce, meat, and peppers.

"I still think it's wild that you can buy kimchi at Costco. And some of these bougie gourmet markets are making their own not-so-good versions," Saachi said. "They're right next to the frozen vegetable biryani."

"Ah, the stinky smell of cultural appropriation."

Mina shared her purple rice with her friend and accepted a bunch of grapes in return.

"Did you watch the last episode of *My Love, My Life*?" Saachi asked. "It was epic!"

Mina blew a loud raspberry. "Stopped watching it."

Her friend gasped. "But why?"

"I'm just so tired of the jerky mean guys as the main love interests."

"Yeah, but they're so sexy," Saachi said.

"Aw, come on! That last drama we watched, the nice guy was even better-looking than the main guy," Mina said.

"But the jerk was way sexier."

Mina put down her drink. "You see, this is the problem with our society! You've been brainwashed into thinking bad boys are sexy. Sometimes they are, but most of the time they're just assholes."

"Ooooooh, who's the asshole? Share!" Megan Sandler appeared, dragging a chair behind her and setting it in front of the bench. Megan, Saachi, and Mina had been best friends since they'd met in middle school. Megan always joked that she was their token white friend.

She sat and proceeded to stare in shock at Mina. "Woman, what did you do to your hair?"

"What, you don't like it?" Mina had spent nearly her entire Saturday at the salon dyeing her brown-black hair a dark silvery gray ombre.

"You're literally a BuzzFeed meme now! You know the one about rebellious East Asian girls and colored streaks in their hair."

Saachi placed a calming hand on Mina's clenched forearm.

"Don't listen to her, Mina. I think it looks gorgeous! Gray is the hottest color," Saachi said with a wink.

"I mean, don't get me wrong, it looks great on you! Makes me want to do something about this boringness," Megan continued, fingering her own mop of curly light brown hair. "But what did your dad say?"

"I don't know, he hasn't been home to see it." Mina shrugged. "So, if you're looking for the stereotype, I guess you found me. Rebellious teen dyes hair gray in act of defiance against overbearing lawyer father who wants her to give up art. But you know, stereotype or not, I love it. And I think it suits me. And if you don't like it you can go—"

"Okay then," Saachi said as she covered Mina's mouth. "No need to shout."

"Aw, you should have let her keep going! She was on a roll." Megan laughed.

Saachi shrieked and snatched her hand away. "She bit me!"

"Serves you right," Mina smirked as she wiped her mouth with her sleeve.

"You did ask for that." Megan nodded as she began to eat her lunch. "And you know she bites."

Saachi grabbed a small bottle of antibacterial liquid and rubbed it all over her hands. "Nasty girl."

Mina shrugged. "As I was saying before you two weirdos interrupted me, bad boys are always assholes."

Megan turned to Saachi. "What the hell is she talking about?"

"She's still mad that the nice guy didn't get the girl in that last K-drama we watched," Saachi said. "You know, *Pretty Boy Fairy Tale*."

"Oh yeah, but the bad boy was way sexier."

"I know, right?"

"And the shower scenes . . ." Both girls sighed lustfully.

Mina eyed her two friends in disgust. "Well, I for one would like a romance where the nice guy gets the girl!"

"That's so, um, *nice?*" Saachi raised an eyebrow in mock disdain.

Megan busted out in laughter but covered her mouth quickly at Mina's scowling face.

"I don't know why I put up with you two always teasing me. . . ."

"Because you love us . . . ," Saachi cooed, and fluttered her eyelashes.

"Lies. All lies."

"Speaking of lies," Megan said with an imperious wave of her hand, "you promised me a romantic webcomic, but so far it's been a big fat nope. I'm going to stop reading if you don't start heating the romance up for me."

"What's wrong with my webcomic?"

"Two words: bor ing."

"How dare you!"

"Megan's being a little harsh," Saachi cut in. "You know we are your biggest fans . . ."

"My *only* fans . . ."

". . . but the romance has been underwhelming."

"And you know what it needs!" Megan chimed in.

Mina glanced from one grinning face to the other.

"Oh no. There will be absolutely no love triangles!"

"Sacrilege!" Megan shouted. "You can't have a romance without a good old-fashioned hair-pulling, face-slapping, ass-kicking love triangle!"

"Mmmmm-hmmmmm!" Saachi agreed. "I adore love triangles."

"Ha! You guys are so wrong!" Mina crowed. "Plenty of great love stories don't have any love triangle at all."

"Name one!" Saachi demanded.

"*Cinderella*!"

"Pfft! The stepmother and her daughters."

Mina opened her mouth to argue.

"The stepmother plots to destroy the relationship in order to have one of her ugly daughters marry the prince," Megan cut in.

Saachi nodded emphatically. "Definitely counts."

Not to be deterred, Mina continued. "Okay, *Mulan*!"

"First of all, *Mulan* was *not* a romance!" Megan was wagging her finger in Mina's face. "And second of all, Mulan's grandma had the big-time hots for Shang!"

"Ew ..."

"You know it's true...."

"Okay, what about *Snow White*?"

"Puh-lease, that girl was living with seven men," Megan said. "That's not a love triangle—that's a love constellation."

"You are disgusting."

"We've all thought it." Saachi was nodding.

"No, only you two perverts, and maybe pornos."

Saachi and Megan glanced at each other and then bust out laughing.

"Like you'd know," Saachi replied when she caught her breath. "Mina, you little prude. You obsessively watch K-dramas because you get squeamish if there's a sex scene. You can't even watch people French-kissing."

Megan stuck out her tongue suggestively.

Mina made a gagging sound. "I hate you both."

"Give in, Mina. Give me love triangles!" Megan said.

"Nope. My webcomic isn't even supposed to be a romance. It's supposed to be a slice-of-life story. Absolutely no triangles!"

"But why?" Megan whined.

"Love triangles are always so messy. I just want to create a story where everything happens for a reason."

"But what's the fun in that?"

"What do you mean?"

"I mean it sounds like it would be formulaic...."

"Or preachy," Saachi added.

"Ugh, leave Sunday school out of my fiction," Megan said.

"It's not going to be preachy," Mina sputtered. "It's going to be funny and sweet and sentimental. I've got everything planned."

"Okay, but what we're saying is even in fiction it doesn't work if you try to force it," Megan said. "Your characters will revolt."

Mina laughed and waved an impatient hand. "It's my story. The characters are gonna do what I want them to do."

Megan and Saachi looked at each other and then both grabbed one of Mina's hands.

"Mina, your webcomic needs help," Saachi said. "We say this as your friends. Do something, I don't know. Add magic or sci-fi or fantasy ..."

"Or death and lots of violence," Megan cut in.

"Yeah, it doesn't have to be a love triangle—it just needs to be more interesting," Saachi said.

"Soooooo, my webcomic is boring," Mina said flatly.

Megan stared into her eyes sadly. "Like watching paint dry."

Mina glared at her traitorous friends. "Why didn't you say something earlier? Why now, when I'm ten episodes in? Do you have any idea how long it takes me to create one episode?"

"Well, we kept hoping something exciting would happen," Saachi said.

At her words, Mina's hearing dimmed, and the loud chatter of the students around her became nothing more than white noise. She could hear her breathing and her heart thudding in her head. The courtyard faded as she stared blankly down at her feet. All that work for nothing. She was an utter failure. Feeling the sudden burn of tears, she rose to her feet, unwilling to cry in front of her friends. Before she could step away, Saachi and Megan jumped to their feet and sandwiched her into a big hug.

"We're sorry," Saachi said. "We didn't mean to hurt your feelings."

"We love you," Megan chimed in.

"Mina, you are incredibly talented," Saachi said. "Your art is brilliant. And that's what you've been focusing on. You need to put as much attention into your story now."

Mina rapidly blinked away tears as her friends suffocated her in their embrace and made weird comforting noises. She sat on the bench, pulling Saachi and Megan down with her. They continued to cling to her like barnacles.

Mina thought about her conversation with Christina that morning. She'd said she loved Mina's art, but she'd made no mention of the story.

"I guess you guys are right." Mina hiccuped. "I mean, I've been uploading it all summer and nobody likes it. I have no regular readers besides you two."

"People love your art," Saachi said. "That's really important."

"But they aren't interested enough to keep reading." Mina nodded. "Even though it goes against everything I stand for, I'll think about changing it up."

Megan pretending to collapse in fake relief annoyed Mina so much she shoved her friend off the bench. Megan screeched as she dramatically sprawled onto the ground.

"Bravo," Saachi drawled. "All those drama classes are really paying off."

Megan stayed where she was, uncaring that she was blocking the pathway. "That was Oscar-worthy, right?"

Rolling her eyes, Saachi shook her head at Megan.

"I am an unappreciated genius surrounded by the opposite of geniuses." Mina sighed.

"HEY!" This time Saachi pushed Mina off the bench and Megan caught her in a hug.

Mina had to laugh. She could always count on her friends to cheer her up. Digging into her bag, she found her instant Polaroid camera and gestured for Megan to get up.

"First day of senior year, let's commemorate it!"

The girls took a bunch of selfies together and waited as they developed, laughing at some of the sillier ones. When Mina's mother was alive, she loved taking instant photos. She said that it was the best way to memorialize moments in time, better than taking photos on a cell phone. It was why Mina carried her Polaroid camera everywhere with her—so that she could continue her mother's tradition. There was something very immediate and permanent about Polaroids.

"Pick whichever ones you want," Mina said. "My dad bought me tons of film." She opened her bag to show them several packs of instant film.

"Speaking of your dad," Saachi said, "I thought he threatened to take your tablet away if you didn't raise your SAT score?"

Mina scowled. Her father hated when she worked on her art. It reminded him too much of her mother.

"He signed me up for an intense SAT prep course that starts next Saturday morning," Mina said. "Dr. Yee's SAT. High scores, guaranteed."

"Hey, cute jingle!" Megan said. "Never heard of it."

"That's 'cause you're not Asian," Mina retorted. "He's famous in our community."

"Yeah, I think I remember hearing about him from my mom," Saachi said. "But he's kind of far, right?"

"I have to go all the way to Rockville, Maryland."

Her friends gasped. "But you don't drive!"

It wasn't because she couldn't drive; she just hadn't managed to take the road test yet. If she was being honest, Mina had been too lazy to schedule it.

She shrugged. "It'll take me two metros and a bus if my dad can't drive me. Over an hour one way. I can take a car in bad weather."

"Damn, your dad is mean," Megan said.

"Just take the online one with us, Mina," Saachi said. "I'll have my mom talk to your dad about it."

Mina shook her head. "Won't help. He says I have to go to a physical class to actually learn it, and my komo—you know, my dad's annoying older sister—was the one to tell him about Dr. Yee's SAT. My cousin Sam took it last year and got nearly a perfect score."

Megan snorted. "Your cousin is a dweeb."

"An Ivy League dweeb."

"That's what your dad wants, not what you want."

"I know," Mina sighed. These were the moments when she intensely ached for her mom's presence. If her mom were still alive, she wouldn't let her dad force her to do something she didn't want. She would understand Mina's need for art. She wouldn't force her to go all the way to Maryland to take an SAT class.

"Mina, you've got to tell him you want to apply to art school," Saachi said.

The thought of bringing it up to her father stressed Mina out. Any conversation about art ended in a fight. Mina felt like her relationship with her dad was tenuous enough. It hadn't always been like this. Her father had been different before.

"Not yet," Mina said. "I'm not ready. I need my webcomic to get some traction. Have real fans, not just you guys. Maybe then he'll believe in me."

"Mina, he may never accept your art," Saachi said gently. "But you have to do it anyway."

Before she could respond, Mina was relieved to hear the bell ring.

"Gotta go! Catch you later!" she said as she and her friends gathered their bags to join the throng of students reentering the school.

CHAPTER 3

Alone Again

Mina punched in the six-number passcode to her front door and entered after the loud click.

"I'm home," she announced. But no one answered.

No one ever answered anymore.

She'd begged her father for a dog, but he refused, saying that he wouldn't be able to take care of it when she went to college. She would have willingly gone to a local college if it meant having a dog, but her father wouldn't agree. He didn't understand how lonely the house was because he was hardly ever home.

Mina changed out of her shoes into her house slippers and then trudged into the kitchen. She took off her backpack and poured herself a mug of tea. Mrs. Song, the Korean ajumma who cooked and cleaned for them, always brewed a fresh pot of barley tea for Mina.

Mina's stomach rumbled. Since her dad worked late every night except Sunday, Mina had gotten into the habit of eating early. When her mother was alive, her father would try to make it home for dinner at least a few times during the week. But now the only meal Mina ever had with him was on Sunday nights, unless he was traveling.

Otherwise, she was usually eating by herself. She'd gotten used to it, but she didn't enjoy it. Luckily, Mrs. Song was a great cook.

Mina opened the fridge to pull out small Tupperware boxes full of banchan, Korean side dishes. Opening the rice cooker, she inhaled the scent of steaming hot, freshly made rice. She heaped a big serving into a large metal bowl and then piled on the vegetables, shredded beef, and a spoonful of gochujang, Korean red pepper paste. She drizzled in sesame oil and mixed everything with vengeance until the rice turned red. Sitting at the kitchen table, Mina shoveled a huge bite into her mouth and thought of her mother.

She remembered when she was eight and insisted she could make it all by herself.

"Mina, what do you want to eat?"

"Bibimbap!"

"That's all you ever want to eat!" Her mom laughed.

"I'll make it, Mama!"

Her mom passed the big mixing bowl to her and Mina piled everything in but made the mistake of using too much gochujang.

"Ah! Too spicy! I'm sorry."

"That's okay, honey. All you have to do is add some more rice."

They remixed the bibimbap and ate every bite. It became their weekly ritual. Mom made the rice and fried a runny egg; Mina mixed it all up with the vegetables and sauce. And then they would devour it straight out of the silver mixing bowl. Just like she was doing now.

An ache in Mina's throat caused her to choke up. She pounded her chest as she felt the acid rise and give her the slow pain of heartburn.

She opened her phone to a photo of her mother painting. Mina could almost smell the curious mix of pleasant linseed oil and harsh paint thinner that always reminded her of her mom. Her dad had hated the smell, which was why Mina's mom had started digital painting, but Mina loved it.

As if he could sense she was thinking of him, her phone suddenly rang.

"Hi, Dad," Mina answered.

"Hey, honey, how was your first day of school?"

"Okay."

"Great, do you like your teachers?"

"For the most part, I guess."

"Good." Her dad paused for a long moment. "Sorry I was gone all weekend. I'm on a big case and I'll have to do more traveling back and forth to New York this week."

Mina sighed loudly. "Fine."

"Halmeoni invited us to dinner Saturday night. Do you want to go?"

"You have to ask?"

"Yes, I have to ask," he retorted. "She's your grandmother."

"Hardly," Mina muttered. She was not fond of her paternal grandparents. They never approved of her mother because she was an artist. That disapproval had passed on to Mina. Dinner was a constant nag fest of criticisms, and the food was bad. Her halmeoni was a terrible cook and her harabeoji was just mean.

"Mi-na." Her dad dragged her name out when he was getting irritated.

"I don't want to go, Dad. Tell them you're busy. You probably will be anyway and I won't go by myself."

There was a heavy silence before he responded.

"All right. I'll ask Mrs. Song to stay late the rest of this week and keep you company."

"Yeah, thanks." Her tone was surly, but she was relieved to hear she wouldn't be completely alone.

"Oh, and by the way, your komo mentioned that she'd be dropping off some books to you today."

"Does she have to?" Mina whined. "I'm not in the mood for her lectures."

"Be nice," her dad replied. "She's just trying to help."

Mina rolled her eyes and didn't respond.

"Okay, I'm going to be pretty late tonight, but I'll make it up to you later," her dad continued. "Don't stay up too late."

" 'Kay, bye."

Mina polished off the rest of her bibimbap and cleaned up. Before she could head upstairs, the doorbell began to ring insistently. Mina's heart sank. The only person who was that annoying was her komo. She opened the door and watched as her aunt swept into the house in a cloud of expensive floral perfume.

"There you are, Mina—what took you so long? I've brought you these SAT prep books," Komo said as she slipped off her shoes, put on the guest house slippers, and marched into the living room. She plopped a big canvas bag onto the coffee table before sitting down and looking at Mina with an expectant arch of her eyebrow.

"Would you like some coffee?" Mina asked grudgingly.

"Yes, milk, no sugar," Komo replied.

Suppressing a groan, Mina slunk into the kitchen to turn on the coffee maker and cut up some fruit. Her mother's lessons had been ingrained in Mina since she was little. Anytime a guest came over, you had to serve fruit. Mina took a Korean pear from the fridge and peeled and cut it. On another plate, she added her favorite ginger cookies. Komo had a wicked sweet tooth that she never admitted to. After adding milk to the coffee, Mina put it all on a tray and served it to her aunt.

Ignoring the peeled fruit, Komo went right for the cookies and dipped them in her coffee.

"Now, Mina, your dad told you about Dr. Yee's SAT program, right?" she asked. "Starts next Saturday and it's excellent! Sam got a perfect score on his second try. That's how he was accepted into all the Ivy Leagues."

"Yeah, Dad told me," Mina replied. "How come Sam went to Stanford? I thought you always wanted him to go to Harvard."

A look of resentment crossed her komo's face before she fake smiled. "You know how much Sam hates snow," she said airily. "He just really wanted the warm California weather."

Mina bit back a smile. She was pretty sure Sam went as far away from his controlling parents as he could.

"Anyway, you really should have taken this program over

the summer, Mina. In order to make early decision applications, you have to take the October SAT, which only gives you a month to prepare!"

"I was thinking of taking the November one and applying regular admission, Komo," Mina responded.

"Absolutely not! You need to apply to your top schools early decision or early action."

As her aunt droned on about the program and when to take the SAT, Mina tried to contain her frustration. She wished she could just tell her aunt that she had no interest in applying to Ivy League schools. That the schools she wanted to apply to didn't even require the SAT. But it would start another lecture she didn't want to hear.

"Just in case your dad is too busy as usual, I'll come and pick you up to take you to dinner at Harabeoji and Halmeoni's house this Saturday."

Mina's lips flattened as she did her best not to scream. "That's okay, Komo, I'm not going."

Komo put her cup down with a loud clink. "And why not? Everyone's going to be there! This is Sam's last dinner before going to college. You're refusing to go to family dinner?"

"I thought we already had family dinner for him last month?" Mina asked. It had been a terribly uncomfortable affair as usual. The only saving grace was that it had been in a Korean restaurant, so the food was good and her grandparents' awfulness was tempered by the fact that they were in public.

"That was to celebrate his graduation," Komo said in an aggrieved tone. "This is his going-away-to-college dinner."

"What's the difference?" Mina snarked.

"Mina, this is family. Everyone will be there."

Even more reason not to go, Mina thought. Her father was the black sheep of the family just because he'd gone to law school instead of med school and had further compounded the sin by marrying an artist. Her father's older brother was a doctor, and her komo had married a doctor, and so they were the favored ones. Mina's four cousins were all male and older than her. One was already married with kids. She had nothing in common with any of them. Sam, who was the closest in age to her, was an obnoxious jerk.

"Komo, dinner will be better without me," she replied. "Besides, you know I'm their least favorite grandchild."

"That's not true. . . ."

Rolling her eyes hard, Mina sank down in the armchair. "It's okay, Komo, you don't have to say that. It doesn't hurt my feelings anymore."

"Your grandparents are just not good at expressing their emotions," Komo tried to explain.

"I don't know about that," Mina snorted. "They were always really good at showing how much they hated my mom."

Komo was quiet. Mina could see the slightly guilty look on her face. Her aunt hadn't been nice to her mother either. But at least she had the decency to feel bad about it.

"Your grandparents love you," Komo said. "You're their only granddaughter."

"They sure have a funny way of showing it. Last time I saw them, they complained that I was just like my mother, wasting time on art."

"They are just worried about your future."

"They even blamed my mother for dying and causing my father so much trouble, like having to take care of me."

Once again Mina had made her komo gape in shock. "They didn't mean that," she replied weakly.

"Don't try to excuse them, Komo," Mina said. "They couldn't have said a worse thing to me."

Her aunt frowned. "Mina, you have to understand, they're old and they have a very different perspective."

Mina swallowed back a lump of tears and let out a harsh laugh. "You know when my mom was alive, she would always make excuses and laugh off their comments, just like you're doing. But I can't handle their nuclear toxicity anymore. I'm very close to saying something unforgivable to them. So it really would be better if I don't go."

It had been like this since she could remember. Her halmeoni with her powdery perfume and her habit of passive-aggressively saying bad things about her mother right in front of both of them.

"Aigoo, what kind of mother sends her poor child out in the cold without gloves and a scarf?" she said, even though it was Mina who lost them.

"Such an unfortunate child to have a lazy mother who forgets to pack her a lunch box," Halmeoni said with fake sympathy when Mina told her she'd bought school lunch once.

"Oh, my poor son! Look how thin he is! What kind of wife is too lazy to cook for her husband?" she said in front of the entire family.

Once when Mina raged about it, her mother just laughed and told her it was the Korean way.

"She doesn't mean it," her mother said. "It's just what all grandmothers say."

"Well, I don't like it and I don't like her!"

"Don't say that, Mina," her mother admonished her. "It'll hurt your father's feelings. She's your grandmother. She's your family."

But her mother wasn't here anymore, her halmeoni wasn't hiding her dislike and contempt, and Mina wasn't in the mood to be the good Korean granddaughter.

Komo got up to leave with a heavy sigh. "I'm sorry you feel this way, Mina," she said. "Eventually, I hope you will learn to let go of your bitterness. They are your grandparents."

Don't hold your breath, Mina thought to herself.

After her aunt left, Mina grabbed her bag and went up to her room. Immediately she was filled with the warmth of her mother's memories. Mina's walls were covered with all the art and photographs that once hung throughout the rest of the house. Before her father decided that looking at them was too painful. As if he was the only one to suffer. Mina missed her mother every day. It was like an open wound that never healed. But she didn't want to hide her mother away like her father did. There was only one painting that Mina couldn't bear to hang up. The last one her mom painted. It was of a mother and daughter laughing in a field of sunflowers. The bright blue of the sky against the rich shades of yellow of the flowers reminded Mina of summer and sunshine and her mother's laughter. It sat tied up in acid-free paper and bubble wrap in her closet, waiting for the day it wouldn't tear her heart apart to look at it.

Mina sat at her L-shaped desk; one side was for schoolwork and the other side held her mom's old Wacom Cintiq drawing tablet. It was the best tablet on the market ten years ago. But it still worked well and Mina loved it.

She reached into her bag and pulled out the instant photos she'd taken earlier in the day. On her favorite, she wrote "first day of senior year" across the white frame and pinned it to the large board full of Polaroids. One corner of the bulletin board was for friends, one was for her mom, and the others were filled with random photos of things Mina would draw.

After turning on the tablet, Mina stared at the blank page for several minutes, trying to come up with a new idea for her webcomic. For a moment, she deeply resented her friends for telling her their opinions. Did she really want to know how much it sucked?

"Yes. Yes, I did," she said out loud. "What's the use of spending all that time creating a webcomic if no one reads it?" Being alone so much, Mina would often talk to herself just to break the silence of the house.

As she slumped in her seat, she was suddenly startled by the text tone from her phone.

"Auntie Jackie!" Mina smiled as she grabbed her phone.

Auntie Jackie: Mina honey!!! Taking train down tomorrow. Dinner?

Mina: YES

Auntie Jackie: 5pm. The usual.

CHAPTER 4

Monthly Dinner with Auntie Jackie Young

Tuesday, August 30

"Mina, honey, why is your face so gaunt? Have you not been eating well? Sleeping well? Are you getting any sunlight at all, dear girl?"

Mina was bombarded with questions even as she was enveloped in the warm embrace of her mother's bestest friend.

"I'm fine!" Mina exclaimed. Auntie Jackie was a slight Asian woman whose stylish black hair had a narrow swath of pure white framing her oval face. Her wide mouth and high cheekbones were made for smiling, especially because of the deep dimple on her right cheek.

Auntie Jackie was more family to Mina than anyone on her father's side. It sucked that her mom was an only child and Mina wasn't close with her paternal relatives. But Auntie Jackie made up for it all. She was also the coolest person Mina knew. Auntie Jackie was such a big celebrity in the bridal fashion industry that people came from all over the world to have her design their wedding dresses. Her flagship store in New York, like her fashion line, was simply named Jackie, with locations in Los Angeles, Chicago, and Washington, DC.

Mina sat down just as the waiter appeared with their double order of soup dumplings. He took off the bamboo lid, letting the steam and the delicate aroma of the pork-and-chive mixture waft into Mina's nostrils. Auntie Jackie always came early and ordered so that Mina never had to wait long to eat.

Before she started eating, Mina pulled out her instant camera and took a picture of her auntie smiling down at the steaming hot dumplings.

"Still taking Polaroids," Auntie Jackie said. "Just like your mama. Now, let me take one of you!"

Mina passed over her camera and then carefully picked up a delicate dumpling and shoved it into her mouth.

"Ah, hot!"

Auntie Jackie chuckled and snapped a Polaroid. "I've been watching you eat xiao long bao for all your life and you always burn your mouth on the first one. You never learn your lesson."

"I can't help it! They're so delicious."

"Even after the roof of your mouth is all blistery?"

"Yep, even after it pops and leaves the skin hanging until it finally rips off in agonizing pain."

Auntie Jackie shook her head with a smile. "As long as you enjoy it, I guess."

That was what Mina loved about Auntie Jackie—she

never judged her and always accepted her for who she was, and not what she could be.

"So tell me about your art, hon—what are you working on? You haven't shown me anything in a while."

Mina was quiet for a moment, debating whether or not to share her recent project.

"I'm working on a webcomic," she said slowly.

"That's brilliant! I love them!" Auntie Jackie clapped her hands in excitement. "My favorite one right now is the makeup one. I swear I'm getting some great tutorials from it! Okay, so tell me what yours is about. Do you have your story written out?"

Mina shrugged. "I had started one but apparently it was really boring, and Saachi and Megan said I had to either make it more exciting or start all over again. I'm not sure what to do."

"Can I see it?"

Mina shook her head. "I don't want you to waste your time on something boring."

Auntie Jackie squeezed Mina's hand. "I love everything you do, but I won't press you to show me. I'll wait until you are ready to share it," she said. "In the meantime, I went shopping!"

She passed Mina a big black bag with a famous department store name embossed in gold. Auntie Jackie's shopping habit was why Mina's closet was the envy of her friends.

"Open it!"

Inside was a long hooded jacket in camouflage green.

"A camo jacket?" Mina asked in surprise.

"Try it! It's perfect with what you've got on. It gives

simple classics a cool edgy vibe. And it goes really well with your new gray hair. Your hairstylist is a genius!"

"Well, he was your hairstylist first," Mina replied as she took the jacket out of the bag. She put it on over her black jeans and simple white top. As usual, her auntie was not wrong.

"Oooooh, I had no idea. But I love it!" Auntie Jackie beamed at Mina. "I remember your mom wearing something similar when we were young and wild. And now you look more and more like her every time I see you," she said. "You remind me of when we were in high school, ready to go off to NYU. We did almost everything together. I mean how many best friends end up pregnant at the same time?" She chuckled and then let out a shaky sigh. "I miss her every day."

They were both silent, caught up in the immensity of their losses.

Auntie Jackie cleared her throat. "How's school been?" she asked. "This is a big year for you. Have you given any thought to what colleges you want to apply to?"

Mina sank back into her seat. "Dad is being a butt."

"Is he still on that Ivy League kick?"

Mina nodded glumly. "And it's all Komo's fault. She got him to sign me up for this expensive SAT class because they said my score wasn't good enough. They don't care that I'm not interested in the schools they want me to go to."

Auntie Jackie folded her hands and rested her chin on them. "Where do you want to go?"

Leaning forward, Mina smiled. "I want to study art like Mom. And NYU Steinhardt is definitely on my list."

Auntie Jackie clapped her hands. "I think you'd love it." She started tearing up again.

"What's the matter?" Mina asked.

"Just thinking about your mom and Jin." She sighed. "Your mom would be so proud to hear you talking about applying to college, and I'm so sorry Jin isn't here for this journey with you."

She wiped her eyes as the waitstaff came to clear away their empty plates and fill up their pot of hot tea. Mina poured the tea into the ceramic cups and then grabbed her auntie's hand. She'd been too young to console Auntie Jackie when she'd lost Jin. He'd been only six years old.

When Auntie Jackie's boyfriend abandoned her, she'd left New York and moved down to Washington, DC, to be with Mina's mother, Emma. They gave birth within a few months of each other. Mina and Jin became the best of friends, just like their moms.

When he died, Mina had been heartbroken. Her mother had been there for Mina and Jackie, supporting them both, letting them grieve. Auntie Jackie then threw herself into her work and became famous. But when Mina's mother died, it had been Auntie Jackie who consoled Mina in ways her own father was unable to. Auntie Jackie was not just Mina's second mother; she was her partner in grief. Their shared sorrow and trauma formed a deep and powerful bond that went beyond love and friendship. It was this bond that healed their broken hearts.

"Did you know that your mom was with me when Jin died?" Auntie Jackie asked.

Mina nodded. "I remember Dad telling me you needed her more than I did."

Jackie nodded. "I did. And so did Jin. Emma told him not to be afraid. That he would be in a place where he would be strong and healthy and not hurt anymore. And though we would miss him terribly, we would see him again. Everything I should have said but couldn't because I was too devastated."

Tears coursed down Mina's face as she thought of Jin and her mother.

"I remember there was a terrible thunderstorm at the time," Jackie whispered. "We sat on both sides of him, holding his hands when he passed. At that exact moment, multiple large lightning bolts crashed so close to us, it lit up everything in a white haze for several long moments. I don't even know how many strikes there were—it felt like it went on for ages. And then everything went dark and the emergency lights went on and Jin was gone. It was as if the storm took my little boy away."

They were quiet except for the sniffling and nose blowing. Mina wiped her face and let out a ragged breath.

"All my memories of being little have Jin in them," she whispered. "I miss him and Mom so much. Why did they have to die?"

It took several long minutes before they were able to speak again. Jackie pulled out a compact mirror and moaned at her reflection.

"Look at me! I've cried all my makeup off." She laughed. "Did I ever tell you that your mom and I had this dream that you and Jin would date and one day get married?"

Mina smiled. "Did you guys secretly betroth us as babies?"

Jackie nodded vigorously. "We were hoping to be in-laws.

Although your dad always thought we were weird." She chuckled and wiped her eyes again. "It didn't matter anyway. You've become as much my child as Jin."

Mina moved to the seat next to Aunt Jackie to hug her.

"I love you, Auntie Jackie," she said, her voice cracking. "I don't know what I would do without you."

"I love you too, Mina."

CHAPTER 5

The School of Secrets

As soon as Mina got home, she turned on her mom's old Wacom Cintiq and patiently waited through the long reboot.

She was still processing all the criticisms that her friends had given her, knowing they were right. New readers might click on her comic, but they would never keep reading. They seemed to like her art, but nobody stuck around. Mina sighed. How could she blame them? Maybe her webcomic was just a boring journal about a high school where nothing happened.

But what if, in the same high school setting, there were people with special gifts who had to hide themselves from those who would exploit or kill them?

The story idea popped into her head, and she knew she had to write it down. Spinning away from her Wacom, Mina turned to her laptop and opened a new document.

She called her new webcomic *The School of Secrets* and began to establish a storyline where a teenage girl was the secret hero in a school of bullies and spies who made it dangerous to be a student with a special gift. Mina snorted. Lots of mean kids at her school she could choose from.

Mina paused and chewed on her lower lip. Was this storyline too cliché? Hadn't it been done so many times before? Would Megan and Saachi still complain that it was boring? Would other readers criticize it for being unoriginal? Then Mina shrugged, remembering something her mother had said long ago.

"The thing about art is that there will always be someone somewhere who will criticize your work. And that's okay. Your art is not for everyone. Your art is for you to have fun creating it and for those who appreciate it. So don't think about what people will say. Just make it."

Okay, Mom! Let's do it!

If her main characters were high school kids with special gifts, then who was her villain? Someone at the school, definitely. Someone who was always on the lookout to expose the Gifted and send them to a shadowy government group that experimented on those with gifts. But the real intent of the group was to turn the Gifted into unbeatable soldiers.

Mina stopped typing. Weren't shadowy government agencies a total cliché? With a frustrated sigh, she deleted the entire paragraph.

She tugged at her hair as if it would make her brain think harder. A military group that captures the Gifted to copy their talents to make the ultimate mutant weapon? Ugh, that was too Wolverine.

What if it was a private corporation that wanted to capture and sell the Gifted to the highest bidder? Wait, wasn't that like Deadpool?

Mina groaned and banged her head on the desk. Why was this so freaking hard? After several hours of writing and rewriting, she finally settled on her villain's backstory.

The ultimate villain is a multibillionaire, Rowan Mercer, former CEO of a shady hedge fund and a climate change denier who has always been fascinated with the Gifted and wants powers of his own. He's the head of an unethical science corporation called Merco, which studies genetically modified humans. He has a private army on payroll and orders them to kidnap the Gifted and bring them to Merco labs, where they are subjected to horrific surgeries that remove their talents. Unfortunately, the Gifted then fall into comas and most of their talents are lost. But Mercer successfully extracts a fraction of talents that are then genetically transfused into his DNA. He wants more, and he won't rest until he creates a lasting powerful talent of his own. He forces his scientists to work on stabilizing the transferal. But he doesn't realize that the gene editing and transference are mutating him into a monster.

Pleased with what she had so far, Mina decided to work on her other characters.

In her previous webcomic, she'd been too focused on re-creating the look of her mom's art. But that wasn't really Mina's style. She didn't need her webcomic to look realistic, like photographs. She loved the Korean manhwa style, with its vibrant expressions and mix of drawing styles. Plus it was easier and faster for her to create.

Hearing the voices of her friends in her head, Mina knew she had to draw a great love interest. But she refused to include a love triangle in her story. No, she would give her webcomic the perfect boyfriend.

Immediately a face came to mind, and she turned to her tablet to draw a serious-looking boy with dark hair that hung over dark brown eyes and a wide mouth with one deep dimple in his left cheek. He looked familiar but Mina couldn't place him. Maybe he was a K-drama or K-pop star she'd seen online? She had this overwhelming feeling that she knew his face. For a moment, she considered drawing a different character. But no—he was so good-looking he was likely to appeal to a lot of readers. Brushing aside her concerns, she drew him over and over, in different poses and different clothing until he felt comfortable, like an old friend. Happy with his look, she finalized his character design and gave him a large wristwatch that glowed. Next to it, she wrote, "can stop time." At the last moment, she wrote the name "Jin" over his head. In honor of her old best friend, who also had one deep dimple in his left cheek.

Now to draw the rest of the characters.

Images began popping up in her head. She started creating first drafts of the cast for her new story.

A pretty half-Asian girl with light brown hair and eyes and electric sparks shimmering around her hands. Mina wrote the name "Sophia" over the girl's head. Next she drew a few more characters: a Latina girl named Kayla with wavy dark blond hair that flew up around her face as if she were in a wind tunnel; Jewel, a fair-complexioned redhead with the bluest eyes that stared serenely, her expression the very epitome of soothing calmness; and a Black boy named Mark with a short fade and a solid build. He had his hands outstretched and balls floating above them. Mina wrote, "telekinesis."

She marveled that their names came so easily to her. It was as if they were real people. When creating her first webcomic, Mina had the hardest time naming her characters.

After several passes each, Mina had clean drafts of her main characters, and then she methodically began to ink them. Usually when she inked, she was so caught up with perfecting her lines that she would mess up constantly, leading to hours of frustration. It was why she hated the inking process. It was tedious and difficult. But this time her hand was steady and sure with no hesitation. Her inking was fluid and her lines smooth.

After she drew her main cast members, she worked on her villains. She drew the first image that popped into her head: the sharp, cold features of a very blond older woman with glasses and red lipstick. Mina giggled as she recognized her physics teacher, Ms. Sarah Allen, her least favorite teacher of all time. If she was being honest, it was more that she disliked physics. Ms. Allen had been all right. For her webcomic, she named her Ms. Alexander and made her the assistant principal at Sophia's high school. Ms. Alexander was someone without any abilities who believed that the Gifted were a threat to society. Next, Rowan Mercer, the ultimate bad guy. What would he look like? Mina could think of many real-life people she disliked, but none who she thought actually looked evil besides some politicians and criminals. Suddenly, she thought of a has-been actor, a racist bigot who had been in several sleazy sex scandals. Mina grinned. Tim Woods. Everybody hated him and he had the face of a true villain. He'd be perfect.

It was well past midnight when Mina took a break. She blew out a loud, frustrated breath as she realized how much work she had to do. She'd intended to have her webcomic done in time for college applications, but at the rate she was going, she wouldn't get half the story done before the first deadline. If one episode had at least thirty to fifty panels to sketch, ink, color, and letter with dialogue, it would take over a week to do and it would take at least forty episodes to complete the entire story.

Mina closed her eyes and pondered how to shorten the process. Aside from writing the outline and script and storyboarding the entire plot, the most time-consuming and labor-intensive part was inking and coloring. Since the setting was a school, it didn't make sense to draw new backgrounds. Might as well use all the background settings she'd already created for her previous webcomic. And if she shortened each episode to thirty panels instead of fifty, that would save her a lot of work. While there was no way around inking the characters, if Mina kept her coloring simple, one shadow or highlight for each base color, it could save her considerable time. Her colors might be flat, but if people liked her story, it could work.

Satisfied with her plan, Mina switched off her tablet and stretched. She would tackle the first episode tomorrow and then see what Saachi and Megan thought.

"And there will be no love triangles! Says the conquering hero," Mina crowed as she headed to bed.

CHAPTER 6

Disappointing Dad

Wednesday, September 7

A week later, Mina had finished the first episode of her new webcomic and part of the second. It was the fastest she'd ever worked in her life, but only because she'd pulled several all-nighters in a row. Simplifying the coloring had been a tremendous time-saver, but the inking process was still tedious. Her hand was a throbbing painful mess, but she felt excited for the first time in a long while. It was four in the morning, and she was exhausted but eager to surprise and impress her friends. She sent the title page and a few panels with a message.

> **Mina:** Sneak preview invite.

Mina then took a one-hour power nap but still managed to be late to school. On the way, she checked her group chat and found new messages.

Saachi: Woah! Mina! Way to go! Can't wait to read it!

Megan: Love triangle potential????

Mina: No 🖤

Megan: Fun killer

Saachi: 💀💀💀

Mina had to laugh. She felt a strong surge of gratitude for her friends. They kept her humble and also were her strongest supporters. She was so lucky to have them in her life. Without Saachi and Megan, she might not have survived school after losing her mother. They'd made sure to keep her busy and to stay by her side, even when her father threw himself back into work.

The day flew by, as Mina spent most of the time in her classes thinking up new story ideas for her webcomic. When the last bell rang, Mina found her friends waiting for her outside her classroom.

"We're coming home with you today," Megan announced as she draped her arm over Mina's shoulders.

"Says who?" Mina asked.

"Says your bestest friends," Saachi replied, walking close on her other side, forming a Mina sandwich. "Seeing the sneak preview on our phones was not enough—we need to see it on your big tablet screen. And we want to know what's going to happen next in your thrilling new webcomic."

"How about some personal space," Mina groused.

"Like this?" Megan threw her arms around Saachi to complete the Mina sandwich.

"I am a sardine trapped in the smelly armpit of life."

"That's right, stinky!" Megan laughed.

Mina groaned and complained but didn't push them away. The idea of not being alone at home filled her with a warm glow she hadn't felt in such a long time.

"Okay, I guess," Mina said. "Although I know you're only coming to eat all of Mrs. Song's food and my Korean snacks."

"Well, duh," Saachi replied.

The friends holed up in Mina's room, hovering over the tablet as they read the first episode and gushed over the character sketches.

"Their gifts are great, but how come you don't have a super strong character?" Megan asked. "You know, like Superman!"

" 'Cause then all you would need is Superman to defeat everyone and the story would end," Mina replied.

"What are you talking about? Every strong hero has a weakness! That's what makes them interesting!"

Mina laughed. "Okay, if I add a new character, they'll be super strong, just for you."

"Good! But make them a girl!"

Mina nodded.

"So what happens next?" Saachi asked excitedly.

"I don't even know," Mina responded. She tapped her cheek absentmindedly as she furrowed her brows in thought. "I'm trying to plot out my next few episodes."

"How long will it take?"

"Can we see it first?"

Before Mina could answer, she heard the front door slam shut and her father's voice calling up to her.

The three girls traipsed down the stairs to greet him.

In the kitchen, Mina's dad placed a bag of fried chicken and sides on the table, along with a box of specialty doughnuts from the local gourmet shop.

"Hey, Mr. Lee!" Saachi said.

"Thanks for the food," Megan chimed in.

Mina's dad smiled, softening his severe face.

"Since I was coming home early for once, I wanted to make sure you all had enough food." Glancing at Mina, he sighed. "I still can't get used to your hair, Mina. Were you trying to match me?"

Her father had a bright shock of white hair on the top of his head but otherwise didn't look his age. He had wrinkles around his eyes only when he smiled, which he rarely did anymore.

"This is cool silver, Dad," Mina snarked. "Your hair is old-man white."

"I think your dad rocks it," Megan said with a double thumbs-up.

"Mr. Lee, gray is such a great color," Saachi said. "Mina might be after the trend, but I think she looks gorgeous."

"It's never too late if I'm doing it," Mina joked as she side-eyed her father warily.

He shook his head and gave a conciliatory smile. "Mina, trend or not, you always look beautiful," he said. "So now that you're all seniors, what schools are you thinking of applying to?"

As her friends talked about the schools they were

interested in, Mina's dad served them food and juice and listened intently as they all ate.

"I'm going on a road trip with my parents tomorrow to see schools up north," Megan said. "And Saachi's flying west to look at some California schools."

"School visits? I've been so busy with work I didn't even think of that," Mina's dad said with a wince. "Mina, should we try to see some schools also?"

Mina shrugged and Saachi shook her head. "We both tried to get Mina to come with us but she refused."

His eyebrows shot up in surprise. "How come you didn't mention it to me, honey? That might have been good for you."

"I hate traveling," Mina replied. Technically, it wasn't completely true. She loved the idea of traveling, but it just didn't agree with her. Both flying and driving made her terribly motion sick.

"Dramamine always worked well for your mom when she had to travel," her father said. He gave Mina's hair a gentle tug. "I'll clear up my schedule so we can go see a few schools."

Mina bit her lip to stop herself from saying what she really wanted to say. That he wouldn't take her to see the schools she was interested in. That she had no intention of studying science or English or math or going to medical or law school. All she wanted to do was make art. That was what she was most passionate about, what she loved doing. But her father wouldn't allow it.

"I have to do some work before my business trip tomorrow, so I'll be in my office," Mina's dad said as he got up from the table. "Let me know if you need anything, girls."

After dinner, Saachi and Megan headed home, and Mina went up to her room to continue working on her webcomic. She was so absorbed in it that she didn't hear her father at her door until he spoke.

"Mina, do you have a minute?"

She jumped in surprise. "Yeah, Dad. What is it?"

Her father walked in and looked around her room. For a moment, a pained expression showed on his face as he glanced at the art hanging on the walls. Mina could feel a matching hurt in her heart. She knew how hard it was for him to see her mother's art.

He walked to Mina's side and peered over her shoulder at the character sketch on her tablet. Mina could smell his cologne, citrusy, slightly spicy, and always a clean fresh scent. Her mother had bought it for him, an iconic Japanese brand she had loved. Even now it was the only cologne he wore. Mina bought it for every birthday and Christmas because it was one of the few things she knew he actually used. It suited him in a way that no other scent could. It was simply Dad.

"What are you working on?" he asked.

"Just practicing," Mina replied. She wasn't ready to tell him about her webcomic. She needed it to be successful first. To prove to him that she could do it. Make a career out of art.

"Shouldn't you be doing homework?" he asked.

Mina tightened her grip on her tablet pen. "I finished already."

Her dad stepped back and sat on the armchair next to the window.

"I'm going to be doing some heavy traveling this

weekend, and Mrs. Song isn't available to come by. Are you going to be okay all alone?" he asked.

"Dad, there's this thing called online ordering and delivery? I promise I won't starve. Besides, Mrs. Song usually makes a lot of food on Friday for me to last the weekend."

"Yeah, but I thought your friends would be around to hang out with you."

"I'll be fine," Mina said sharply. She hated when he treated her like a child.

Her dad rubbed his eyes as if he had a headache. "You're right. I'm sorry. I just worry about you, that's all."

"I'm not a baby, Dad. I'm seventeen! And don't call and text me all the time! I hate when you do that! Like I'm a prisoner you have to check up on. I'm busy too!"

He laughed. "Don't worry. I'm going to be on planes most of the weekend, so I won't be able to bother you too much."

"Good," Mina replied.

"Anyway, I was thinking about the SAT class, and I realized I was being a bit harsh about making you take public transit," he said. "Maryland is not like DC or New York. It would take you far too long to get there. Just use your car app. It'll save you a lot of time and walking."

Mina frowned. "Okay, thanks."

Her father sighed. "I know you don't want to go, but it's the best program in the area. It'll really help you raise your score."

"Dad, a lot of schools aren't even requiring the SAT anymore. . . ."

"That may be, but a good score on the SAT is still the best way to make your application stand out and help you get into the best college possible."

"But what if that isn't what I want?"

Her father pressed his lips flat, his face turning stern. "Mina, I'm worried about your future. You need to be able to get a job and take care of yourself."

"I don't get it. Mom was an artist—why can't I be one too?"

"Your mom never made any money off of her art," he replied. "I don't want that for my daughter."

"Mom didn't make money from her art because she didn't really try," Mina retorted. "She was more focused on being your wife and my mother."

"That's your auntie Jackie talking. . . ."

"But she's right!" Mina yelled in frustration. "I remember how much Harabeoji and Halmeoni put down Mom's art. They always said it was a waste of time and she should focus on her family first. She never had a chance. . . ."

"Even if she did, what kind of career would it have been?" her father cut in sharply. "The starving artist isn't some myth—it's a reality. And I don't want that for you!"

Mina was shaking her head furiously. "It's different now! There's so much more to art than you think, Dad. It's a business like any other career! Artists can be successes or failures just like any other career people out there. But they have to at least try!"

"There are some jobs that people can always make a good salary from, like doctors, nurses, accountants. . . ."

"Ugh, no, Dad! I don't want to do any of that!"

"Don't be closed-minded, Mina. You won't know what you like until you go to college and try out some classes."

Mina could feel her frustration rising, and she wanted to scream.

"I want to go to art school!"

"Absolutely not! I'm not paying for you to throw your life away."

"It's my life!"

"But I'm the one paying for your college."

Mina gritted her teeth to keep from responding with all her pent-up snark. She didn't want to blow up this fight.

"Mina, if you go to a good liberal arts college, you can still study art. But you can also take other courses, open yourself up to other opportunities. It's the best of both worlds! Something you won't be able to do at an all-arts school. And that will give you a wider range of career options," he said in a milder tone. "I need you to have a stable career so your future is safe. I don't want to have to worry about you if something happens to me."

Mina remained silent.

"I know this isn't what you want to hear, but you'll thank me when you're older."

At his words, Mina rolled her eyes so hard her eyelids fluttered with disdain. "You'll thank me when you're older" had to be the most annoying phrase parents said to their kids.

"Maybe I will, but what if I don't?" Mina complained. "What if when I'm older I resent you because you were wrong? Then what, Dad?"

"Then I'm wrong and you should follow your dream, but at least you'll have a strong educational foundation to fall back on."

Mina clenched her fists and swiveled her chair to face

the wall. She didn't want to cry in front of him. He refused to understand how she felt about art. She was just like her mom. Art was her life. But as unhappy as her father's words made her, she also knew just how hard he worked and how much he missed her mother. It was what kept Mina from being mean to him. She loved her dad; she just didn't agree with him. After a long moment, she heard her father close the door.

She was so tired of hearing him say the same things over and over. Art wasn't a profession. She had to choose a wise career, like doctor or accountant or teacher. Blah, blah, blah. Just thinking of what he always said irked her. She would work hard on her webcomic and build a big audience and possibly make some money off it. Then she would show him that art was a career she could pursue. Because if it wasn't, what did she have to look forward to?

Mina worked late into the night, not stopping until the sun began to rise and her alarm for school rang. Her second episode was almost complete. She was having so much fun making Sophia a badass superhero who used her powers to save another gifted student from being taken by Merco. Mina colored Sophia's electric bolts a bright blue against a stark white background for maximum effect and was pleased with how it looked.

Exhausted, she fell into bed and slept, only managing to mutter that she didn't feel well when her father checked up on her.

"It's a little early for senioritis, don't you think?" he asked as he poked at her.

Mina growled and pulled the bedcovers over her head.

"All right then. Just rest. I have to go on my trip, but I'll have Mrs. Song come early to check on you."

She woke up at noon to the sound of soft but persistent knocking.

"Come in," she said, her voice still groggy from sleep.

Mrs. Song entered. She was a grandmotherly type with short permed salt-and-pepper hair and a round face that radiated warmth.

"Are you all right?" she asked in Korean.

Mina barely spoke Korean, but she understood quite a lot from her maternal grandparents, who lived in Korea, and from watching K-dramas.

She nodded. "I'm just tired," she replied in English.

Mrs. Song brought over some hot tea and sliced fruit and sat next to her on the bed. She patted Mina's head gently and offered her the mug.

"I'll make you lunch, but have this for now."

Drinking the hot tea cleared the sleep from Mina's brain and got her ready for another day of creating her webcomic. Only stopping briefly to wolf down the meals and snacks provided by Mrs. Song, Mina worked tirelessly on her creation. Mina realized writing and drawing each panel of her new project was easier and faster than ever before. There was something about these characters that motivated her and compelled her to bring them to life. It was as if they were creating themselves.

In honor of Saachi and Megan pushing her to make her story more interesting, she decided to draw herself and her two best friends walking in the hallway behind the main characters. She wondered if they'd even notice.

By 10:30 p.m., Mina was finished. Happy and proud of

what she'd done, Mina uploaded both episodes onto Toon-webz and gave her cramping hand a well-deserved break by binge-watching several episodes of her latest K-drama. When she finally went to bed, she dreamed that her comic characters had come to life and were wreaking havoc at her school.

CHAPTER 7

Mean Girls

Friday, September 9

After a restless night of sleep, Mina felt like one of the walking dead. She contemplated not going to school again but knew her dad would not approve. In every class, she found it hard to keep her eyes open, and without her friends around, she was bored and lonely.

Although both were out of town on school visits, Saachi and Megan were still texting in the group chat about the first two episodes.

> **Saachi:** Webcomic! 💜 💜 💜 💜 💜 💜 💜
> But needs a new cool character like this

Below her text popped up a picture of Saachi posing dramatically in her hotel room.

Megan: LOL
No, more like this

Megan's selfie was just as dramatic but with pouty lips and crossed eyes.

Mina snickered and then typed her response.

Mina: Hell No

Saachi: whyyyyyy

Megan: mean

Mina: don't want real people in it
too weird

Megan: youre weird

Mina grinned. Her friends still hadn't noticed that she'd drawn them into the webcomic. She wondered if she should tell them or try again and see if they caught on. She loved her friends and already missed them. But she hoped they were having a good time. Megan was checking out Wesleyan in Connecticut because her idol, Lin-Manuel Miranda, went there, and Saachi was driving up and down the Pacific Coast Highway. Although she'd been sending more pictures of the beach than of any colleges.

Since Christina was also absent and there was no one in school Mina really wanted to eat lunch with, she headed to the art room. She could use her mobile tablet to work on the third episode of *The School of Secrets*. It had not even been a day since uploading the webcomic, but she already had two hundred likes on the first episode. That was more than all ten of her previous episodes combined. For the first time ever, Mina was getting comments from new readers who were excited for more episodes. She didn't know how they were finding her story, but it was critical for her to post regularly so they wouldn't lose interest.

She was looking at her tablet as she neared the art room. As long as she was connected to Wi-Fi, she could access her cloud files and her webcomic account. Mina was so glad her father had agreed to buy her the mobile tablet for her birthday. She'd made the argument that it was for school more than for art, but truth was, she used it only for drawing.

"Watch it, stupid!"

Mina hadn't been paying attention to where she was going. Now she realized she'd bumped into the mean popular girls. Bailey Keller, Madison Tipton, and two more lookalikes whose names Mina could never remember. Ashley? Tiffany? Whatever, it didn't matter, since it was Bailey who was holding some overpriced specialty drink. Mina tried not to panic. Bailey was notorious for being the meanest girl in the entire school, and she hated Mina.

"Sorry about that, I didn't see where I was going." Mina eyed the girls cautiously; she didn't know what mood they were in.

"Bitch, you made me spill my kombucha. What're you gonna do about it?"

Damn, they were in a fighting mood. She eyed the tiniest of drops on Bailey's luxury-brand shirt and apologized again, bracing herself for what was to come as the girls circled her. The first shove was expected. It sent her flying into Madison behind her, who then shoved her forward even harder. Back and forth, several times, until finally Mina fell to her knees.

"I'm gonna make sure you watch where you're going from now on," Bailey said as she proceeded to pour the stinky kombucha all over Mina's head. They laughed raucously as Mina sat on the floor, hugging her precious tablet to her chest to protect it from the liquid. Tears of rage mixed with the nasty-feet-smelling fermented drink that coursed down her face. She couldn't believe Bailey would drink something that smelled like it had gone completely bad.

As usual, there were no teachers or security guards present when you needed them. Amid the snickers and outright laughter around her, Mina kept her head down and raced to the bathroom.

Trying to clean up the mess was no use—the smell was overwhelming. Giving up, Mina ditched school and ran home, surprising Mrs. Song, who was in the middle of cooking.

"Mina! What happened? Are you okay?" Mrs. Song asked in Korean.

But Mina couldn't answer, trying not to cry. She rushed upstairs and locked herself in her bathroom.

After showering and changing, Mina came out to find a large serving of sliced and peeled pears and red grapes on her desk. Ignoring the offering, she sat on her bed and hugged her knees.

A knock on the door, and Mrs. Song appeared with a

mug of hot barley tea and a plate of roasted goguma, Korean sweet potato. They were Mina's favorite. Purple on the outside and pale yellow on the inside, they tasted nothing like the American versions—more like chestnuts. She'd been eating them since she was a baby. They reminded her of her mom and her maternal grandparents. Of warmth and comfort, which she needed so much at the moment.

Wiping away her tears, Mina reached over and took a goguma and broke it in half. Steam rose into the air as she smelled the sweet nutty aroma. Peeling back the skin and taking a bite flooded her with contentment. Goguma was a healing food.

"Feeling a little better?" Mrs. Song asked.

Mina nodded and managed a small smile.

"I don't know what happened. But you are a beautiful, kind young lady and you deserve only the best," Mrs. Song said as she pressed the cup of tea into Mina's hand.

Mina thanked her and took a long sip. It was hot and soothing, chasing away the last of the coldness that had seeped into her bones.

"Sleep now," Mrs. Song said. "You'll feel better. And I will cook a delicious dinner for you."

Mrs. Song patted Mina's head and got up to leave. Mina wished she could tell her that the delicious dinner was never as good when you had to eat it all alone. But it was beyond her Korean abilities. Emotionally drained, Mina curled herself under the covers and fell asleep.

A few hours later, she woke up ravenous and ran downstairs to find that Mrs. Song had laid out a feast of Korean delicacies. A small pot of spicy shredded beef soup was on the stove, and hot rice was in the rice cooker. All that was missing was her dad. As if he could sense her thoughts, a text popped up on Mina's phone.

> **Dad:** Mina, heavy rain in the forecast. Take car service round trip. I'll be back Sunday.

> **Mina:** k

No other person she knew texted with full punctuation and complete sentences like her dad did.

Mina heated the soup and ate her meal in the quiet stillness of the house. She found it hard to eat around the lump in her throat, which seemed to grow bigger until she gave up and put everything away. She missed her mom so much. It would've been a relief to have told her about her horrible day. Instead, Mina had no one to talk to. She could call her friends or Auntie Jackie, but the effort seemed too much. Phone calls lacked warmth and intimacy. If her dad had been home, she could have told him about it. But he was never home.

Despondent, Mina slowly trudged up to her room. Maybe she'd work on her webcomic. She turned on her tablet and pulled up the latest episode. She'd been working on a storyline where Sophia saves another gifted student from being exposed. But suddenly, Mina felt hot with rage. The anger she'd been holding in ignited, and she began to furiously sketch out a new panel. She found herself drawing the exact scene that had happened at school today. The bump, the spill, the circling, the pushing and shoving. She drew each of the bully girls in perfect detail. Their sneering faces twisted ugly with hate. She paid particular attention to Bailey, the ringleader. Exaggerating her thin lips and sharp features. Mina used ice blue for Bailey's eyes as the only shock of color in her pale face. The coldness accentuating her cruelty.

Even in grade school, Bailey had been mean, as if being born into wealth and privilege had left her an empty shell of a human. But she'd really had it out for Mina since middle school, when Devon Chapman asked Mina to the eighth-grade fall dance. If only Mina had known Bailey liked Devon. She wouldn't have gone with him and made herself a target for the rest of her school career. Just the thought of it all made her so mad. Mina only went with Devon at the urging of her friends. She hadn't liked him. But it was also the first time she and her mom went shopping for a party dress. The first time her mom helped her do her hair and makeup. The first time her mom had told her that she'd grown up into a beautiful young woman. The first and last time. Her mother had died a year later.

While she drew the bullies in full detail, she left the victim's face vague. Drawing her mostly from the back and sides, her features slightly obscured. The only clear defining characteristic was her long dark hair with ombre gray shading, similar to Mina's own. Any more and Megan and Saachi would probably tease her mercilessly.

Since this was her webcomic, she could do anything she wanted.

I'll get Sophia to come and have my revenge.

Mina grinned. She drew Sophia and her friends observing the scene from a short distance. In the next panel, Mina wanted to show Sophia stepping in to stop the bullying. But when she tried to draw Sophia, the screen kept glitching. The pen wouldn't work no matter how hard Mina pressed. It was as if her webcomic was rejecting her idea. She focused on the background and drew in all the details, but the figure in the center, where Sophia should be, was a blur of squiggly lines. Frustrated, Mina erased the figure and began drawing someone else. She let the scene control the flow of the story. She didn't force the narrative. Instead, she let her pen and her imagination take over. When she was done, she was surprised to see that she'd drawn Jin snatching the bottle away before Bailey could dump it on the girl's head.

"What are you doing?" Bailey's dialogue bubble said as she looked shocked.

"Stopping you from being an asshole," Mina wrote in for Jin's first response. She had drawn him giving Bailey a cold glare. "But it's probably too late," read the second bubble.

In the next panel, Jin was leaning down and offering his hand to the no-name character with a smile.

Mina ended the episode showing Jin from behind, his arm draped protectively around the girl's shoulders, guiding her away from the bullies.

By the time Mina finished inking and lettering, it was past midnight and she was exhausted. It was a short episode, but it gave her a keen sense of satisfaction. She uploaded it and went to bed.

• • •

In the morning, Mina woke up late to the sound of thunder. She'd slept fitfully due to vivid dreams and she was still tired. She looked at her alarm clock and cursed. Checking her phone, she saw that her father had texted her another reminder to take a car to her SAT course. That gave her exactly fifteen minutes to get ready. After brushing her teeth and taking the fastest shower in the world, Mina pulled on her ripped black jeans and a cute top. She reached for her messenger bag but paused when she heard another crack of thunder. Instead, she grabbed a black leather fanny pack just big enough to hold her mini tablet, digital drawing pen, and a small notebook and pencils. She strapped it across her body, ordered a car, and ran downstairs.

After pulling on her new boots and lacing them up, she took an umbrella from the closet and peered out the window to see a torrential downpour and strong winds blowing the rain sideways. An umbrella would not be enough. She looked in the closet again but didn't see her raincoat. It must be in her room. She checked her phone—the car was still five minutes away. Glancing down at her boots, Mina groaned at the idea of retying them. Her dad would kill her if she walked in the house with her shoes on, but he wasn't home to stop her. And her boots were brand new, out of the box.

Mina kept them on and ran up to her room. She searched everywhere but couldn't find her raincoat. Then she spotted the hooded camo jacket Aunt Jackie had given her and quickly put it on over her fanny pack, stuffing her phone into a zippered pocket. As she brushed by her desk, her tablet clicked on and a strange static sound filled the room. Concerned, Mina turned back to see her webcomic page glitching.

"What the hell is going on?"

Mina tried to turn her tablet off, but it didn't respond.

The image on the screen warped badly. She wondered if it was because of the storm and was trying to search for help on her phone when, all of a sudden, the screen blacked out and the tablet restarted. It automatically reopened to her webcomic page, but Mina was stunned to see a new scene with her characters on the screen.

"I don't understand," Mina muttered. "I didn't draw this!"

The scene depicted an angry Sophia glaring at Jin as he helped the no-name character. Blue sparks of electricity surrounded Sophia's hands, a telltale sign that she was about to use her powers.

Crap! Is somebody hacking into my account?

Mina tried to delete the scene, but it didn't work. In desperation, she attempted to erase the entire episode, but the system wouldn't respond. It was like she was locked out of her own creation.

Her phone beeped, and Mina realized her car was waiting in front of her house. She was furious and didn't want to leave, but her webcomic would have to wait. She'd take care of it when she got back from SAT prep. Her father would be so mad if she missed class. Mina went to try to turn off her tablet again, but just then the screen stopped glitching and pulled up a blank page. A black-and-white sketch began to appear at high speed, right before her eyes. Someone was drawing Sophia. An angry Sophia with a hand outstretched. A long bolt of electricity streaked out from Sophia's fingertips, across the screen and into the back of the no-name character, sending her bag up in flames. Mina wasn't sure what she was seeing until the first shot of color appeared on the screen. Blue electric bolt. Mina always colored Sophia's electricity in blue.

"NO!" Mina frantically pounded the erase key and used her tablet pen to try to scrub out the scene, the electricity.

The screen was flashing erratically again, but the bolt stopped progressing. Mina didn't know what was happening. Was it something weird in her computer, or was it someone trying to sabotage her? Regardless, she knew she couldn't let this scene upload. She couldn't let Sophia become a bad guy. And she was going to save her no-name character, no matter what. She might not have anyone to help her in real life, but she wasn't going to let anything happen to her webcomic world. Because in her webcomic world, she was in control.

Mina attacked her screen, erasing the newly created scene. Whatever she was doing was working! Slowly, the pictures were disappearing. Mina would not let anyone destroy her creation. She would fight off the hacker who was ruining her story.

But now the screen was going berserk and sending off flashes of light, as if the tablet was self-destructing from within. Suddenly, the thunderstorm outside exploded with multiple lightning strikes and thunder so loud that Mina turned to look at the window. Her room faced the back of the house, where there was a small fenced patio. The sky brightened as another spectacular sequence of jagged bolts rocked the house when they hit the patio and sent a searing jolt of electricity through Mina's body. A high piercing sound assaulted her ears. Mina threw her arms over her head and fell to the floor, paralyzed by the pain.

Then, as abruptly as it all started, everything stopped and the sound was gone. Mina opened her eyes but couldn't see anything but bright white light. Her hearing was muffled, as if she had a bad ear infection, but she could hear people murmuring. What was going on? Blinking at the brightness, her eyes abruptly adjusted and brought her sight back.

Vibrant exuberant color deluged her senses. Mina gasped in complete shock. She was not in her room but in the hallway of a school, with people surrounding her, and everything looked too bright. As if she'd come from a dark room into direct sunlight. Like she was Dorothy entering Technicolor Oz.

Mina took in the circle of faces peering down at her. There stood Bailey and her crew of mean girls, just like Mina had drawn them in her webcomic. And in front of her, holding a bottle of kombucha, was a boy that looked exactly like her character Jin.

"Hey," he said, concern on his handsome face. "Are you all right?"

Mina nodded.

He offered his hand with a smile, his dimple deepening. "Here, let me help you up."

As he bent closer, Mina's eyes bulged in shock. How could this be real?

Behind him, Mina could see a girl whose narrowed eyes and deathly scowl were aimed straight at her. More horrifying were the blue sparks that surrounded her hands.

Sophia. The main character of Mina's webcomic. The hero of her story. Was trying to kill her.

Grabbing the boy's hand, Mina jumped to her feet and ran for the exit, as if lightning were at her heels.

CHAPTER 8

Down the Rabbit Hole

Outside, the sudden reality that she was no longer in her house made Mina's legs go weak, and she stumbled. She let out a small squeak of alarm and would've fallen flat on her face, but someone caught her from behind and twirled her upright.

She blinked in surprise to see Jin's smiling face again.

"Careful now," he said.

"Why are you following me?" Mina asked.

Jin's smile faded to a look of concern. "You seemed shook up. Wanted to make sure you're all right."

She was definitely not all right. There was something wrong with her. She couldn't look at him. It made her feel like she was losing her mind.

"I think I must be dreaming," Mina said to herself. "Yes, this is just a dream. Wake up, Mina." She started slapping herself in the face.

"Hey, stop that," Jin admonished. He gently grabbed

her wrists. "Tell me what's the matter. Do you need to go to the nurse?"

Mina stared at his hands. They felt real. He looked real. But this had to be a dream, right? She let out a dismayed whimper.

"I'm sorry," he said, alarmed as he quickly released her and raised his hands. "I didn't mean to touch you! I just didn't want you to hurt yourself."

She blinked at him and rubbed her eyes hard, making them water. Maybe he was a hallucination. But why could she feel him touch her? She took a step back and opened her eyes wide. He was still there, a vivid, bright, real-life boy who was almost glowing in the sunlight. Sunlight? It was raining just before. Yes, it was raining at home. This was not real—this was a vivid hallucination.

Leaning forward, Mina poked him hard in the chest.

"Ow," he said in surprise. "I guess I deserved that."

Mina was more surprised than he was. His chest was solid. He felt real. She stared at her finger. "What's wrong with me?"

His eyebrows furrowed. "Are you sure you're all right? You kind of look like you might faint."

Mina turned away from him and bit her lip. If this was a dream, it was too realistic. It frightened her.

She heard the bell ring and saw students walking back into the school. This was her school as she had drawn it in her webcomic. She knew this courtyard; it was situated right behind the school. It looked the same and yet different. More vibrant. More vivid. As if to make up for the simple coloring she'd used in her webcomic.

A sudden ringing in her ears sent a wave of dizziness through her. Her legs buckled and Jin caught her again.

"Whoa, let's sit down."

He led her to a bench in the now empty courtyard, and she collapsed onto the seat.

Mina moaned and buried her head in her hands and curled over into her lap.

"I'm having a nightmare," she mumbled.

"You sure you don't need to see the nurse?" Jin asked.

"I need a psychiatrist, not a nurse," she said, still mumbling.

"Sorry, I can't hear you."

Mina raised her head, took one peek at Jin, and moaned again. "I'm losing my mind." She yanked at her hair in disbelief, as if the pain of it would wake her from this all-too-vivid dream.

"You're gonna go bald if you keep that up," Jin warned. He got to his feet. "Wait here, let me get you some water."

Mina watched as he ran back into the school.

"Wake up, Mina, wake up!" She pinched herself hard on her thigh and yelled in pain. "Damn it! That really hurt!"

Blinking away tears, Mina took a deep breath.

Okay, what happened to me? I was supposed to go to Dr. Yee's SAT course. The car was waiting. My tablet was glitching, and someone drew a new scene into my webcomic. I should've just left it. But no, they were ruining the story. And I was trying to erase the new scene when my tablet exploded. . . . That's it! I must have been hurt in the explosion. Maybe I'm in a coma. And now my brain thinks I'm in the world of my webcomic. That's what this is. I'm just dreaming. . . .

She watched as Jin reappeared, holding a bottle of water.

"Here, drink this," he said. He twisted off the cap and gave her the bottle.

But why does this feel so real?

"Thanks," Mina said in a daze. She drank the water and found herself downing it all.

"You must have been dehydrated," Jin said. "By the way, I'm Jin Young Kanter."

The water bottle slipped out of her hands and onto the ground.

"Good thing it was empty," he said with a smile as he picked it up.

This time, Mina leaned so close she could smell him. He smelled like lemon cookies and soap. His pupils dilated wide in surprise, but he didn't move, just sat perfectly still. Mina could see the crinkles at the corners of his eyes, the small pimple on his chin, the slightest of freckles that made clear he was a real-life boy, not a cartoon.

"Is there something on my face?" he asked as his one dimple flashed in and out. Mina was struck by a familiarity that seemed to rest in an old memory she couldn't quite recall.

"Your name is really Jin Young?"

He tilted his head to the side and scratched it, an endearing move that felt like déjà vu. She'd never drawn his character doing that, and yet she'd seen him do it before. What was this weird sensation?

"I don't know, are you really Mina?"

She gasped. "How'd you know my name?" she asked suspiciously.

Jin chuckled. "You've been talking to yourself a lot."

"Oh yeah." Mina's thoughts were a jumbled mess that she couldn't make any sense of.

"So, I feel like you're new here, but you look really familiar to me." Jin studied her face carefully. "Do we know each other?"

Yes, I drew you into my webcomic. You have the ability to stop time.

"No," Mina said, and smiled weakly.

This time, Jin inched closer. "Are you sure? I really feel like we've met before."

Mina leaned away, shaking her head hard.

"But you *are* new here, right?"

Unsure of what to do, Mina just nodded.

"Okay then, you seem really lost. Bellington can be a really confusing place."

"Bellington?"

Did I ever name the school in my comic? No. So it took the name of my real school?

"Yeah, aren't you supposed to be here?" Jin said. "It looks like you have our school schedule."

"Schedule?" Mina asked.

"It's orange like that piece of paper sticking out of your pocket." He smiled encouragingly. "May I see it?"

Mina looked down and was surprised to find a dull orange paper folded neatly. She handed it to him wordlessly.

"Hey, you're in my AP Psych class!"

He gave the paper back to her and she tried to focus on it. Her name was on it. Her address was correct. But her classes and teachers were all different.

"So where did you transfer from?" Jin asked.

Transfer? This is my school.

"Bell ... Bell Academy," she replied in a daze.

"Where's that?"

Right here. This is my school, isn't it?

"Hello, Mina?"

She blinked several times in wonder. This boy was Jin. From her webcomic. Except he was real and talking to her in person. It was dizzying to look at him. In her mind, the comic version and the real boy kept morphing in and out, like some optical illusion. Mina could feel the rising anxiety inside her and was barely keeping her desire to scream in check.

"Sorry?"

"I was asking you where you were from."

Mina stared at Jin's deep dimple. It reminded her of Auntie Jackie who had a dimple just like it. "New York," she replied.

He nodded, looking pleased. "That's what I thought. You have a New York vibe to you."

Mina pressed two fingers to her forehead, feeling the beginnings of a stress migraine. She reminded herself that she was in a dream or hallucinating. This boy was not Jin from her webcomic. He merely looked like him. And had the same name. And the same dimple. *Dear God, help me!*

"You seem really frazzled. Did something bad or strange happen to you?" he asked carefully, with a look of concern.

"Yeah." Mina laughed nervously. "You could say that. This is the weirdest day. One minute I'm home and then the next I'm here, surrounded by strange people and a girl who was ready to electrocute me, and then you ..."

She stopped and clamped her lips shut. He would think she had lost her mind. He was already looking surprised.

"Hold up," Jin said. "You saw Sophia Parker?"

Mina's mouth dropped open. "You know who I'm talking about?"

Jin raked a hand through his thick black hair. "You said 'electrocute,' and that has to be Sophia. Who else has that kind of power?"

This was all too much. He was literally talking about her webcomic character.

Mina stood up. "I need to wake up now."

Before she could walk away, Jin stopped her. "Listen to me, I know it sounds wild, but you need to be careful and avoid Sophia. She's not a nice person."

What was he talking about? In her webcomic, Sophia was his girlfriend. The hero of the story. How could she not be a nice person?

"Wait a minute, isn't she your girlfriend?" Mina blurted out in confusion.

"Hell no! Where'd you hear that?" Jin demanded.

Mina waved a vague hand. "The way she was acting," she replied. "Like she wanted to kill me just because you were helping me."

"That's why it's never gonna happen. No matter how much she wants it. No matter how much everything around me seems to push her at me. I won't do it!"

His sudden anger jolted Mina out of her weird daze, and she stepped back quickly and tripped on a tree root behind her. Jin caught her by the hand and pulled her into a half embrace, leaving her completely breathless.

I couldn't have made that more K-drama-y if I wanted to. Megan would love it.

"Sorry about that," he said as he gently released her.

"Sophia upsets me. She's mean, self-centered, and dangerous. And if she's after you, then you have to be careful.
Whatever you do, stay away from her. She really can electrocute you. She's one of the Gifted."

Suddenly, Mina felt like crying.

"I don't get it. Everything is messed up," she whispered
as she sat down again. "Why would she want to hurt me?
I'm not special."

Looking concerned, Jin sat next to her and awkwardly
patted her shoulder. "I think it's my fault," he replied. "The
more I refuse to go out with her, the more jealous she acts,
like I'm her possession or something. I can't even talk to
another pretty girl without worrying about what she'll do
to them."

"That heinous bitch," Mina said matter-of-factly, trying
to ignore the warmth in her cheeks from the pretty girl
reference. "She needs a serious ass kicking. But from behind, so she doesn't electrocute us first."

Jin choked on a laugh and began coughing. Mina
pounded him on the back.

"Ow, ow, I'm okay! You sure hit hard."

Mina pulled her hand away quickly. "Sorry about that."

Jin frowned. "I think you dislocated my shoulder."

"Yeah, right!"

"No, really, I can't lift up my arm. Look." He flailed his
left arm as if it was useless. "Uh-oh. Now it's my neck. I
can't turn it." Jin moved his whole body toward Mina with
an alarmed expression.

Mina suppressed a grin and raised her fist. Jin ducked.

"You seem okay to me," Mina sniffed.

"Almost made you smile." Jin grinned.

"No."

"I saw it—you had to bite your lip."

"I was holding in a burp."

"Aw, so polite. But next time let it out. It's natural."

Mina relaxed as they fell into a lighthearted banter. This part felt surreal as they talked.

I knew this had to be a dream.

The bell rang, and the loud bustle of moving students filled the air. Mina wondered why she still hadn't woken up and what she was supposed to do now. Alarm filled her again. Her head was throbbing and she was strangely exhausted.

"Hey, give me your phone number," Jin said.

Without thinking, Mina recited her number. Jin punched it into his phone and texted a message. "You should have mine now. If Sophia approaches you or bothers you, call me. I promise I won't let her hurt you. But in the meantime, try to avoid her."

The late bell rang. "I have to go to class," Jin said. "Are you sure you'll be okay?"

Mina nodded and waved as he got up to leave. He looked worried, so she gave him a weak smile. "Thanks. I'll be all right."

"If I don't see you later, then I'll catch up with you in Psych tomorrow morning, okay?"

Mina nodded absently and watched as he headed for the building. At the door, he turned and waved one last time, looking less real and more like her webcomic character.

Once she was all alone, Mina looked up at the sky and said, "Hello, I'm ready to wake up now, please!"

When nothing happened, she closed her eyes and slouched down. Her hand caught in the strap of her fanny pack. She slowly opened it and saw her mini tablet. This whole dream sequence started because of her webcomic. Turning the tablet on, she saw the battery was down to 25 percent. She clicked the Wi-Fi signal and pulled up *The School of Secrets.* Mina's eyes bulged as she rapidly scrolled through the latest episode. This was not what she'd drawn and uploaded the night before. This was an entirely different story, starring a brand-new character who looked exactly like her, wore the same clothes she had on, and had the same thoughts she'd been thinking.

"Holy crap," Mina whispered. Everything that had happened to her this morning was chronicled in her webcomic. From the glitching tablet and the lightning strikes to the moment she saw Jin and Sophia. The last panel was of her sitting on the bench, looking at her tablet.

Furious, Mina let out a frustrated yell and grabbed her digital pen. She pressed the eraser function and tried to delete the scene. Suddenly, the bench she was sitting on crashed to the ground, and she fell off with a painful thud. She stared in disbelief. The right legs of the bench were gone, as if someone had erased them from existence. On her tablet, the image of the bench was also missing the right two legs, correlating to the marks she'd made with her pen. With an unsteady hand, she hit the undo button. Immediately, the bench returned to its original state.

"What the heck?"

Resisting the urge to fling her tablet away, Mina deliberately made the bench disappear and reappear again.

"Oh, crap! I gotta get out of here!" she shrieked. This

was all too much for her to take in. Either she was dreaming or she'd suddenly developed magical abilities.

No, she had to be dreaming. But what could she do to wake herself up? She just wanted the nightmare to end.

Shoving her tablet and pen back into her bag, Mina ran out of the courtyard and onto the street. The only thought in her head was to go home. She could barely see due to the excruciating pain of the migraine that pounded inside her skull and the nausea roiling her stomach.

She needed to get into her bed and sleep. The streets were familiar; she knew her way home. Maybe she was in the hospital and they'd prescribed narcotics that were causing trippy visions. She couldn't hold the thought; she felt violently ill. And a frigid wind was now blowing into her face, making her shiver uncontrollably. She didn't understand why it was so unseasonably cold.

Mina soon found herself in front of her town house. With a sob of relief, she punched in the security code and entered. After kicking off her boots, she pulled herself up the stairs and into her room, where she collapsed into bed and passed out.

CHAPTER 9

Through the Looking Glass

Mina opened her eyes to the incessant ringing of an alarm. Her room was dark. She looked over at her clock. Six a.m. Why would she set her alarm so early on a Sunday? Was she supposed to do something? No—there was nothing special happening today. Puzzled, she sat up in her bed and thought back to her weird dreams.

"What was that all about?" she said out loud.

They were the most vivid dreams she'd ever experienced in her life. She wondered if they had something to do with the horrible migraine she'd suffered all night. It was probably why she was still so tired and thirsty. As much as she hated to get up, she needed to get some cold water or, better yet, some of Mrs. Song's barley tea. She dragged herself out of bed and looked for her slippers but couldn't find them. Puzzled, she walked by her desk to check the bathroom—only to freeze in horror. Her Wacom Cintiq tablet was gone.

Mina shrieked in alarm. Telling herself not to panic, she tried to remember what happened yesterday. Her tablet was malfunctioning. Was it broken? Maybe her father had taken it in for servicing? Mina ran to his room, but it was dark and empty. She bolted downstairs, shouting for her father, but there was no one home.

Mina sagged; she shouldn't have been surprised. Her dad was never home. She ran back up to grab her cell phone and call him.

Her fanny pack was on the bed in a tangle of sheets, but her phone was not there. Thinking hard, she remembered stuffing her phone into her jacket pocket. Spying her jacket on the floor, she unzipped her pocket and found her phone. It was dead.

After plugging it into the charger next to her bed, Mina saw a slew of text messages from Saachi and Megan. She ignored them and tried to call her father. The call wouldn't go through. She tried again. There was no ringing. Something was wrong with the phone service, but texts were coming through. That was odd. She switched to her messages and could see that Saachi and Megan were still texting her in the group chat.

As she scrolled through the messages, a rising panic assailed her.

> **Saachi:** Mina you creep! I can't believe you put yourself in your own webcomic but refused to put me or Megan in it! Some friend you are!

> **Megan:** We are disappointed

Saachi: However, I must give you an A+ on the love triangle, even though it is kind of creepy that its YOU!

Megan: It's creepy and I love it love it love it I didn't think you had it in you, Mina Lee! And way to throw everyone off on who the real hero of the story is!!! Hint: it's not scary blue fingered Sophia! I never liked that girl . . .

Saachi: She made herself a main character!

Megan: Kind of awesome, not gonna lie.

Saachi: She refused to put us in it!

Megan: Yeah, that's uncool! Expect you to include your new main character/love interest's best friends in your webcomic or else . . . 😵

Saachi: But how are you posting all this new content so quickly? And aren't you in your SAT course right now? Did you schedule them?
Mina?
Mina?

Megan: Mina is ignoring us . . .

Saachi: She probably forgot her phone at home again

Also, Megan, why are you awake before noon on a Saturday? What happened? Alien invasion?

Megan: I'm traveling with my parents

Saachi: Oh right LOL

Mina dropped her phone on the bed and sat down hard. *What the hell are they talking about?*

A terrible thought had her reaching to turn on the light on her nightstand. Immediately, Mina saw what she'd been afraid to see. Her room was not her room. Which was to say, it was her room, but void of her personal belongings. No art on the walls, no books or clothing thrown around haphazardly. Mina crawled back into bed and pulled the covers over her head. She could hear how loud her breathing was over the rapid beating of her heart. She must still be dreaming.

"Wake up, Mina! Please wake up!"

She couldn't breathe under the heaviness of the covers. Sitting up, she reached for her mini tablet and turned it on. It opened immediately to the last scene: her falling asleep in her bed, clothing still on and everything. She scrolled up and once again saw the disappearing bench. Only this time, the scene right after was of her running, panicked, down the streets until she entered her house. This was not just someone hacking into her webcomic. This was some surreal science-fiction crap messing with her brain.

A warning popped up on the screen signaling the battery was at 18 percent. Plugging the tablet in with trembling fingers, Mina felt overwhelmed with emotions. She couldn't brush this off as a dream. She was too awake. She was scared and confused. What was happening to her? She'd thought she was dreaming about her webcomic world, not living in it. But now even her house was just a webcomic setting.

As her eyes panned across her room, Mina went over to her walk-in closet. She turned on the light and squinted her eyes against the brightness. This was her closet but not. It looked neat and tidy, exactly how she would've drawn a generic closet. No paintings leaning against the walls. No piles of clothing all over the floor. No overflowing drawers that couldn't be closed.

Everything was organized and easy to find. Generic dresses, tidy shirts, basic sweaters, brand-new designer jeans, and lots of black pants. This was not her wardrobe. These clothes had never been worn before.

This is my house and yet not my house. This is my closet but not my clothing. This is all so bizarre.

She turned on the light in her room, grabbed a book off the desk, and slammed it on her head. It hurt less than she thought it would, but she did feel dizzy. She wasn't dreaming.

"Okay, so if the webcomic is the problem, I'll just delete it. See, problem solved!"

She picked up her tablet, toggled to her account page on Toonwebz, and tried to delete all the episodes of *The School of Secrets,* but an error message kept popping up.

"Why won't you let me delete this!"

She threw herself onto the bed and buried her face in her hands. She was trapped in her webcomic, and she didn't know what to do.

Mina took a deep breath. What she needed was a hot shower and food, in that order. Maybe that would help clear her head.

Everything in the bathroom was also new and untouched. Generic brands of soap, shampoo, conditioner, toothbrush, toothpaste. She felt like a stranger in her own house, which wasn't her house.

After showering, she dug through all the drawers until she found a decent pair of jeans and a slouchy, off-the-shoulder black sweater.

Her stomach started gurgling. Mina realized she hadn't eaten lunch or dinner. She was both starving and thirsty, although her thirst seemed to be bothering her more. She picked up her phone from the bed, then ran downstairs to the kitchen and opened the fridge. The shelves were practically empty. No Korean food prepared by Mrs. Song. Nothing to make a sandwich. Not even any yogurt. All she could find was eggs, butter, lactose-free milk, and jam.

Lactose-free milk? So this world knows I'm lactose intolerant?

She checked the rice cooker. It was cold and empty and looked like it hadn't been used, ever. What in the world was she supposed to eat? Closing the fridge, she noticed a bunch of takeout menus clipped to a magnet. Mina opened the pantry door and found granola bars, rice, cereal, bread, peanut butter, and cans of tuna fish.

Gross, I hate tuna fish.

Because Mrs. Song did all the shopping and cooking,

Mina had gotten used to eating mostly Korean food. But here, there weren't even any instant noodles or Spam, staples in most Korean kitchens. She would have killed for a bowl of her favorite spicy ramen. There was nothing healthy or Korean in the pantry. Not that ramen was healthy.

Mina pulled out the peanut butter, bread, and jam and cautiously opened them all. They looked and smelled fine. The bread wasn't even stale.

She quickly made a peanut butter and jam sandwich and ate it with some skim milk. When she put the glass down, she noticed a new cell phone and wallet on top of a laptop.

Inside the wallet, she found a wad of cash, a student ID, a credit card, and a driver's license with her picture on it.

"Well, that's another thing this world got wrong." Mina sighed, looking at the driver's license. "Although it would be nice to have one."

She was relieved to see the money and cell phone, grateful that the webcomic world was providing her with the basics she would need to survive. This thought immediately reminded Mina of her father.

Mina put down the phone and went back to her father's bedroom. When she opened the closet door, her heart sank to see it was completely empty. Since she hadn't drawn her father into the webcomic, did it mean he wasn't in this world with her?

For the first time in her life, Mina felt completely alone. While her father was hardly home, he was still always checking up on her and taking care of her.

"I am trapped in the prison of my own creation," she whispered.

She returned to the kitchen, picked up the cell phone, and found that it unlocked with facial recognition.

"Oh my gosh, this character really is me," Mina marveled aloud. Trying not to freak out, she looked for the calendar and nearly dropped the phone. The date was Wednesday, October 12.

"That can't be right! It's only September!"

She opened the calendar app to find a neatly organized schedule of her classes.

First period, AP Calculus, Whitman, Rm 257

Second period, AP Psychology, Chen, Rm 156

Third period, AP English Literature and Composition, Meiers, Rm 109

Lunch

Fourth period, French 6, Martinez, Rm 142

Fifth period, AP Environmental Science, Tran, Rm 221

Sixth period, AP Studio Art, King, Rm 335

Seventh period, Ceramics, Tippie, Rm 340

Dang, this schedule is too intense. This is what Dad would want me to take. Closing the calendar app, Mina noticed the time and gasped. The cell phone read 7:15 a.m. How could over an hour have passed so fast? The first bell was at 7:39. Should she go to school or stay home and figure out how she'd gotten here? No—the house was empty, and when she'd been pulled into this world, it had put her in school.

Might as well go and search for answers there.

Turning around, she knocked the glass to the floor, spilling milk down the front of her pants. Mina cursed in annoyance and then yelped when she stepped on a shard. Luckily, she was wearing socks, but her foot hurt and was starting to bleed. She would have to clean up the mess and change her clothes, and she was already so late. Staring at the broken glass, Mina was reminded of the bench in the courtyard. She wondered what would happen if she erased the cup. She limped up to her room and unplugged her tablet, even though the battery had charged to only 21 percent. She opened it to the most recent scene. Using her digital pen, she erased the broken glass off the floor.

She felt a bizarre rush of air around her body, and before she could even blink, Mina was back in the kitchen, her tablet and pen clutched in her hands. On the counter stood the unbroken glass of milk, just like before. And her clothing was completely dry, no sign of a spill anywhere. She peered down at the bottom of her foot. There was no blood and no pain. She took off her sock and found no cut.

Whoa!

When Mina checked the tablet, she realized that the scene had deleted itself, resetting the webcomic to the previous scene, before she knocked over the glass. She had just teleported herself back in time.

"Holy shit!" Mina was stunned. This was an incredible gift to have. She wondered if it meant she could reset the entire episode, scene by scene. Sitting at the kitchen table, Mina tried to delete the earlier scenes, but again the error message flashed across the screen.

This must be a rule of the world, Mina thought. *I can only reset a scene right away, maybe within a few minutes.*

She decided to test the theory by spilling water on the table and timing how long she could wait before the scene wouldn't reset. It ended up being exactly one minute. Mina wondered how useful it could be to change something that happened only sixty seconds ago. But it was better than nothing.

A sudden longing to be safe at home, talking to her friends and eating Mrs. Song's delicious food, filled Mina. This new world was too strange and stressful. The messages in the group chat showed that her friends hadn't noticed she was gone. She pulled out her real-world phone and looked at the time stamp on the last text. It was September 10, Saturday morning.

Mina looked at the other phone. The date and time were completely different. How could this be? She calculated that she'd arrived in this world around noon yesterday, a Tuesday. It was now 8:15 on Wednesday morning. At home, she'd been waiting for the car service to take her to SAT prep. She checked the car app and saw a notice for a cancellation fee. Her ride had left at 8:20 in the morning. Her real-world phone was now reading 9:10 a.m. So all the time she'd spent here was not even an hour at home? None of this made any sense. Mina could feel her head begin to throb again. She couldn't think too hard about what was happening. She didn't want to trigger another migraine.

On the chair next to the laptop was a gray messenger bag just like the one Mina had at home. She picked it up, shoved her tablet, wallet, and phones into an inner compartment, and zipped it closed.

In the foyer, she put on her boots. A quick peek in the shoe cabinet showed sneakers, heels, and a few other basic shoes. Not much of a selection. Mina was also struck by the fact that there were no men's shoes. At home, the cabinet held both her and her father's footwear. Here, there weren't even any house slippers. A reminder that her dad wasn't in this world.

Taking several calming breaths, Mina stepped outside and was immediately hit with a blast of cold air. She shivered and went back into the house and opened the coat closet. Inside were a few coats and jackets. She threw on a warm black coat and started walking to school.

Outside, the skies were clear and bright. Mina avoided looking at the buildings and people around her, confused by the similarities and differences of the neighborhood. The tree in front of her house was the same dogwood that she'd grown up with. But everything else seemed slightly off.

Mina pulled up her class schedule. She checked the time and realized that first period was almost over and she would have to rush to make it to second period. Mina ran the last few blocks and stopped abruptly at the sight of the building. It was Bellington, but a version interpreted from her webcomic. The school banner was a different color. The tall stately trees out front had been a bit boring to draw, so Mina had drawn dogwoods, cherry blossoms, and even a few magnolia trees instead. Just having different trees made the school look unfamiliar and off.

She found her second-period class but hesitated uneasily at the door before walking in and greeting the teacher. Mina did a double take when she recognized him as a real teacher from her school.

"Nice to meet you." Mr. Chen smiled. "There's an open seat right over there for you."

He gestured to a desk next to a girl with long black

hair and a friendly smile. She also seemed vaguely familiar to Mina.

"Hi, I'm Lauren!"

"Hey, I'm Mina."

"This is Abby and Diana." Lauren pointed to the two girls right behind her. "I love your hair! It is so cool!"

Abby and Diana scooched closer to gush their compliments.

Mina slid into the open seat next to Lauren and blinked in shock at the other two girls. She'd definitely seen them at her real school. What was going on?

"Where'd you get your hair done? I wanna get silver highlights also!" Abby, who was white with dark blond hair, raved.

"You'd have to do your whole head if you wanted the silver to show," Diana said. She was a very attractive Black girl with cool glasses and long braids. "So, Mina, did you just move to the area? Where from?"

What had she told Jin?

"New York," she replied.

"Where in New York?" Diana pushed. "I go there often to visit relatives."

Auntie Jackie's apartment was in Brooklyn. What was the neighborhood again?

"Windsor Terrace in Brooklyn. Closer to Prospect Park."

"Oh, I don't know Brooklyn at all," Diana said, disappointed.

Mina let out an internal sigh of relief.

"Since you're new here, you haven't made a lot of friends yet, right?" Lauren asked.

Mina nodded, her head whirling in confusion.

"I know how hard it is to be new and know no one," Lauren said with her sweet smile. "Here, I'll give you my number."

"Us too!" the other girls chimed in.

Mina was surprised at how friendly they were. She held up her phone and let them type in their info. Just as she got her phone back, the bell rang and the teacher started attendance. It was still shocking when he called her name. She really did write herself into this reality.

As the class began a discussion on abnormalities of the brain, Lauren texted Mina.

> **Lauren:** So have you met anyone else here at school?

> **Mina:** I don't know, maybe?

> **Lauren:** I was just wondering if you'd met Jin Young Kanter because he's been staring at you this whole time.

Immediately, Mina glanced around. Jin was sitting on the other side of the room, staring at her. He smiled and gave her a slight nod. Mina flushed and looked away.

Her phone vibrated in her hand.

> **Lauren:** So you do know him!

> **Mina:** Yeah, I met him yesterday.

> **Lauren:** I think he likes you!

Mina rolled her eyes.

> **Mina:** No, he's just very nice. He helped me out yesterday when I had a run in with some mean girls.

> **Lauren:** Oh no! What happened? You have to be really careful. There are some scary people here

"If I see anyone texting, I'll be keeping their phone, and a parent will have to come in to sign for it," Mr. Chen said loudly as he came to stand right in front of Lauren and Mina.

The girls quickly pocketed their phones. Mina's head was spinning from the normalcy of taking notes in class in a school that wasn't real. It didn't help that she was hyper-aware of Jin sitting on the other side of the room.

At the end of class, Jin walked over to Mina's desk.

"Hey, Mina," Jin said. "How come you didn't reply to any of my texts?"

"You texted me?" Mina asked in surprise.

"Didn't you get them?"

She took out her phone and was scrolling through her texts when she abruptly remembered she'd given him her real-world number. Mina realized that texting between the two worlds wasn't possible.

"Oh, sorry, I think I gave you my old number. I can't remember this one so well," she said.

Jin took her phone and inputted his number and texted something.

"Now I have it." He smiled. "Don't forget to call me if you need me."

With a little wave, he left. Lauren nudged Mina in the shoulder.

"Told you!" Lauren laughed. "I heard he doesn't have a date to Homecoming. Maybe you can go with him."

"I just met him," Mina protested.

"So?"

The other two girls crowded close to Mina as they all exited the classroom.

"Don't listen to Lauren," Diana said. "Jin's nice, but any girl he pays attention to gets hurt. It's not worth it."

Lauren frowned. "That's right, we need to warn you about Sophia. Listen, we gotta run now, but come meet us for lunch. I'll text you where we'll be."

The three girls rushed off, and Mina winced in pain. The migraine she'd been worried about crept up her head. The jostling of bodies and the sheer volume of noise made the migraine intensify. Her head hurt so much she was starting to shiver. And the light was making it worse.

Mina walked slowly in the crowded hallway, keeping her eyes down, until she reached the nurse's office. All she wanted was to curl into the fetal position and sleep the pain away.

CHAPTER 10

My Best Friend Jin

Wednesday, October 12

Mina was ten, watching her mother sketching a portrait, referencing a black-and-white photo. The boy in the picture looked very familiar to Mina, but she didn't know why.

"Mom, who is that?"

Her mother put down her pencils and turned to face Mina with a serious expression.

"Mina, you know how hard it's been for Auntie Jackie since Jin passed away?"

Mina nodded. They used to see Auntie Jackie every day, but since her move to New York, it was only once a month.

"It's been hard for her, seeing you growing up and missing Jin," her mother continued. "Last time we visited her, she cried to see how big you'd gotten."

Mina remembered that. It had made her cry also.

"Jackie realized that more than anything she just wanted

to know what Jin would look like as he grew up. An age pro-gression photography company created pictures of Jin at ten, fourteen, and eighteen."

Each photograph showed an older Jin, but there was a strange warped effect about them.

Mina looked at her mother doubtfully.

"I know what you're thinking," her mother said with a sad smile. "Is this really a good idea? Won't it make Auntie Jackie more upset to see these photographs, knowing Jin is no lon-ger with us? And these photos are not great. They don't do Jin justice—he was such a beautiful boy. I asked her to give them to me and let me do portraits instead."

She opened her sketchbook and showed Mina the dozens of drawings she'd done of Jin.

Mina could feel the tears threatening to spill over at the sight of her old friend. These sketches showed Jin laughing and smiling just the way she remembered him, but slightly older at ten, and then as a handsome teenage boy with a dimpled smile.

Mina woke up suddenly. She took off her sleep mask and sat up. Nothing had changed. She was still in the web-comic world.

She placed a hand on her head. At least her migraine seemed gone, but she was still so fatigued. She checked the time to see that she'd been sleeping for thirty minutes. But it felt like only five.

"How are you feeling now?" the nurse asked. "Do you need to go home?"

Yes, desperately.

"I feel a little better," Mina replied. "Resting with the sleep mask really helped."

The nurse nodded. "It might be useful to keep one

on you to help block the light when you feel a migraine coming."

Mina thanked the nurse and wandered out into the hallway. It was not quite lunch period, but there wasn't enough time to go to fourth period. Instead, Mina headed to the courtyard. Sitting on the bench, she took out her tablet to see what had uploaded since she'd learned of her reset power. The battery had drained down to 16 percent, and Mina made a mental note to charge it as soon as she could.

She scrolled through the episode and saw that the web-comic had captured only those scenes that were relevant to the storytelling, which Mina would've found fascinating if she hadn't been in the story herself. Most of the panels were from second period. Mina could feel herself flushing. The webcomic made it seem as if Jin was really interested in her instead of just being concerned.

"Jin," Mina marveled. At least now she knew why his face seemed so familiar. He looked just like her childhood friend, only grown up and healthy. The Jin her mother had drawn for Auntie Jackie.

That must have been the connection.

She should've been happier. This was her old friend brought to life. But if anything, she was more afraid than ever. She was stuck in the world of her comic. How did it happen? Why was she here?

At that moment, a breeze sent the leaves above Mina fluttering, and she caught the play of light on the ground. She watched it for a long moment, absorbed in its rhythmic motions. It calmed her. There was a Japanese word for this. Her mother had taught it to her.

Komorebi.

It was why she loved her studio. The way sunlight would weave through the leaves of the dogwood tree in front of their house. That was what komorebi meant. Mina remembered how she would sit at her mother's feet in the warmth of the sunshine as her mother created beautiful, realistic paintings that looked like they could breathe.

As she stared at the rays of light dancing in the air before her, she suddenly had a clear memory of her mother consoling her.

"Mina, I know you are sad about losing Jin, but I want you to always keep him in your heart. Nobody is ever gone as long as you remember them."

There was never any chance that she'd forget Jin. Every year, she celebrated his birthday with Auntie Jackie by going to his favorite Chinese Korean restaurant and eating jajangmyeon noodles. Mina still remembered what a messy eater he'd been, getting the sauce all over his face and even in his hair. The memory made her smile. She missed Jin so much.

Just then, she became aware of someone calling her name.

"Mina, I texted you but you didn't respond! But here you are!" Lauren beamed as she urged Mina to join her at a nearby table. Abby and Diana were already there, as well as another girl named Tracey, whose long black hair, dark brown complexion, and big brown eyes reminded Mina of Saachi.

The girls immediately pulled out their lunches and started eating and gossiping. Mina tried to follow along but was distracted by all the food and her rumbling stomach.

As if she knew what Mina was thinking, Lauren handed her a bag of carrots.

"Here, eat this," Lauren said. "You look like you're gonna pass out."

In the space of less than a minute, Mina was gifted with cheese sticks, potato chips, cookies, fruit, and even a can of sparkling water.

"You all are the best." Mina was sincerely grateful for their kindness and generosity. If she really did go to school here, she'd happily be friends with all of them. For a few minutes, she ate the food and listened to the other girls spilling tea about people she didn't know, and then Lauren finally pounced.

"So, tell us what happened with Jin," she demanded.

Mina looked at the circle of curious faces around her and suppressed a groan.

She then carefully explained what had happened when Jin saved her from the bullies, but didn't mention Sophia's electric sparks.

"Wow, so your very first day here, you come in at lunchtime, get bullied, get saved by Jin, and then go home, without making it to any of your classes. Harsh," Diana said with a sympathetic look.

"I think it was a great first day! Jin clearly likes you," Lauren whispered loudly.

"Sophia will have a cow," Abby with the blond hair and freckles cut in. "She scares me."

"She scares everyone," Diana said. "Didn't she send Jane Powell and some other girl to the emergency room? It's been weeks and no one's seen Jane since."

"Nobody's sure," Lauren replied. "Those are just rumors."

"Aw, come on, she has a fight with Sophia and ends up in the emergency room!" Diana continued. "Mina, that girl is bad news. Here, someone show her a picture so she can avoid her."

"I know what she looks like," Mina said.

"What? How?" Everyone was speaking in hushed whispers and had moved closer together. Mina told them how Sophia had stared at her as if she wanted to kill her.

Diana reached over and grabbed Mina's hand. "You need to be careful. There are some strange rumors about her. The kids that got hurt. They were burned badly. Severe electric burns. But nobody reports her because everyone is too scared. And she's obsessed with Jin. You might need to stay away from him."

Everyone was silent as they stared worriedly at Mina.

Mina chewed on her lip. Maybe avoiding Jin wasn't a bad idea. Not only was he the main character of her webcomic, but she had no idea why she was pulled in to this world.

"Yeah, you're probably right," she said. "I'll try not to get too close to him."

Lauren looked disappointed. "Poor Jin," she sighed. "I feel so bad for him."

The girls were quiet for a moment, then Tracey, who had not spoken much at all, suddenly nudged Diana hard.

"We have to warn her about Merco," Tracey whispered.

Lauren and Abby both shook their heads. "It's just an urban legend," Abby said.

"I don't think it's a good idea for us to spread it," Lauren said.

"No, Tracey's right—Mina should know about Merco," Diana responded seriously. "We don't know what's true and what's not. It's like warning her about Sophia. Better for her to know everything so she can be extra careful."

Diana gave the others a look, which made them all nod.

"There are stories that soldiers who work for a corporation called Merco have been rounding up kids with gifts," Diana said flatly. "I don't know how true it is, but the reality is that nine students have disappeared and nobody knows why. Their families are gone. They vanished."

"What do you mean gifts?" Mina asked cautiously. In her webcomic, it was a secret. How much of the truth was actually known?

"Those rumors about Sophia? If they're true, then she is one of the Gifted, kids with superpowers."

Mina looked at all their faces after this pronouncement. Their expressions were a mix of fear, excitement, and curiosity.

"You're kidding, right?"

Lauren patted her arm. "I know it sounds too weird, but that's what the rumors are about. And maybe there's nothing to it, but strange things keep happening at school."

The girls began to describe several events that Mina had created for the webcomic, causing her to choke on her food.

"When did this all start?" she asked.

The girls looked blank for a moment. "I have no idea," Diana answered. She glanced at the others.

Tracey shook her head. "I feel like it started at the

beginning of this semester. I mean no one had even heard of the Gifted or Merco before this year. Who knew that there were people with actual superpowers? And if it wasn't for those Merco soldiers, the Gifted wouldn't have to hide their powers."

"Sh! Lower your voice, Tracey," Lauren whispered. "We never know who could be listening."

Tracey's eyes grew round, and Lauren quickly changed the subject to college applications.

If these things started happening not too long ago, then this really was Mina's webcomic story. But did she create the webcomic world? Or was this a world she'd written her webcomic into? Also, Sophia was not the hero Mina had intended her to be, but instead she was probably the villain. If this was Mina's story, nothing was turning out the way she had imagined.

As she noted the nervous and awkward way her new friends had changed the subject, she could sense their underlying worry. Whatever was happening here was related to her. Maybe this was why she'd been brought into this world. To fix what she'd done before it was too late.

CHAPTER 11

A Dangerous Story

After lunch, Mina spent fifth period hunkered down in a hidden corner of the library so she could charge her tablet. She sat on the floor next to an outlet and dozed off again. She woke up to realize sixth period was over. It was weird how fast time had flown by. Almost as if the day had sped up.

Entering the staircase, Mina heard a familiar voice. From around the bend, she caught sight of Saachi laughing and talking with Megan as they walked up the stairs together. Mina blinked and rubbed her eyes, but her best friends were still there. She froze midstep and gaped at the approaching girls. She'd missed them so much! Saachi and Megan eyed her curiously as they passed.

"What's her problem?" Megan asked Saachi.

"Clearly overcome by my stunning beauty," quipped Saachi. They both laughed and continued up the stairs, not giving Mina another glance.

The person behind Mina shoved past her with a loud curse word. Dazed, Mina walked down to keep from being trampled.

She'd drawn her two best friends into the webcomic world, but they didn't know who she was. The rush of happiness at seeing them was crushed by overwhelming misery. She missed her friends and Mrs. Song and her dad. She desperately wanted to go home. She wandered out onto the third floor as the late bell rang and meandered down the hallway for a while before deciding to cut class. The way her day was going, she wouldn't be surprised if she drew something and it came alive in front of a class full of strangers.

Mina wondered why she was even at school when she should've been trying to find her way back to her world. The real world. Determined to leave, Mina headed to a narrow staircase in the farthest corner of the building that was usually empty at her real school. It was dark and cramped and always smelled vaguely of cigarette smoke and skunk. Opening the stairway door, she found it to be exactly the same. She heard raised voices two floors below. Mina silently peered down the stairwell. Sophia, Kayla, and Jewel were arguing.

"Did you find anything out about that girl?" Sophia was angry. "I've never seen her before. Why did Jin go off with her?"

"I don't know and I don't care," Kayla responded. "Let it go already. And leave Jin alone. You're the worst kind of stalker."

"What are you saying?" Sophia's voice was hard.

"He doesn't like you, Sophia!"

"Shut up! You don't know anything! I just need to find her...."

"What for?" Kayla asked. "So you can hurt her too? Send her to the hospital? Or what, kill someone this time? You're going too far and making it dangerous for everyone."

From her vantage point, Mina could see the blue electricity sparking from Sophia's fingertips. Mina bit her lip. Kayla and Jewel were Sophia's friends. Sophia wouldn't hurt them, would she?

Jewel stepped between them and put her hands on their arms.

That's right—her gift is calming people and persuading them, but she has to touch them for her power to work. Pretty impressive, Mina thought.

"Sophia, you should listen to us," Jewel said in a low, melodic voice. "There've been a lot of rumors about you lately. You need to stop bringing attention to yourself. Merco kidnapped some students a few weeks ago."

"And that was your fault also!" Kayla cut in. "You nearly killed Jane Powell in chemistry lab. If Jewel hadn't been able to persuade everyone it had been an electric short, and if that poor Ryan kid hadn't healed her so quickly, you would've been the one who disappeared, not him."

"That was not my fault. Jane was being a total bitch to me," Sophia retorted.

"You've got to control your temper." Jewel put both hands on Sophia, as if to try to contain her anger.

Sophia threw off Jewel's hands. "Don't use your gift on me, Jewel. Don't try to control me."

"Damn it, Sophia! What's wrong with you these days?"

Kayla burst out. "You're not the same as you were before you got your gift. It's gone to your head."

"What about you, Kayla? Just admit that you're jealous of me because I'm more powerful than you and your stupid wind tricks."

A sudden gust whooshed up the stairwell, sending papers flying through the air.

"Jealous? Of you? You've become a dangerous fathead who thinks nothing of hurting people to get what you want. And you're fixated on Jin! But guess what, he doesn't like you. He doesn't want anything to do with you. I mean, it's pretty obvious that he hates you!"

"Shut up!"

Jewel attempted again to intercede. "Sophia, what's wrong? You've never been like this before about Jin. You've always liked him, but this feels weird. You can tell us."

There was a long pause, and Sophia's voice was so low Mina had to strain to hear what she was saying.

"I don't know," she said. "I can't control myself when I'm around him."

"Can you tell me why?"

"Because I'm supposed to be with him." Sophia got loud again. "We're meant to be together. No matter how much he fights it, he can't fight our destiny."

"What are you saying? You sound crazy!" Kayla's voice was filled with frustration and disbelief. "Snap out of it. He's not your destiny."

"Yes, he is! I had a vision. We're the perfect couple. A power couple. We belong together!"

That stupid webcomic!

Mina wanted to scream. She'd actually written those words about Sophia and Jin. That they were the perfect power couple. Sophia's obsession was because of Mina's webcomic.

"Sophia, as your friend, I'm telling you this honestly," Kayla said. "You need to see a psychiatrist. This behavior is obsessive and dangerous and not like you."

"I'm not obsessive! I just know this is the right thing to do, and I have to convince him to be with me!" The last part was almost a shout.

"No, you don't! You're deluding yourself!"

"Stop talking to me! I don't want to hear it anymore!"

"You're being an idiot!"

Mina could see that the girls were in each other's faces, both holding back their powers.

"Enough, guys! Someone could hear us!"

Jewel was trying to get between the two of them and push them apart.

"I said don't touch me, Jewel!" Sophia shoved Jewel, but Kayla caught her before she could fall down.

"You've changed, Sophia," Kayla said bitterly. "I don't know who you are anymore. But I know I don't want to be around you."

"And you're no friend of mine! You hate me because my gift is stronger!"

"I hate you because you're a raging bitch!"

It happened so fast Mina almost missed it. The flash of electric blue lightning, Jewel shouting "Look out, Kayla!" and pushing her out of the way. Kayla's scream and Jewel's soft sobbing. The stairwell door slamming shut as Sophia ran off.

"Jewel, Jewel! I'm so sorry! I shouldn't have fought with her!" Kayla was crying. "Let's go to the nurse now! It looks really bad."

"No," Jewel said. "Ms. A won't let us go if she sees this. She'll come after Sophia...."

"I don't care about her! I care about you!"

"If she gets caught, we all get caught—you know that." Jewel whimpered in pain. "But she's so out of control."

Mina couldn't bear to hear Jewel's sobs. She turned on her tablet and found the last panel: Jewel crying over the burn on her arm. Mina was well within the time to reset the scene, but she didn't want to bring Sophia back. She grabbed her digital pen and carefully erased the burn on Jewel's arm. As soon as she was done, a new panel appeared, showing Mina holding the tablet and erasing something.

That means it worked, right?

"What the hell?" There was complete silence in the stairwell.

Mina peeked over the banister and was startled to see Kayla and Jewel staring up at her in shock. With a squeak of alarm, Mina started to run up the stairs, but a blast of wind stopped her in her tracks and Kayla appeared in front of her.

"It's you! The girl Sophia is mad at, right?" Kayla said, excitement coloring her voice. "You have a gift. You healed Jewel." This last part she whispered just as Jewel caught up to them.

"Thank you," Jewel said as she enveloped Mina in a warm hug. Keeping hold of Mina's arm, Jewel guided her downstairs and toward the exit. "Let's get out of here and go get something to eat and chat?"

Kayla grinned. "I'll drive."

Caught between the two girls, Mina felt she had no choice but to leave with them. But maybe this was a good thing. She needed information, however she could get it.

Kayla drove them to a coffee shop. They bought drinks and sat in a secluded corner in the back.

The two girls leaned toward Mina with similar looks of anticipation and determination. Mina was instantly on the defensive. They weren't being nice just because she healed Jewel; they were trying to find out everything they could about her. Given that Sophia was not the person Mina had written her to be, she was extra concerned about being alone with Sophia's best friends. She had no idea who they really were.

"Tell us all about it," Kayla said. "When, where, what is it?"

Their intensity made Mina anxious.

"When, where, what about what?" she countered.

Jewel placed her hand gently on Mina's arm. "Don't be nervous. We won't hurt you. We're on your side, I promise."

She's trying to use her gift on me.

Mina was very curious to know what Jewel's power would feel like. She looked into Jewel's bright blue eyes and could sense the warmth she exuded. It made Mina feel like she could trust her. Something about Jewel's personality itself was calming. It reminded Mina of being at the beach with the warm sand sliding through her toes and the sound of the ocean waves lapping nearby. But she couldn't tell if that was the gift or if she just liked Jewel.

Mina stretched, moving her arm out of Jewel's reach. Leaning back in her chair, she realized she had to be cautious. There was no way she could tell them who she really was. She didn't know what the ramifications of such a revelation would be, or if the girls would even believe her. She was only now seeing how much unintentional harm she had caused in this world in her quest to tell an entertaining story.

"I still don't understand what you're asking," she replied.

Kayla sighed. "Okay, I get it. You don't completely trust us. Can't blame you. We've been Sophia's best friends for years. But I swear we would never hurt you, and we won't tell anyone else about your gift. We both have them too. You might have noticed I have the ability to channel wind. Jewel has this amazing ability to calm people down and can even persuade people to do things when she turns up her power. She could make you talk, but we want you to trust us."

Assessing the gazes of the two girls, Mina could sense their sincerity. She already knew that they were not like Sophia. But there was still no way she could tell them everything.

"When did you get these gifts?" Mina asked.

"Hmm, not exactly sure when. Before the beginning of the school year, maybe?" Kayla responded.

"Thirty-four days ago," Jewel answered.

Why thirty-four days? Mina tried to remember the timeline of the story. She had skipped forward a few days and even a week, as most comics tended to do. Had she actually sped up time in this world? Was that why everything felt so fast and rushed here? She calculated the math. This morning, her real-world phone was showing that one hour at home was somehow twenty-four hours here. She had uploaded the first episode on Thursday night at ten thirty. She'd been transported to this world on Saturday morning at eight thirty, thirty-four hours later. She nodded. They got their gifts when she first uploaded the new webcomic. And the webcomic had sped time up to correlate with the story. Wow, she was both awed and horrified.

"I don't even remember how it happened," Kayla said. "It was just suddenly something I could do. Shocked the hell out of me, that's for sure!"

Jewel laughed. "Me too."

Kayla leaned her head on Jewel's shoulder. "Thank God I had Jewel. I was so freaked out I couldn't control it at all, but Jewel kept me calm."

Jewel caressed Kayla's hair, a loving smile on her lips. "You weren't that bad. Although you did leave my room looking like a tornado had hit it."

"I'm so sorry about that." Kayla sat up to look at Jewel. "I broke so many things."

Jewel shrugged. "Nothing important, fortunately. Although the smell of all the perfume that got smashed is still lingering on my bed."

They both laughed, and Mina felt the awkwardness of intruding on what felt like an intimate moment. She cleared her throat loudly.

"What about Sophia? She must have really been spooked."

They separated and turned to face her, their cheeks rosy.

Kayla ran a hand through her thick blond hair. "Sophia was a mess. If it wasn't for Jewel, she might have burned the entire city down!"

"Like she did to her piano?" Jewel said.

The two friends glanced at each other sadly.

"What happened?" Mina asked.

"Sophia is an amazing pianist. Her dream is to play in big concert halls all over the world," Jewel said. "But when she got her power, she accidentally destroyed her piano, and her parents refused to buy her a new one. She was devastated and furious. She felt like her parents weren't being supportive, and I think that's why she's changed so much."

Kayla snorted. "Puh-lease! Bad things happen. But it doesn't have to change you into a murderous asshole. And besides, her parents didn't tell her to stop playing. They just didn't buy her a brand-new grand piano because it costs over thirty thousand dollars!"

Jewel patted Kayla's arm, and Mina could see Jewel's gift working on the other girl. There was something hypnotizing about Jewel's rich and soothing voice. Mina wondered how much was the gift and how much was just Jewel's natural charm and calming personality.

"Your talent must have been harder to discover," Mina said thoughtfully. "I bet Kayla didn't even notice you had one, am I right?"

Kayla shook her head. "I had no idea. Jewel is always such a calming force." She looked at her friend. "How did you find out?"

"I knew right away," Jewel responded. "I felt different. You guys always thought I was so calm all the time, but the truth is I was stressed. I just hid it well."

"What?" Kayla's mouth gaped. "I don't believe it!"

"No, it's true," Jewel continued. "But when I got the gift, it was different. Suddenly, instead of just trying to look calm, I actually was."

"Whoa, amazing," Kayla exclaimed. "And you didn't tell

me about it until we found out Jin and Mark had developed powers also."

"Kayla!" Jewel gave her a warning look, and Kayla gasped, covering her mouth with both her hands.

"Um, Mina, can you please pretend I didn't say anything about Jin and Mark?"

They both looked at Mina with worried expressions. Mina had to fight the urge to apologize to them for creating this superpower storyline and foisting it on their world.

"Don't worry, I would never tell anyone about this. I have as much to fear," Mina assured them.

They looked relieved, especially Kayla, who leaned forward with an expectant expression. "What about you? When did you discover your ... talent?"

"I didn't have any until this morning," Mina replied cautiously, trying to be as truthful as possible. She owed them that much. "I still don't know to what extent it is. I do know I had a cut this morning, and I was able to make it vanish. I wanted to try it on you, Jewel, because you were hurting so bad."

Jewel grasped Mina's hand gratefully. "Thank you so much. The pain was the worst I'd ever felt in my life. But you can't tell anyone about your healing gift, not even your best friends. It's dangerous being a Gifted, but especially for healers."

Kayla was nodding grimly. "Two kids with healing powers have disappeared recently. Both times, it was right after they publicly helped someone that Sophia hurt. Word is some big important type needs healers to keep from dying."

"I'm sorry, what?" Mina was confused. "What do you mean to keep from dying?"

"There are lots of rumors," Jewel said. "The one that we think is true is pretty messed up. Rowan Mercer, who's, like, a multibillionaire and the CEO of Merco, has been kidnapping the Gifted and experimenting on them to steal their powers for himself. But something went wrong, and now he needs healers to fix the damage."

Kayla slammed her fist on the table. "Bastard," she seethed.

The first part correlated with what Mina had created before she was brought to this world. But where was the "healers fixing Mercer" storyline coming from?

"Can you tell me exactly what happened to the last healer?" she asked.

Jewel nodded. "It was an accident in chem lab."

Kayla did a double take. "It was not an *accident*—it was all Sophia's fault. She's not rational when it comes to Jin!"

Letting out a calming breath, Jewel agreed. "It was Sophia's fault. She started a fire in chemistry lab, and this girl named Jane got burned pretty bad."

"I feel like you are leaving out some of the important nuances of the story, Jewel," Kayla interrupted. "Like the fact that Jane was Jin's partner on a group project and Sophia saw them at the library together. Even though Jane has a boyfriend, Sophia was jealous. And Jane has—well, had—beautiful curly black hair."

Mina's eyes widened in shock. "She burned her hair?"

The two girls looked at each other grimly.

"If it wasn't for the healer—his name was Ryan Tran—it

would've been far worse," Jewel said. "He was able to heal most of her burns, but she lost all her hair.

"Too many people saw what he did," Jewel continued. "Ms. A probably reported it to Merco, because the next day, there was a rumor that Ryan had been transferred to a school for the Gifted that nobody knows anything about."

"School, hah!" Kayla spat out. "More like prison. All thanks to Ms. A and her spies."

"Spies?" Mina asked.

"You have to be really careful—she's got a lot of students doing her dirty work," Kayla said.

"Who's Ms. A?" Mina asked.

"The assistant principal. But everyone calls her Ms. A because she used to be the physics teacher."

"Is that Ms. Alexander?"

Kayla shook her head. "Nah, that was the previous assistant principal. But people kept getting them mixed up so she goes by Ms. A."

Mina had a strange feeling. "So what is her name?"

"Sarah Allen," Jewel replied.

Mina was shocked. Sarah Allen was the name of her old physics teacher. The one Mina had based the evil assistant principal on.

"It was so weird. One day she was teaching physics, and the next day she was an assistant principal," Kayla said with a shrug.

Mina winced internally. In the real world, Sarah Allen also went by Ms. A. But she was still a physics teacher. In the last episode, Mina had briefly touched on the assistant principal being a spy for Merco, without naming her.

In retrospect, the whole evil administrator idea was not great. But maybe if she looked into what Ms. A was doing, she could find out what was now going on in the web-comic.

"That happened two weeks ago, and nobody's seen Ryan since," Jewel said.

"And Sophia?" Mina asked. "What about her? Everyone seems to know about her power, but she's still walking around, no problem! Why is that?"

Kayla and Jewel exchanged worried glances. "We don't know," Kayla said. "She has exactly the kind of power that Mercer was kidnapping Gifted for when this whole mess first started. He has to know about her."

"How many Gifted have disappeared besides the two healers?" Mina asked. This storyline was troubling her. She'd created only three episodes and had not gotten deep into the Mercer storyline yet. Whatever was happening with him now was all new to her.

"Maybe six or seven," Jewel said. "But we don't really know."

"You said Sophia has the type of power Mercer would have wanted. So if he knows about her, why hasn't he taken her?"

"Maybe he already has someone with electric power and doesn't need her?" Kayla shrugged. "Maybe she thinks she is strong enough to fight anyone who comes for her? Or maybe she's just a stupid jackass?"

"No, none of that makes any sense." Mina bit her lower lip hard. She had no idea what was causing the diverging storylines.

They were all silent for a minute, deep in their own thoughts.

Mina was trying to make connections between all the storylines. "Was Sophia the reason the other healer got transferred also?" she asked.

Kayla nodded. "See what I mean? Stupid jackass."

"But every time she hurts someone, a healer gets outed . . . ," Mina said slowly.

Jewel gasped and covered her mouth while Kayla shook her head hard.

"No, not even Sophia would sink that low," Kayla said emphatically.

"But you said so yourself, she's changed. She's a monster. . . ."

"I said no!"

The friendly atmosphere had shifted, and Mina felt an uneasy awkwardness with the others. Even seeing the evil Sophia was doing, they couldn't bring themselves to give up totally on her. Was this because of Mina's original storyline? She'd cast Jewel and Kayla as loyal best friends to Sophia. So maybe they couldn't break from her because the world was restricted by the rules Mina had made. And now they were all in real danger from a subplot she hadn't written.

I am the ultimate villain of my own superhero story.

This was an absolute nightmare.

CHAPTER 12

Finding Jin Again

Back at home, which was not her real home, Mina made a beeline upstairs and collapsed on the bed. The day had flown by so fast; she felt like she'd been trapped on a bullet train that never stopped. It was the sensation of not having enough time in a world that was speeding ahead. The stress was overwhelming. She just wanted to sleep and give her head a rest.

But sleep was impossible with her brain still on overload, and hunger gnawed on her insides. She needed food, and a lot of it. This she could do something about. Mina pulled up a grocery store app and quickly ordered instant noodles, frozen meals, pizzas, and snacks.

Bored with no one to talk to, or at least no one she felt safe talking to, Mina found herself doodling on some scraps of paper. Before she knew it, she'd sketched a picture of Jin, his dimple flashing next to his warm smile. His eyes stared straight at her. He was so incredibly attractive.

The loud ring of her phone startled her. She was shocked to see Jin's name on the display.

"Hello?" Mina answered cautiously.

"Hey, I was just thinking of you," Jin said.

OMG, did drawing Jin's face cause him to call me?

"I looked for you after school, but you were gone," he said. "Are you okay?"

"Oh, I'm good, thanks," she responded. For some reason, she felt nervous talking to him. "You could've just texted me."

"Why, is it weird talking on the phone?"

"Yeah, I guess." Mina could hear the smile in his voice, which made her think of his dimple, which made her stutter. "I—I—I'm not used to talking to anyone here yet."

"Hopefully I can change that," he replied.

Mina could feel heat rising up her face and was really glad they weren't video chatting.

"Is everything all right?" he asked.

"I don't know." She laughed awkwardly. "This has been the shortest, longest day of my life."

There was a pause.

Argh, he must think I'm so weird!

"I'm not making sense . . . ," Mina said.

"No, actually I get exactly what you mean," he replied. "Lately, every day has felt like that."

Huh, so it isn't just me. The days are going too fast. Another rule of the world, or something I did? Mina's mind was whirling again.

"So what were you calling about?"

"Did you see Sophia or her friends today?"

"Why are you asking?"

"I heard that Sophia and her friends were looking for you and I got worried."

Mina became very aware of how loud her heartbeat was. He was worried about her. She covered her face in embarrassment. This was ridiculous. She couldn't have feelings for him. None of this was real, no matter how much she might wish it were.

"Um, thanks. But you don't have to worry about me," she said. "I can take care of myself."

"I'm not saying you can't. I just want you to be careful. I don't think you understand how dangerous things are around here."

If only she could tell him how much she really understood.

"I know all about the strange things happening," she said. "Jewel and Kayla filled me in on everything."

He was quiet again. "What exactly did they tell you?"

"That the school is filled with dangerous people and strange disappearances and maybe I shouldn't have come here," Mina quipped.

"Well, I'm glad you did," Jin replied simply.

Gah! He's so sweet! Mina thought.

"Thanks, I think," she said.

The doorbell rang.

"Listen, I have to go," she said. "My dinner is here."

"Can we have lunch tomorrow?" he asked.

Internally, Mina told herself to calm down. "Sure?" she answered.

"Cool, meet me in the courtyard."

"'Kay."

"See you tomorrow."

After making herself something to eat, Mina prowled around the house trying to distinguish what made it feel so wrong. It was the same building. The same interior, mostly. There were things missing. Furniture that she couldn't remember except for its absence. And then there were changes that seemed to have materialized just recently.

All the paintings and photographs that, in the real world, had been locked away when her mother died were on the walls and tables. In the living room, Mina stared at the painting of the mother and daughter laughing in the middle of a sunflower field. She remembered watching her mom paint it. They'd gone on a family trip to a local sunflower farm. They'd packed a picnic basket, and her father had driven them there. Her mom had taken a lot of photos of the sunflowers, but her father had captured a picture of Mina and her mom dancing around the flowers. Her mom had loved it so much she'd painted it. It was Mina's favorite of her mother's paintings, and the one most painful for her to look at. At home, it remained in Mina's closet. But here, it was displayed prominently.

"Mom's sunflowers," she said out loud.

This was a memory of home before her mother died. The home she longed for so desperately. But memories couldn't stop the ache of loneliness of an empty space. The paintings were reminders of a deep and irreplaceable loss. That was why her dad had locked them all away.

But as she gazed at her mom's sunflowers, instead of loss, Mina remembered the laughter and warmth of that long-ago moment. She could almost hear her mother's voice calling her name, telling her how much she loved her. Mina closed her eyes and let the memory flow over her, and here in this empty house, she could feel her mother's presence once again.

"Mama, I miss you so much. I wish you were here with me," Mina said. "I'm so confused. I don't know if I'm dreaming or I'm delusional or I'm really in another world. I think it's all my fault and I have to fix it. But I don't know how to put things right."

"Mina, art is real."

Mina sat down and buried her head in her hands. She was thinking so hard her brain hurt. It was all too confusing. She had to write it down. She grabbed the small notebook from her fanny pack and jotted down her thoughts.

Tablet malfunction
Webcomic hijacked
Transported into webcomic world that is
    similar to my real world
Webcomic main characters are all here
Superhero powers
Bad guy storyline
School is my school but not
Saachi and Megan are here but don't know me
Dad not here
Jin is Jin?

She crossed that line out. It was too outrageous. Her best friend Jin was dead. This Jin was just a character in the webcomic world. He wasn't real.

But why does he feel so real? she thought.

Mina closed her eyes and pictured Jin with his adorable dimple and gorgeous smile. She shook her head and focused on her list.

> Sophia not a superhero
> Jin doesn't like Sophia
> Characters stuck in roles but rebelling?

The key was her webcomic. Jewel and Kayla said that everything changed at the beginning of school. Exactly when Mina uploaded her first episode of *The School of Secrets*. That meant this world existed before her story. So she'd somehow brought her webcomic story to life in this world. Her characters were real people following a script that she'd made for them, but they didn't know it. And the only way to delete the files was to go back to her own world and access them there.

It dawned on Mina that if this world was real, then that had to mean Jin was real too. He wasn't just a character. But was Jin her Jin? Mina mentally swatted away the distracting thought and tried to come up with a plan of action.

Frustration brought her back to her feet and all the way upstairs to her room. She paced around and then opened her closet door. Mina heaved a long sigh. This wardrobe was so disappointing. When she'd drawn the bullying scene, she had based the character on herself but vaguely. And that was what she got. A character with no real backstory, no real substance. Her character wasn't meant to be deeply developed. But the house was evolving the longer she stayed. Her mother's paintings now adorned the walls. So in theory, her own clothing should be here also. She stared at the closet for several long moments, wondering if just thinking about her clothes would make them materialize. When this failed to do anything but hurt her eyeballs, she slid to the floor with a pout.

An idea struck her, and she reached for her mini tablet. Turning it on, she saw that it still had almost a full charge. She then drew her black leather jacket and a few favorite items that Auntie Jackie had gifted her recently.

She had just finished the sketch and was about to color everything in when the pieces began to appear one by one in the closet.

For a split second, Mina worried that she'd moved her real clothing from home, but when she examined the items, she realized they were all brand new.

"With great power comes great accessories!" Mina clapped her hands gleefully.

She drew earrings, jewelry, bags, even house slippers, and marveled when they all appeared in front of her.

"Well, since I'm either trapped in a dream or another world, might as well make the most of it!" She felt light-hearted for the first time since all the weirdness began. For now, she could pretend she was dreaming and just having fun.

"I wonder what would happen if I invented something instead of drawing it from memory?" Could she create things? She decided to draw a ruby ring studded with tiny diamonds. It appeared before her, but it looked fake. Mina laughed and put it on. It was vibrantly gaudy and too old for her. That was the problem with drawing from her imagination. She quickly drew a sketch of herself wearing a butterfly bracelet. When it appeared, Mina was intrigued. It was beautiful and delicate and precisely the size she wanted it to be. But it looked otherworldly. Almost too good to be true.

She wondered what else she could do. Could she make living things? She drew a small cactus and watched it materialize on her desk. But when she tried to create a dog, all that appeared was a stuffed animal version of her sketch. She even tried to draw an ant and got a plastic figure instead. When she erased the ant from her screen, the plastic version disappeared.

Another rule of the world: she couldn't draw live animals. That was a good thing. It also meant she couldn't create humans. So the only people who could exist in this world were already here. Good to know she wasn't some kind of god.

Drawing on the mini tablet was hard on her hand. She missed her Wacom. As soon as the thought occurred to her, she began to draw one. Mina was elated to see it appear on her desk. Switching it on, she saw that it was newer and faster than her real one. Now that she had a large tablet, she wondered how creative she could get within the realm of her imagination. Could she create things that hadn't been invented yet, or magical items?

On the blank page, she started doodling without thinking about what she was creating. Sometimes the best things came from her freestyling. As she drew, she realized she was sketching a cute little silver robot on wheels, with movable arms that could pick things up for its owner. The robot face had big round light-up blue eyes that could open and close and a mouth that could form a smile, frown, or straight line. On its chest was a small screen that could display answers to questions. Music notes and beeps showed how the robot could communicate. She then sketched it scooting around the floor, tidying up after the Mina character. And when it was resting, it rolled itself into the size of a tennis ball, which her character then placed into her jacket pocket. Putting down her pen, she smiled in anticipation.

A sudden beeping came from behind her. Whirling around, she found a tiny robot waving at her, smiling as its screen unfolded into a panel that flashed *Hello*.

"Hello there." Mina beamed. "What's your name?"

Cute beeps emanated from the robot as a question mark appeared on its screen.

"Hmmm, well, I always wanted a dog that I could call Bomi. So how's that?" Mina asked.

A big heart lit up the robot's screen, and then it began to twirl and do a funny dance, making Mina laugh. "I'm not going to be so lonely with you here, Bomi."

Watching as Bomi zipped around the room beeping noises of contentment, Mina couldn't help but feel conflicted. Bomi was adorable. She was excited to have created them. But she shouldn't be here in this place. She didn't even know what *here* was.

"Is there really such a thing as an alternate reality?" she asked out loud.

Bomi stopped beeping and rolled in front of Mina.

A computer-generated voice that sounded like a young child answered her.

"Alternate reality. Parallel universe. Multiverse. 'Many world' interpretation of quantum physics. Multiverse: a theoretical reality that includes a possibly infinite number of parallel universes."

"Wow, did I just create a genius robot?" Mina asked.

"My programming is directly connected to Janus, a supercomputer. I have an eighty-five percent probability rate of accurately answering Owner's questions," Bomi replied as they gave a happy little twirl, their lights flashing.

"Why only eighty-five?"

"I am limited to what data is accessible from the super-computer. That is only information based on the known world. It cannot provide data on the unseen world, the alternate world."

"Bomi, explain about the alternate world."

"Science of the multiverse. Big bang theory, string theory, quantum theory."

The explanation was so long, detailed, and complicated that Mina had a hard time following it all.

"Bomi, speak English!"

"I am speaking English," Bomi responded. "Did you want me to use a different language?"

"I mean use simpler terms so I can understand."

Bomi's lights flashed for a moment before they continued. "The big bang theory explains how our universe came into existence. It is believed that it was triggered by random quantum fluctuations and that there could have been many events like it, which would cause multiple universes."

"Multiple universes?"

"Yes, based on quantum theory. Every time a quantum event happens, the universe splits. Or as string theory suggests, matter is composed of infinitely small vibrating strings or loops of energy, which lead to infinite solutions that could each be a different universe."

"I am the creator of my own destruction," Mina groaned.

A question mark flashed on Bomi's screen.

"Bomi, I don't understand anything you are saying. Just tell me, if I am from an alternate world, how did I get here? Do you have a scientific explanation for what happened to me?"

The robot cocked their head. The screen flashed *Input*.

Mina launched into a full explanation of all that had happened to her before and after entering the webcomic world. Bomi sat completely still, listening, their screen flashing.

"Plausible answer," Bomi responded in a bright voice. "Possible quantum event at the time of friend's death in Owner's world caused an alternate timeline where friend did not die. Owner's connection to friend opened a channel between the worlds when they created webcomic using likeness of friend. Owner inserted a membrane over the alternate world, causing an anomaly and corrupting it. So chaotic was the anomaly that it brought Owner into the alternate world, where they are now proceeding in this new timeline."

"Did you say an alternate timeline where Jin is alive? My friend Jin? How's that possible?"

"Quantum event caused alternate timeline...."

"Right, but what is a quantum event? Is it like the big bang?"

"No one knows for sure."

Mina thought about what had happened to her right

before she came here. She remembered looking out the window and seeing multiple lightning strikes near the house. She gasped. Auntie Jackie said there had been a thunderstorm and repeated lightning bolts when Jin died.

"Bomi, could a major electrical storm and multiple lightning strikes in one spot cause a quantum event?"

"It is plausible."

Then Jin really could be Jin? A shiver went down her spine.

"Bomi, how do I get rid of the problems I've created here?"

"First option, see through the completion of the storyline."

Mina shook her head vehemently. "That's a bad idea."

"Second option, Owner takes control of the storyline within this world. Third option, Owner returns to her world and deletes the anomaly."

"How do I go home to my own world?" Mina asked.

Bomi made a frowning face. "Not enough information to compute answer at this time."

"Maybe I should draw myself out." Mina sighed but then blinked. "Wait, can I do that?"

On her tablet, she drew her bedroom wall, added a door, and labeled it "real home." In another panel, she sketched herself opening the door to her real bedroom. As she was drawing, a door materialized just as she'd depicted it. She jumped to her feet, dashed over, and opened the door—only to find a solid wall behind it.

If she couldn't draw her way out of the webcomic and she couldn't delete it, maybe she could end the story safely and quickly. All she had to do was take control instead.

Mina began a new episode that opened with the Mercer character being healed in surgery. She drew Merco being disbanded. In an explanatory panel, she wrote that the Gifted were no longer powerful and could go back to normal. But no matter how many times she tried to upload the new episode, it failed.

Defeated, Mina sank low in her chair. There would be no easy solution to her predicament.

CHAPTER 13

Memories and Sadness

Thursday, October 13

Emma Lee was in her studio, the sun pouring in and brightening the room with a bright yellow light. Her easel held up a large unfinished piece, while smaller canvases leaned against the walls. Emma was concentrating on her Wacom tablet.

Laughter filled the room, and Emma turned around with a huge smile.

Little Mina and Jin ran in, and Emma swept them both into a hug and spun them around, their voices bubbling over with joy.

"Mama, can we get a puppy?"

"No, honey, your dad is allergic to them."

"Aw, but what about the ones that are hippollergic?" Mina asked.

"Yeah, hippollergic," Jin piped up. "Means they don't make people sneeze and stuff."

Emma laughed. "I know what you guys mean, but even

those dogs can still cause allergies. It would be terrible to bring one home only to have to give it away, right?"

"I know," Mina said with a mischievous smile. "Let's give Daddy away instead."

"Mina!"

Emma looked shocked, but Jin was giggling with his little hand over his mouth. Mina pouted.

"Well, he's never home anyway," Mina explained. "Maybe he should live somewhere else and we can get a dog!"

"I want another dog, but my mom said we can only have one. But Mochi is no fun. All he does is sleep and eat and sit on my mom's lap." Jin heaved a big sigh. "Mina, when we growed up, we can get married and have lots of dogs, I promise!"

"Like ten?" Mina clapped her hands.

"A hundred!"

They burst into giggles as Emma knelt down to hug them again. "I tell you what—just because we can't have a dog in the house doesn't mean you can't have one."

"Huh?"

"We can have a dog?"

Mina and Jin began to squirm in delight.

Emma nodded and called them over to the tablet. "What kind of dog do you want?"

"I want a great big one that's brown with spots and I can ride it like a horse!" Jin jumped up and down in excitement.

"Okay, but first let's start them as puppies." Emma quickly sketched a cute puppy with a little boy who looked like Jin holding it.

"What about you, Mina?"

"I want a short stubby dog with a big head and ears like we saw at the store the other day!"

Emma laughed. "You mean a corgi?"

"Yes! And her name will be Cookie!"

"Mine's Horse!"

"Jin, you can't name a dog Horse! He's a dog, not a horse!"

"Then you can't name a dog Cookie!"

As they squabbled, Emma finished the sketches and colored them in and printed them out. She labeled them "Jin and Horse," "Mina and Cookie."

"There's no such thing as 'can't' in art," Emma said.

Mina woke up with a smile. She'd forgotten about that day. She and Jin had bugged her mom for many more pictures of Horse and Cookie. They even created a picture book of their own about Horse and Cookie and their adventures trying to catch the ice cream truck every day. Mina wondered if the book was still somewhere in her room.

The memory also gave her some thoughts.

There's no such thing as "can't" in art.

The answer was in her art. She created the problem; now she had to make the solution. School seemed to be a good place to find more information and enlist help if at all possible. So that would be her plan.

Stepping out of bed, she heard a series of beeps as Bomi woke up and rolled over to greet her.

"How'd you get up here?" Mina asked in surprise.

Bomi extended their legs and made a climbing motion. Mina laughed. The robot was quite resourceful.

She took a quick shower and dashed into the closet to pull out a pair of strategically ripped dark blue jeans, a gray sleeveless hoodie shirt, and her camo jacket. She grabbed a pair of black velvet sneakers with thick black satin ribbon laces.

Just as she was about to leave her room, Mina noticed her tablet lying by the side of her bed.

"Can't forget you," she sighed. Her fanny pack and everything in it were the only things that came with her from her world. She had a suspicion that in order to return home, she would need it. She put her tablet and real cell phone into her pack, slung it over her head, and ran downstairs. Mina could hear the robot slowly following her, but didn't stop to help them. She looked at the clock and realized she had to leave immediately. Mina grabbed a chocolate doughnut and gulped it down with a glass of milk.

She tied her shoes and left the house just as Bomi finally made it all the way down. They beeped a sad farewell.

Outside, she was surprised to see Jin waiting on the sidewalk. He straightened up with a smile at her approach.

"Hey, thought I'd walk you to school," he said.

Flustered, Mina blurted out the first thing that came to her mind. "How'd you know where I live?"

"I looked you up, and when I realized we live so close, I thought I could see you in the morning," he responded sheepishly.

His dimple flashed at her as he grinned, and Mina could feel the heat rising in her cheeks.

"So what did you want to talk to me about?" she asked, trying not to look at him.

He didn't respond right away, just matched his long stride to Mina's. His hand brushed against hers, as if he were trying to hold it.

OMG, where'd that thought come from?

She shoved her hand into her jacket pocket and walked faster.

Jin gently tugged at her arm. "Slow down, we've got time."

You can actually stop it, if you wanted to. Mina wondered if she should tell him she knew he was a Gifted.

"Sorry, I guess I'm a fast walker," she replied.

"For someone with short legs," he teased.

She shot him a dirty look and started walking faster, leaving him behind again.

"You remind me of my old dog, Mochi. He was this small Westie mix with a fat belly and little stubby legs."

"Your dog?" Mina asked, shocked. He was describing Auntie Jackie's dog, who was now fourteen years old.

"Yeah, when he walked, his little legs would go super-fast, and it was the funniest thing to see."

Mina stopped and narrowed her eyes at him in warning. For now, she pushed aside the question of how he seemed to know Mochi.

He then proceeded to mimic an exaggerated version of her walk.

Mina raised her fist, as if to punch Jin in the arm.

"But he was really cute, like you!" he protested laughingly.

She threatened him again.

"Okay, you don't remind me of a dog!"

She lowered her fist.

"Maybe more like a fat cat?"

"That's it!" Mina went after Jin, who ran around in circles, laughing. He let out barks and meows whenever she slowed down, causing her to chase him hard again. He finally turned to face her with his hands clasped in front of him.

"I'm sorry! Please forgive me!"

Mina smacked his arm and kept walking.

"Ouch." He frowned. "You know it's your fault for being so damn cute."

She looked up to see his smile and the laugh lines around his shining eyes. *He had no right to be so gorgeous!*

"Victim blaming, strike number two," she said. "One more and you're dead to me."

Jin staggered with his hands over his heart. "Unfair! Take one back! I'll do anything as long as it is legal, doesn't cost a lot of money, and is not so humiliating that I have to transfer to another school."

"Well, that's no fun!" Mina teased.

"I promise you, I'll make it fun," he responded.

His voice had turned serious. Mina tried to fight back the blush she could feel heating her neck. He made her all squirmy inside.

"So you have a dog named Mochi?" she asked casually.

The smile on his face faded as he looked away. "Used to," he replied.

They walked in silence for several minutes until Mina couldn't stand it anymore.

"Didn't you want to say something to me?"

Jin smirked. "I think I'll make you wait until lunch."

"What? Then why bother walking with me this morning?" Mina was peeved. She needed to think, and he was too much of a distraction.

"I'll take any excuse to spend time with you," he said.

Surprised, Mina spun around to face him. "Huh?"

Jin leaned closer. "You had a chocolate glazed dough-nut with milk for breakfast, didn't you?"

She gaped at him. "How'd you know?"

He reached into his pocket and pulled out a packet of tissues. "You left evidence all over the corners of your mouth."

Flushing red with embarrassment, Mina took a tissue and scrubbed her mouth.

"Easy! You're leaving little bits of tissue on your lips," he said. Using another tissue, he gently wiped away the resi-due. Mina stared at his face, mesmerized, until he was done. He gazed down at her, a serious look on his usually smil-ing countenance.

"Do you feel it too?" he asked.

Her face grew hot under his intense stare. "Feel what?" she asked cautiously.

"This connection," he said slowly. "I've never felt this sensation before. It's almost like I've known you all my life."

Shock caused her to flinch. This was the last thing she'd expected. Jin pounced on her reaction, his eyes going wide.

"You do sense it, don't you," he continued.

Mina backed away. "I don't know what you're talking about. But I gotta go right now. I'll catch you later." And with that, she fled.

At school, she decided that her search for answers should begin with Ms. A. In her webcomic, Ms. A was a vil-lain who provided Merco with information about all the Gifted. Mina needed to go to her office and snoop around. But the stress of getting caught terrified her. She wished

Jin were with her. He could stop time so she could sneak around without worry. Should she ask him?

Stop being such a baby, Mina Lee! He doesn't know I know!

Mina took a deep breath before heading to the first-floor lobby. The front offices were all glass with three administrative assistants sitting at their desks. Behind them was a hallway where all the administrators had their offices. If this was the same as her high school, then there was a back entrance at the other end of the hall where the conference room was. The hallway was busy with people rushing around. Security guards were also in the main office.

What she needed was a big distraction.

What about a fight? Hmm, that would take care of the security guards, but not the administrators. Okay, what if there's a fire alarm? Then everyone would have to leave. That would work!

Mina ran to the bathroom and tried to find a clean stall and nearly died.

Why are all high school bathrooms disgusting?

She bolted back out and decided to go up to the art hall on the third floor. There was a supply room she could hide in. As she passed the studio art room, she spotted Ms. Ellis talking to a student. Mina paused when she noticed it was Christina Jackson, looking perfect as always. A pang of homesickness surprised her. She missed her art class and Saachi and Megan. She missed Mrs. Song's cooking and even her father's nagging. She missed the boring normalcy of her life.

Clamping down on her emotions, Mina snuck into the

supply room and hid in a far corner. She began to create a scene on her tablet. While it would've been easier to just pull the alarm herself, the school had surveillance cameras in that corridor. Mina didn't want to risk getting in trouble. For a brief moment, she hesitated. Pulling the fire alarm was a serious crime.

But so was taking away people's free will.

What she'd done was far worse. She had no choice except to do whatever she could to fix this world.

She was about to draw someone to pull the fire alarm when she had an idea. Instead of having an unknown student get in trouble, she would just make it happen. She recreated the red fire alarm with its white T lever. Then in the next panel, she copied it, but this time the lever was pulled down. Mina then drew an outside scene of the school emptying as everyone exited the building. Before she could finish it, the fire alarms blared; students filled the hallways and teachers tried to maintain calm.

Within a few minutes, the halls quieted except for the alarms. Mina hurried to the main office, which was now completely empty. She slipped into Ms. A's office and closed the door. She had only a few minutes before the fire department would arrive.

The office had no decorations. Not even a picture frame on the desk. There were boxes in the corner and files piled up on the bookshelves behind her. Mina spotted an open file with her name on it. She paused but moved on. As she was a new student, it made sense for Ms. A to take a look at her file. Nothing questionable about that. Maybe.

Mina wouldn't find answers in a file that was lying

around. She began searching through the desk drawers. Most were filled with junk. The last drawer had only one thing in it: an accordion folder with a thick rubber band wrapped around it. Inside were several pages with pictures attached. They were records of Sophia and nine other students Mina didn't recognize. This was it.

She heard the fire engines roll in outside. She had to go. She took pictures of the documents until she heard firefighters running through the hallways. She shoved all the papers back into the folder, wrapped the rubber band around it, and placed it in the drawer. Sneaking out of the office, she saw that the back door was clear. She raced up the stairwell and into the art supply room.

She began to review her photos of the documents. The first was a detailed record of Sophia's school and personal history, but the pages after were different. Handwritten notes about Sophia's gift. An observation about electricity shimmering around her hands. An incident involving an electric shock of another student, which was considered minor and written off as a fluke, but Ms. A had noted that Sophia was present. It was clear that Ms. A had been keeping a close eye on Sophia and knew about her talent. What was not clear was why it was still a secret. Or were Sophia and Ms. A both working for Merco?

The other documents were about students Mina didn't recognize from her webcomic. Two had healing powers, one was superstrong, another had invisibility power, and another could make fire. Mina assumed the other four were also gifted. All the students except Sophia had been transferred.

What was going on? None of these characters were from

Mina's story. So why were they in Ms. A's file? Was the webcomic story creating its own characters?

Out in the hallway, the clamor of returning students interrupted Mina's troubled thoughts. She could hear people entering the art room. Not wanting to get caught, she pocketed her phone, slipped into the hallway, and headed to class.

• • •

At lunchtime, Mina hesitated at the courtyard entrance. The last thing she wanted was to raise more of Jin's suspicions. But she knew he was somehow related to why she was here in his world. She wanted to ask him about his powers and how those had changed things for him. And what of Merco? Was he scared? There was so much she wanted to ask, but *how* was the question. She took a deep breath and walked out.

Jin was sitting by himself on the bench.

She sat down next to him.

"Why aren't you eating?" she asked.

"Because I'm polite and was waiting for you," he said. "Where's your lunch?"

Mina frowned. "I forgot to pack one." She heaved a sigh and eyed Jin's enormous hoagie loaded with meat and lettuce and even avocado. "Huh, didn't take you for an avocado kind of guy."

"Well, I was *going* to offer you half of my avocado and turkey sandwich, but forget about it now," he teased.

Mina looked up at him with a sad face and whimpered. She had no shame when it came to food.

"You like turkey?" Jin smiled as he handed her half of his hoagie.

"I like food," she said.

Mina took a huge bite of the sandwich and nearly melted in relief. She was so hungry all the time ever since coming to this world.

"Mochi, take human bites!"

Mina swallowed and immediately got violent hiccups. She could see Jin trying not to laugh.

"Not funny!" She unscrewed her water bottle and tried to drown the hiccups away. At first, they seemed to be gone. But just as she relaxed, a very loud and painful hiccup undid her, and Jin snickered.

"Stop! They really hurt!" Mina pinched her nose and held her breath, puffing out her cheeks like a chipmunk. Jin convulsed with laughter, and Mina elbowed him and hiccuped again.

"Ouch!" Jin rubbed his arm.

Mina tried to apologize, but another loud hiccup garbled her words, which made Jin nearly fall over laughing.

"You always got the worst hiccups when you ate too fast and didn't drink any water!"

At his words, Mina's hiccups abruptly stopped. It was a memory from the real world.

"How do you know that?" Mina whispered.

Jin's eyes widened. "It just came to me. This memory of you and me when we were little."

They stared at each other, Jin in confusion and Mina in shock.

"Wait a minute," he said with dawning realization. "I *remember* you! We used to be friends. Best friends."

"What else do you remember?" she asked.

Jin was quiet for a moment, then said, "You used to poke your finger in my dimple and yell, 'Holey hole!' I hated it but you would never stop."

On the left side of Jin's face, he had a perfect hole of a dimple. Mina remembered poking him just to irritate him. She would tell him that she couldn't help it because it was the perfect size for her fingertip.

"But then my mom told you it wasn't a poking hole, it was a kissing spot, and I hated it more," he said.

Mina's eyes grew round. She remembered how funny she had found the idea that his dimple was for kissing. And because he hated that even more, she would go out of her way to ambush him with messy smooches. Sometimes peanut butter, sometimes ice cream, but always something sticky.

He laughed and then stopped short. "I haven't thought of my mom in years. It's all coming back to me now. We used to see each other almost every day because your mom and mine were best friends, right?"

Mina didn't know what to make of this. Her mind was absolutely blown. She had no idea what was the right thing to do or say.

She nodded slowly.

"When my mom abandoned me, I never saw any of you again. But why am I just remembering this all now? It's like I had amnesia or something."

There was a dazed expression on his face, as if he was coming out of a fog.

"It's *you*, isn't it," he said. "You're making me remember everything I'd forgotten. Or maybe I suppressed it all."

"Abandoned you? What do you mean by that?" Mina asked.

He was quiet, his face stiff with the pain of an old wound. "I was sick and Mom took me to the hospital. But when I woke up, they told me she'd left me there."

Deeply horrified by this revelation, Mina couldn't speak. How cruel this world was to leave Jin alone without any family. In her reality, Jin died. But here, when the timeline broke, it left him believing he'd been deserted by everyone.

"Oh my god," she whispered.

"You didn't know?" he asked.

She could hear the bitterness in his voice and see the pain in his eyes.

Mina shook her head, blinking back her tears.

"I guess my mom didn't want me," he said.

"That's not true," Mina said.

"Then why did she leave me?" Jin demanded. "Do you know? Can you ask your mom?"

"She died three years ago."

"Oh, I'm sorry, Mina," Jin said. "But why didn't you say something from the start? Why did you pretend you didn't know me?"

She bit her lip, not knowing what to say, and decided to be honest. "I was told you died."

It was Jin's turn to look shocked. "Is that what my mother said? Is that how she explained not having me anymore?"

This was terrible. This was not what she wanted him to think. But Mina couldn't tell him everything. There was no way he'd believe her.

"I don't know," Mina said. "And I don't know where she is." This was true. Mina wasn't certain whether there was an Auntie Jackie in this world. But the fact that Jin had been left alone meant there probably wasn't.

Jin nodded, but he looked unhappy. "Did you forget about me too?"

"No," Mina answered. "I never did. I missed you terribly."

Mina stared into Jin's sad brown eyes. She wished there was some way to tell him the truth.

"I just want to know why." His voice cracked, and his eyes were watery with unshed tears. "Why did she abandon me?"

Because you died.

Mina couldn't answer. A few tears slipped down her cheeks. She quickly wiped her face with the back of her hand.

He let out a shaky breath.

"It's okay. That wasn't fair of me to put you on the spot," he said. He reached over and thumbed away a tear that she'd missed. "Let's not talk about it now. We were both kids. What did we know?"

His smile was bleak, and it made Mina's heart hurt to see it.

"I need to walk around a bit," he said. "Clear my head. I'll see you later."

As Mina watched Jin walk away, all she could think of was Auntie Jackie. How devastated she would be to know of his unhappiness.

CHAPTER 14

Same but Different

"Mina! Wait up!"

Lost in her thoughts, Mina didn't realize Lauren was calling her until she was tackled from the back.

"Hey, didn't you hear me?" Lauren beamed at her with such goodwill that Mina couldn't be annoyed.

"You look down, Mina, what's wrong?" Diana asked, popping her head around Lauren. "Did anyone bother you today?"

Mina shook her head. "Just tired, I guess."

"And bored, right?" Lauren laughed. "Well, we're going shopping because Diana still doesn't have a Homecoming dress."

"I don't see why I need a fancy dress when I don't have a date," Diana responded.

"What do you mean? You have three dates! Me, Tracey, and Abby!"

Rolling her eyes, Diana nudged Mina gently. "Come

shopping with us, Mina. And if you find a dress, you should come to Homecoming too."

"Yes!" Lauren said. "Then it'll be five gorgeous girls for everyone to cry over."

She and Diana high-fived each other before linking arms with Mina and leading her to the parking lot. In Lauren's car, the radio played songs that Mina had never heard.

"Who is this?" she asked, enjoying the infectious rhythm and melody.

Diana swiveled her body all the way around from the front seat in shock.

"Are you for real? You must be the last person in the world not to know this song! It was only the biggest hit of the summer."

Mina gave a weak smile. "I don't listen to the radio much."

"Well, you should definitely check them out. Sabotage is my favorite K-pop band, and 'You're the Only' is their biggest song to date!"

That this was a K-pop band that Mina didn't know was fascinating; she was a huge K-pop fan. She wondered if Sabotage existed in her world and if their song would release there. It was a great song. The lyrics, all in English, struck the tender spot in her currently fragile heart.

> *You're the only, my one and only*
> *Without you, I'd be so lonely*
> *Baby, don't leave me*

They drove to the closest mall, which Mina knew well from her own world. It even had the same name, the Shops at the Pavilion.

Inside, the layout was exactly the same, leaving Mina with a strange sense of familiarity. She could have been with Saachi and Megan instead of Lauren and Diana. In some ways, the similarity was uncanny. Here, same as home, she was being dragged to go shopping against her will.

Suppressing a heavy sigh, she followed the girls into a large department store and watched them try on too many dresses, gossiping the whole time.

An hour later, they were finally able to narrow Diana's choices down to a sleeveless red dress that made Mina gape.

"That's the dress! You don't need to try any more on!" Lauren exclaimed.

"Lauren, you've said that ten times already," Diana shot back. "Mina, what do you think?"

"You look so gorgeous and hot, like you could tear men's hearts out with your teeth and they'd still crawl on their hands and knees to kiss your feet."

Both girls blinked in amazement before whooping with laughter.

"Damn, I'm buying this dress!" Diana went to change.

"If only you'd said that ten dresses ago," Lauren said.

"It wasn't true until now," Mina replied matter-of-factly.

"Yeah, she will slay in that dress!" Lauren sighed. "Poor Diana. She wouldn't be like this if it wasn't for Mark."

Mina glanced curiously at Lauren. "Explain?"

"Mark and Diana have been flirting since ninth grade, but they were always with other people. But this year it finally looked like the timing was right, and he was getting up the nerve to ask her on a date. Then suddenly he starts seeing Jewel. I mean, it was like out of nowhere. They didn't even know each other that well. It was so weird.

But it really hurt Diana. And she wants to look her best at Homecoming since he'll be there with Jewel."

Mina's stomach churned. She'd been the one to pair Mark and Jewel up in the webcomic.

Thinking about the mess she'd made, Mina didn't hear the incessant pinging until Lauren nudged her.

"Mina, your phone."

Thanking her, she checked her phone and found three messages from Jin.

> **Jin:** Mina, are you home?
> Can we talk?
> Hello?

Mina's heart skipped a beat. She took a deep steadying breath before responding.

> **Mina:** Sorry, I'm out shopping with Lauren and Diana

> **Jin:** When will you be back?

> **Mina:** Not sure, maybe in an hour or two?

> **Jin:** Text me when you're heading back.

> **Mina:** k

Two heads suddenly blocked Mina's phone. The other girls were giggling.

"Who is it?" Diana asked, holding a dress bag behind her back. "Is it Jin?"

"Yep, it's Jin," Lauren crowed. "He really *does* like you! I knew I saw a connection between you two."

Surprised by her words, Mina asked, "What makes you say that?"

"It's this intensity when you both look at each other," she replied. "As if two soulmates have met up for the first time. *So* romantic."

Lauren clasped her hands together and batted her eyes teasingly, making Diana crack up.

"I swear, Lauren, you're either going to be a romance novelist or one of those tarot card fortune tellers who work in tourist areas, luring unsuspecting sad lonely people."

Lauren stuck her tongue out at Diana, then turned to Mina. "Don't you feel it too, Mina? When you're around Jin? Like you were meant to be?"

"I . . . I don't know," Mina responded, causing Lauren to look disappointed. But inside, Mina was shaken. That was exactly how she felt. It was just the first time she finally understood what she was feeling.

They ended their shopping expedition with bubble tea, the highlight of the trip for Mina. Although the shop had a different name, it had the exact flavor she ordered at home, grapefruit yogurt slushie with tapioca pearls. As she sat chatting and laughing with her two new friends, Mina was a bit confused by the normality of it all. She was in another world with dangerous evil villains out to capture and destroy superhero teens, and yet here she was, drinking bubble tea and laughing at cat videos on Lauren's phone.

While there was danger in this world, Mina did not sense any real urgency or fear from anyone around her. It was strange.

Mina thanked Lauren and Diana for a fun afternoon and waved as they drove away from her house. She then walked the five blocks to the local park, where Jin had asked her to meet him. Mina felt a little guilty for not telling Lauren and Diana about seeing Jin, but she didn't want to deal with their teasing. Even though she knew they meant well, Mina was too sensitive and conflicted by all the new emotions battling inside her.

Mina was both happy and nervous to see him again. For most of the afternoon, she'd avoided thinking of Jin too much and had been grateful for the distraction of the shopping trip. Now, with nothing else to think of, she worried about what he would say. What he would ask. And what she could tell him.

Approaching the park, she could make out his form sitting on the top of the monkey bars. As soon as he saw her, he jumped down and started running toward her. Surprised at the smile on his face, Mina shuffled to a stop and found herself caught up in a big bear hug.

"What are you doing?" she asked, her voice muffled against his chest.

"I'm greeting my oldest and best friend in the world," he said into her hair. "I've missed you so much."

Immediately teary from his words, Mina rapidly blinked to fight off the waterworks. She cleared her throat.

Keeping an arm around her shoulders, he walked her over to an old-school seesaw. She hadn't seen one in a long time. They'd replaced the seesaws in her real park because they were considered a safety hazard for children. She sat on the down side and then gasped as Jin sat on the other end, sending her flying high in the air.

"That's not fair, Jin!"

He laughed. " 'It's not my fault being the biggest and the strongest. I don't even exercise.' "

Mina's eyes lit up. "*Princess Bride*! That's my favorite movie!"

"What?" Jin replied. " 'Inconceivable!' "

" 'You keep using that word. I do not think it means what you think it means,' " Mina quoted.

The up-and-down, back-and-forth of the seesaw mimicked the nonstop chatter of two old friends catching up. Finally, they sat balanced, tired from bouncing.

They were both quiet for a moment. Mina chewed on her lip. She was sure he'd ask about his mom again. She just wasn't sure how much of the truth she could tell him.

"Jin, about before . . . ," Mina started. She didn't know what she could say that wouldn't hurt him more. "I . . ."

Jin shook his head. "You don't have to say anything. We were little. It's not our fault what the grown-ups did. All I care about is that you're here with me now."

His words stabbed at her heart, and she had to look away. It had been only two days and also a lifetime. *I don't want to leave him.*

"Hey, it's okay! Don't feel bad," he said. "The whole point of not talking about it is so that neither of us have to feel guilty about what happened in the past."

When she still couldn't look at him, Jin sat all the way back, sending Mina shrieking into the air.

"Hey! I wasn't ready for that!"

"That's better." He smiled.

"What?" she snapped.

"Angry is better than sad."

Mina blew out an exasperated breath through full cheeks.

"Can you please let me down?"

"Only if you do two favors for me," Jin said.

"What are they?"

"First, if you don't have any plans tomorrow after school, then let's go do something fun. We could see a movie, go to the arcade, go to Target...."

"Go to Target? What the heck?" Mina laughed.

"I was just checking to see if you were listening."

"Actually, I like Target," Mina said.

"Are you serious?" Jin asked.

"It's my favorite store."

"You really are serious? You want to go on a date to Target?"

At the word *date*, Mina felt her heart thump again.

"I'm hungry," she said, changing the subject. "Let's go eat."

"Now?" he asked.

Mina paused. "Oh, it's okay if you have to have dinner with your family."

Jin shook his head. "No, that's fine! I'd rather eat with you."

"Cool, let me down!"

"Wait, I haven't asked my second favor yet," he said.

"What is it?" she asked.

"I've never gone to Homecoming before. Never wanted to. But I was thinking that it would be nice if I could go with you," he said hesitantly. "So what do you say? Will you be my date to Homecoming next Friday?"

Mina gasped in surprise. "Me?"

Jin looked around. "There's no one else here."

Mina didn't know what to do or what to say. For the first time in her life, someone she really liked was asking her on a date. A dress-up party kind of date. And she was overwhelmed with a longing for this to be real. But it wasn't. This was not her world. Even though her face was hot and her pulse was racing and she felt like hyperventilating. These feelings couldn't be real. She wasn't supposed to even be in his world at all.

Besides, she wasn't here to date Jin, have a relationship, fall in love.

No, her job was to fix her own terrible mistakes. She shouldn't be sidetracked by anything else.

And yet she wanted desperately to go to Homecoming with him. If only because of the vulnerability in his eyes that made her anxious not to hurt him. He hadn't done anything wrong. He didn't deserve any more pain. For his sake, she should go.

"Okay, sure!"

Jin's shy smile made Mina's heart squeeze painfully. This feeling. She wasn't used to it.

How will I be able to say goodbye to him?

CHAPTER 15

The Real MC

Friday, October 14

Mina sat staring at her tablet in horror. The worst thing possible had happened to her webcomic. *The School of Secrets* had become a romance with a love triangle that seemed to center around her, Jin, and Sophia. That was now the main plot. The one thing she had tried to avoid at all costs.

When Mina had first created the webcomic, she tried to keep the attention on the ensemble cast. But the story had taken a huge shift. There could be no other interpretation. Mina was now the main character.

So shaken was she by the revelation, Mina banged her head on her desk and screamed. Nothing was going the way she'd planned. And now she was stuck, and she just didn't know what to do about the webcomic. The last thing in the world she wanted was to have the story center on her. There was nothing special about her. Saachi and Megan must be so disgusted with this turn of events. How was she ever going to face them? More important, how was she ever going to get home again?

Depressed and exhausted, she decided not to feed the webcomic story and stay in bed. If the main character did nothing, then the plot couldn't advance. That was the only thing she could actually control.

Also, she had to sleep to stop the oncoming migraine.

The constant ringing of her phone finally woke her up several hours later.

"Hello?"

"Mina, are you all right?" Jin sounded worried. "You weren't at school and didn't respond to any of my texts."

"I'm fine, just really tired. Didn't sleep well last night. Bad dreams."

"Hmmm, I should've stayed with you," he said, his voice deepening to a sexy huskiness. "I would've chased them away."

Fully alert now, Mina sat straight up, aware of the flush heating her entire face. "Jin!"

"What did I say?" he teased. "I only meant I would have kept you awake. What were *you* thinking?"

"I'm hanging up."

"No, wait! We still on for our date today?"

Mina hesitated. She didn't want to feed the webcomic, and yet she wanted to see him.

"Are you not feeling up to it?" His voice sounded disappointed.

The thought of not seeing him caused Mina to make up her mind.

"I'm good!" she said quickly. "Just be warned, I'll be very hungry."

"Some things never change," Jin replied with a laugh. "I remember you used to always eat my food too."

"Not my fault," Mina countered. "You eat too slow."

"I'll come pick you up at five, and I promise to feed you."

"Cool!"

Dinner with Jin was so much fun. She asked for a burger and fries and a chocolate milkshake and grossed Jin out when she'd dipped her fries into her shake.

"What? You don't like sweet and salty?"

"Sure, just not together...."

"It's the best combination," Mina proclaimed. "Like chocolate-covered potato chips. Besides, I'm lactose intolerant, so this is the only way I can enjoy milkshakes."

Jin's revolted face made Mina laugh. "That should be illegal."

Afterward, they'd walked around the neighborhood, holding hands and talking about the parts of their lives they'd missed. Jin had been adopted by the Kanter family and liked his parents a lot.

"They're white and don't know much about Korean culture, but they really try hard," he said. "My mom even learned how to make kimchee."

"Kimchee? Hey, that's pretty cool of her!" Mina remarked.

Jin pulled a face. "It didn't taste very good. She doesn't believe in garlic and thinks black pepper is too spicy."

Mina burst into laughter. "Does that mean you don't go to Korean restaurants?"

"No, we do! My dad and older sisters love Korean food. But my mom will order bibimbap and eat everything completely separate."

"No gochujang, huh?"

Jin shook his head hard. "She tried the tiniest drop once and complained that her tongue burned for weeks."

"What are your sisters and dad like?"

He pulled out his phone. "Here, let me show you." He swiped through his pictures until he arrived at a family portrait. It was the stereotypical all-American white family, except for Jin sitting front and center. The parents were attractive with dark hair and warm smiles; the two older sisters were blond and very pretty.

"My dad is a pediatrician, Mom makes her own jewelry, and both my sisters are in college. Anne, the oldest, goes to Oberlin, and Meredith goes to Dartmouth," Jin continued.

"They seem like a really nice family."

He nodded. "I was lucky. My dad brought me home from the hospital as soon as I got better, and they adopted me when it was clear my biological mom wasn't coming back. But they insisted I keep my Korean name just in case."

Mina bit her lip. She wished she could tell him how much Auntie Jackie loved him.

The silence grew awkward until Jin completely changed the subject by launching into a funny story about his sisters dressing him up for Halloween as a slug, complete with slime.

"What about your dad?" Jin asked. "He was always really nice to me. Do you think he'd remember me? Can I come see him?"

Mina could feel her face freeze. "He's never home. Always working. It's like I live all alone." *That's technically the truth in both worlds,* Mina thought bitterly.

"I'm sorry," Jin said.

"It's okay," Mina replied. "My dad and I haven't been on the best terms since my mom died."

"How did she . . . ?" Jin stopped. "I'm sorry. . . ."

"You don't have to apologize. It was a car accident. Sometimes I still can't believe she's gone."

They walked in silence for a few minutes. Mina wondered if Jin would mention his power to her. She wanted to ask him but didn't know how to bring it up.

Mina could feel the beginnings of a migraine creeping up her head.

"Listen, I think I need to go home. I'm getting one of my migraines," she said.

By the time they reached her house, Mina's head hurt so badly she needed Jin's steadying arm around her as they walked.

At the door, she apologized for ruining their date.

Jin hugged her. "You didn't ruin anything," he said. "Are you sure you don't need anything?"

She shook her head. "Sleep is the only thing that helps."

Jin paused. "Do you think you'll be up for going out for pancakes tomorrow morning?"

"I'm not sure," she replied with a heavy sigh. "Sometimes I need a day to recuperate."

"Oh." Jin looked disappointed. "Bummer. My parents are taking me out of town tomorrow afternoon for college visits. I was trying to get out of going, but we'd already bought the plane tickets."

"It sounds like fun! How long will you be gone?" Mina asked, ignoring the sadness his words triggered in her.

"Almost a week. But we take the red-eye on Thursday night, so I'll be in school Friday bright and early!"

"Won't you be exhausted?"

"I'll sleep on the plane and dream of you." He winked.

"My head hurts too much to make the appropriate vomit sound," she replied.

He laughed. "Good night. I'll call you in the morning."

She waved goodbye and went into the house. Bomi let out a series of happy beeps and followed closely at her feet, just like a real pet would do. Mina went to the kitchen for some medicine and a glass of water. Stumbling for the stairs, she heard Bomi beep sadly behind her. She picked the robot up and carried them to her room. Taking off her fanny pack, Mina heard a soft beeping and whirring sound from her tablet. She opened her bag and saw that her tablet was dying. She plugged it in, changed her clothes, and slid into bed, gasping in pain.

Eventually sleep came, but with it, another bizarre dream.

She was in an office with a desk, a computer monitor, a conference table and chairs. Ms. A was sitting at the table, talking to someone Mina couldn't see.

"There were some strange anomalies on your record that I wanted to talk to you about."

Mina couldn't hear any response, but Ms. A seemed to be listening. "Well, perhaps it was a good thing to do," she replied. "It allowed me to gather as much information as I could and try to understand what was happening."

There was another long pause, and then Ms. A spoke again.

"Everything is out of control and getting worse. There's no fixing this from here. You have to go back."

Mina woke up confused. She didn't know what the dream meant, but she knew it had something to do with her webcomic. The strangest thing was Ms. A's vibe. In her storyline, Mina had written her as a cold, nasty woman who was obviously meant to be a bad character. But Mina's dream reminded her of Ms. A's real-life persona. She might look cold, but she was actually quite nice. It was just bad luck that she happened to teach the class Mina hated the most in high school.

The dream was clearly about the webcomic world, but if Ms. A was more like her real self, then she wasn't really bad. And Sophia, who was supposed to be the good character, was not. So there was a flaw in how Mina's story was working in this world. And if that was the case, there had to be a way to get rid of it. Mina just had to figure out how.

CHAPTER 16

Intermission

Thursday, October 20

Mina came home from school after another frustrating day of learning nothing new. The week without Jin had flown by faster than she thought it would, in large part because he texted her constantly, sending her photos of his entire trip. But Mina was busy also. She spent all her time trying to uncover as much as possible about the webcomic world. She talked to anyone who had any knowledge of a rumor and inputted all the information into Bomi for analysis.

All her efforts amounted to nothing helpful. Bomi still could not come up with a solution to her dilemma. At some point, she would have to talk to Jin directly about being a Gifted, but Mina was putting it off as long as possible. They had such a strong connection to each other that she knew she would have to tell him the truth eventually. But she was afraid of hurting him.

Mina was not surprised by how much she missed him. The most interesting part of Jin being away was that it made Mina realize the webcomic had two main characters. Mina was one and Jin was the other. While Jin was away, the webcomic barely updated. Mina's week showed up only as a short summary in which nothing major happened. Like some kind of intermission.

As she thought of Jin, her phone buzzed. It was a text from him asking if she had a dress and what color it was.

A dress! Mina had completely forgotten about Homecoming. She dashed over to her closet. There was nothing she could wear to a dance. She should have bought a dress when she went shopping with Lauren and Diana. But she hadn't known she'd be attending her first Homecoming. The idea of going with Jin as her date was secretly thrilling. She knew she shouldn't be so excited—she might not be in this world much longer—and yet still, it made her happy. She wanted an outfit that would dazzle him. Mina thought back to the most recent Academy Awards presentation. One of the winners had worn a metallic silver mock turtleneck dress—formfitting, sleeveless, backless—paired with strappy silver high-heeled sandals. It was her favorite look of the night. Mina decided to re-create a shorter version of the dress with a flared skirt above the knee. With the image in her mind, she turned on her tablet and drew the dress on a hanger, the shoes on the floor beneath it. As soon as she finished, the dress and shoes appeared in the closet. Eagerly, she tried them on and twirled in front of her mirror. She was pretty sure no one else would wear anything similar.

Mina texted Jin back.

> **Mina:** Silver

> **Jin:** ? What flowers go with silver?

She grinned. "Oh, that's so cute. He wants to get me a corsage!"

> **Mina:** Thanks but no thanks not really a flower girl

> **Jin:** will think of something else

> **Mina:** make it yummy

> **Jin:** Okay Mochi!

> **Mina:** 🙈

> **Jin:** 💀💀💀💀💀💀

Putting her phone down, Mina stared at Bomi.

"What am I going to do about Jin?" she asked the tiny robot.

Bomi beeped, a question mark showing on their panel.

"Yeah, I don't know either." She sighed. "Okay, Bomi, let's do some work."

She looked at all the information she'd scribbled in her notebook and realized it was a big mess that she couldn't follow logically.

"Let's try and make sense out of all this."

She grabbed her tablet and drew a large freestanding

whiteboard with markers and watched it appear in her room. Bomi spun and chirped happily in the background.

Mina began outlining.

School of Secrets characters:
Gifted—Sophia, Kayla, Jewel, Mark, Jin
Villains—Mercer, Ms. A, Sophia?
Main characters—Jin, Me?

Original webcomic storyline:
Unnamed Gifted kidnapped
Taking of powers from Gifted
Transplanting powers into Mercer
Side effects turning him into a monster?

Changes to storyline:
Sophia is bad
Sophia and Jin are not a couple!
Relationships are making people unhappy
   (Jewel, Mark, Diana)
Mercer kidnapping healers to fix his side
   effects

Rules of the webcomic world:
Can't delete episodes from within the webcomic
Can reset a scene within sixty seconds of it
   happening
Can add scenes but cannot change the past
Can create anything that is not a living animal

Questions:

How bad are the side effects?

What will Mercer do next?

What is Sophia up to? Is she connected to Mercer?

How do I fix everything and go home?

Why am I always so tired every day?

How I got here:

Electrical storm shorted my tablet, crashed my webcomic, sent me into the alternate world

Something to do with Jin

How can I go home:

Fulfill a quest?

Fix the world back to normal?

Wait for another electrical storm?

Stuck here forever?

"I am the main lead of my own melodrama." She sighed. "If only I knew how it's going to end."

Writing the information on the board helped her understand all that had happened, and also made clear the enormous impact of the story she'd created. She still had no idea how to proceed, but one thing she was sure of was Jin. He was her connection, the link between two worlds. Had she not created her webcomic, she would not have been pulled into this world and discovered her friend alive and well. That alone was worth everything she'd gone through.

Mina focused on Sophia and Mercer. Sophia had been

out of sight all week, as if Jin being away meant there was no Sophia storyline either. It was weird and it made Mina worry. Was the webcomic just waiting for Jin to return to unleash bad stuff? Something was going to happen; Mina could sense it, even without being in control of the story anymore. If only she knew how the Mercer storyline had evolved. When they said he was turning into a monster, what did that mean?

Depressed, Mina checked her home phone. She'd been in the webcomic world for nine of the fastest days of her life. Even though her dad was always working, he was still a constant presence in her life. A day didn't pass without Mina talking to him at least once. She used to find it annoying; now she missed hearing her father's voice.

It was five thirty p.m. at home. Only nine hours had passed. Her father had texted her at three asking how the SAT class went. Because she'd made a stink about him checking up on her too much, he would probably not call until later in the night. No one had missed her at all. While she should've been relieved, if anything it made her feel terribly alone, in a far worse way than she'd ever felt at home.

CHAPTER 17

The First Attack

Friday, October 21

Mina shuffled into the gymnasium behind Lauren, Diana, Tracey, and Abby. It looked like most of the school was packed in for the double-period pep rally. There was to be a parade of all the athletes and performances by the cheer teams. It was the last place Mina wanted to be.

As her friends looked for a place to sit, she was lost in her thoughts, worried about Jin, Mercer, the storyline, and the whole mess that was all her fault.

"Earth to Mina!" Lauren poked her hard.

"Hmmm? What is it?" Mina asked. Lauren just shook her head and pointed to the end of the bleachers. Mina saw Jin waving her over.

"Go get him," Lauren said with a smile.

As her new friends all giggled and cheered, Mina

crossed the length of the gym to where Jin was sitting, painfully aware of the curiosity in everyone's eyes.

She sat down next to him, still feeling awkward.

"Hey," he said, his eyes warm and bright.

"Hey back," she replied. "You doing okay?"

He nodded with a sweet smile.

A handsome boy with a wide grin pushed Jin aside to look at her. Mina recognized him immediately.

"Well, hello there. I'm Mark. So you're the new girl Jin's been talking about." Mark arched an eyebrow. "It's too bad you didn't meet me first."

"How unlucky of me," Mina teased.

"But your luck has clearly changed now."

"Really? What did I win?"

"Me!" He wiggled his eyebrows suggestively.

"Bummer, I was hoping for a manicure."

Mark reached over and grabbed her hand. "Would that be a pretty in pink or a luscious cherry red, princess?"

"Hey, go flirt with your own girlfriend!" Jin cut in, breaking their hands apart.

Mark laughed and gave Jin a knowing look.

"Wait, I'm not his girlfriend," Mina protested.

"Not yet, anyway," Mark said back.

Mina could feel herself reddening. When she glanced at Jin, she saw he was staring into space, a slight smile showing off his dimple.

That dimple is dangerous. ARGH, what am I thinking? This can't happen.

The thought was depressing. This was not her world. She was here because of her mistake. She needed to investigate what other parts of the story had changed. That was what she had to focus on. Nothing else.

"Mina, hey! What's up?"

Jewel and Kayla had come over and were eyeing her and Jin with concern. Kayla glanced to the side in an exaggerated way, and Mina knew instinctively that Sophia must be there. Suppressing the urge to turn around, Mina smiled and greeted them as Jewel sat next to Mark. They looked awkward together, and Kayla was clearly unhappy. It was an uncomfortable dynamic. And to top it off, Mina was aware of the sensation of Sophia trying to burn holes in her head ... which she could literally do. Just thinking her name sent a shiver through Mina's spine. That girl seemed to be the center of all the bad things that happened at the school. Mina turned around and glared up at Sophia, who was sitting a few rows behind. At that moment, Jin leaned his body against her. Mina saw Sophia's face twist with hatred.

Ugh! This creepy girl has me in a freaking love triangle over Jin!

It made her so mad she wanted to smack the jealousy off Sophia's face.

"Don't look at her," Jin whispered as he turned Mina around. "Can you look at me instead?"

His gaze was warm and affectionate, and even though the gym was loud with screams and cheers, Mina heard nothing but her own heartbeat in her ears.

I don't want to look at you. You make me sad.

Mina broke eye contact and fiddled with her hair. Her fingers caught in a tangle; Jin gently undid it for her and took her hand in his.

"Excuse me, what do you think you're doing?" she whispered even as she left her hand in his.

"Don't you remember? We used to always hold hands when we were together. I have a lot of fond memories of that."

"We were also little," she griped.

"You're still little." He winked at her, and the combination with his smile dried up the words that were stuck in her throat.

"You are too smooth." Mina frowned at him.

"I try," Jin said as he looked back at the festivities in front of them, Mina's hand still in his.

She should leave. She shouldn't develop any feelings for him. Yet her hand fit perfectly in his. She'd missed her friend so much. For now, she'd pretend that she didn't have to be anywhere but right here, next to him. She let herself get caught up in the antics of the cheer team on the floor. The DJ put on a new song, and the crowd roared as the entire football team came out and began to dance with pom-poms.

From the corner of her eye, Mina spotted Ms. A standing with a student who whispered in her ear and passed her something. Ms. A quickly concealed the item in her pocket before guiding the student toward the exit doors.

Now that's not suspicious at all!

This was the webcomic world giving Mina a sign. It was practically screaming at her to follow Ms. A. Maybe this was the lead she needed to find out what might be coming next. But a niggling feeling in the back of her head warned her that this could be a trap. Like when characters in horror movies went toward the murdering psychopath instead of to safety.

Mina gave an internal shrug. What did she have to lose at this point?

"I'm going to run to the bathroom," she whispered to Jin, regretfully slipping her hand from his.

Before she turned away, she could see Jin's eyebrows furrow in concern.

"I'll walk with you," he said, starting to get up.

Mina pushed him. "That would be a no," she said. "I can go by myself."

Mark laughed. "Man, what are you thinking? Girls only go with other girls to the bathroom. That's a sacred law!"

Mina fist-bumped Mark as she slid past him and went down the stairs just as all the spectators erupted in cheers and jumped to their feet. She exited the gym and ran down the hallway, spotting Ms. A and the student heading into a stairwell. Mina caught up with them, silently pushed the door open, and snuck in. She heard voices a floor below. She almost snorted; people talking secretively in stairwells seemed to be this webcomic's cliché.

"I'm telling you it's all on the thumb drive," the student was saying. "Two of them to watch for, and I think there might be another healer."

"Are you sure?" Ms. A responded sharply. "Who is it?"

"I didn't see them, but I'm certain from what happened to the others that there was a healer present. You'll see on the video."

"We need to find them immediately," Ms. A replied. "Send the video to the others and tell them to focus all efforts on finding who it is."

"Why is it so important? Is it because the other two healers disappeared?"

"They didn't disappear, they were taken," Ms. A retorted. "And I have a feeling something will happen during Homecoming. We need to be ready."

Why was she looking for a healer? And what did she think was going to happen during Homecoming?

Mina carefully opened the stairwell door and slipped through it. As she backed into the hallway, she turned right into Jin's chest.

"So did you go to the bathroom in the stairwell?"

Mina could hear Ms. A's heels coming up the steps. Grabbing Jin's arm, she distanced them from the door.

Ms. A emerged from the stairwell. "What are you two doing out of the pep rally?" her brusque voice called to them.

Jin rested his arm on Mina's shoulder and turned her so she was behind him. "On our way back right now, Ms. A," he said with a salute. With that, he pushed Mina toward the gym.

Returning to the pep rally, Mina winced at the boom of the speakers as the MC shouted along with the crowd. She and Jin stood at the edge of the court, right next to the amps. Mina tripped over the maze of wires connecting the amps to the power sources and was caught by Jin before she faceplanted. He held her close and smiled down at her. The spectators reacted with loud appreciation before starting to chant "Kiss her!" over and over again.

Mina could feel herself turning red. She pushed Jin away when she saw a furious Sophia stand up and start walking down the bleachers toward them, her hands sparking with electricity.

"What is wrong with her?" Mina was stunned.

Then it wasn't just her hands but her entire arms that rippled with electric sparks. Mina's eyes widened in horror as she watched Sophia shoot a huge surge of electric bolts directly at her. Before Mina could scream, the entire gym went completely silent. The quiet was so overwhelming compared to the din beforehand that she thought she must be dreaming again. Blue-white bolts hung frozen in the air, inches from her body. As she stared in disbelief, Jin picked her up to move her.

"What are you doing?" she yelled in surprise.

"Holy crap! You're not frozen!" Jin almost dropped her as he moved her out of harm's way. "Look. We have to talk about this later. I only have sixty seconds before time starts up again. I have to move all the amps or there is going to be a major explosion."

Mina peered behind Jin and saw that there was nothing to stop the electric bolts from hitting the amps and power sources. She looked around the crowded gym. It would be a bloody massacre.

As Jin moved all the equipment, Mina grabbed her mini tablet and deleted the last two panels, resetting the scene. Suddenly, she and Jin were back in the hallway with Ms. A. Jin stood blinking wordlessly at Mina and her tablet.

"Well?" Ms. A said. "What are you waiting for? Go in already!"

This time it was Mina who took Jin's arm and led him

into the gym and to a far corner, behind a group of athletes.

"H-how?"

"Not here," Mina cautioned. She looked up at the clock on the board. "Period's almost over. Let's go now."

Jin snapped his fingers, and once again the gym went quiet. He grabbed Mina's hand and weaved them around frozen people, into the hallway, down the stairs. Once through the front doors, Mina was amazed to find that the entire world had stilled. Birds in midflight, cars stopped on the road. *His power is formidable.* Within a second of the thought, everything shifted back into movement.

"Whoa," Mina said. "That was really cool!"

"I've never shared that experience with anyone before," Jin said with a smile. "But that was so much more fun with you!"

Mina found herself smiling back at Jin when she suddenly remembered what happened in the first place.

"Hey, so thank you," she said in a serious voice. "You saved me."

Jin stopped walking. "That was one of the most frightening moments of my life. If I'd been a second too late . . ."

They both went quiet.

"But what is your power?" he asked. "What exactly did you do with that tablet?"

Mina bit her lip. She wanted to tell Jin everything. But there was no way to say that she wasn't from this world without him thinking she was delusional.

"I can rewind time by a minute," she said.

"That's an incredible power!" Jin raved. "It's similar to mine in that we both manipulate time!"

Not really, Mina thought to herself. She worried she was making a mistake by not telling him the whole truth.

"I don't know," she sighed. "It's only been a week or so since I got it. I'm still learning what I can do." This was all true.

"A week?" Jin raised his eyebrows. "I've had this thing for several weeks now. Still not used to it, and I have no idea why I have it. But you saved everyone just now, and they don't even know it." Jin shook his head in amazement. "Even Sophia. You saved her from outing herself."

"That was so strange," Mina agreed. "Why did Sophia risk exposing herself like that?"

"I don't know. She was acting as if she had nothing to lose," Jin replied.

Mina was reminded of Ms. A's files. Ms. A knew all about Sophia's power. It was an open secret. Sophia was walking around without any repercussions; meanwhile, two healers had disappeared. There had to be a connection. Mercer needed healers to fix him. Sophia outed healers. No matter how much Jewel and Kayla wanted to believe otherwise, Sophia looked suspicious.

"Hey, Mina, you okay?"

She blinked to find Jin bent over, looking her in the face. They'd stopped near an empty playground.

"I'm sorry, I got lost in my thoughts," Mina said.

Jin led her to the swings, and they both sat down.

"What were you thinking about so hard that you looked like your brain hurt?" he asked teasingly.

"Sophia doesn't seem to even care if everyone knows about her power," she said. "Merco supposedly has kidnapped students with gifts. But why haven't they taken her?"

Jin shook his head. "I've wondered the same thing."

"And where can those healer kids be? Are they in danger?"

"The truth is we're all in danger, Mina," Jin replied. "That's why you can't tell anyone about your gift. I know what Merco does with the Gifted. And it's horrible."

"Wait a minute, how do you know?" Mina asked. *Especially when I don't even know,* she thought.

"Mercer owns land out near the river where the old warehouses are. There's a newly built facility with heavy security. He's been experimenting on the Gifted there."

Mina eyed him suspiciously. "And you know this how?"

"Me and a friend went snooping, and we saw some things."

Mina chewed on her lower lip. His friend must be Mark. He was supposed to have telekinesis. "Is it the science experiments like the rumors are saying?"

"It's so much worse," Jin replied. "Mercer's doctors operate on the Gifted. They harvest all their bone marrow to get their stem cells, and then they leave them in hospital rooms that are more like jail cells, hooked up to life support, barely alive. And then the scientists make a serum and inject Mercer with it. They tested first on soldiers and it worked, but the powers only last for a short time. Mercer decided he wanted more than one power, but the side effects were so bad, it's turned him into a mutant."

"Mutant, how?"

Jin paused. "It's the strangest thing, but it's almost like he's disappearing."

"Good. I wish he would disappear!"

"The Merco scientists can't do anything. That's why

they've been trying to find healers. Only healers seem to stop the advancement of his mutation."

Mina felt a rush of anger. "He's evil. I have to do something to stop him."

"What do you mean *you* have to?" Jin asked sharply.

She bit back a groan. She hadn't meant to say that out loud. "I just wish we could help, that's all," she said, backtracking.

Jin's eyes narrowed as he studied her face. "Just because you have this rewind power doesn't mean you can take on Merco. Promise me you won't do anything dangerous."

Mina nodded. "I have no intention of doing anything dangerous."

He held up his pinky, and Mina had to smile. She remembered they used to always pinky swear and thumb stamp all their promises.

After pinky promising, Jin smoothly held Mina's hand.

"I'm looking forward to a party for the first time in my life," he said. "Can't wait to see your dress and have you take my breath away even more than you already do."

Blushing, Mina rolled her eyes. "I'm sure you clean up nice also."

"I promise I'll shower just for you."

"Wow, thanks."

She stood up and pulled him to his feet. "Since I have so much pressure to look nice now, I'm going to have to go home and get ready."

Mina was struck by how seamlessly Jin had switched from talking about the horrifying things Mercer was doing to talking about the dance. As if the dangers were more urban legends than true fears. Was it because Mercer was a cartoonish villain Mina had created? Or was it because the Mercer storyline had been forced on everyone and therefore their reactions weren't genuine? Were they following a script, speaking the lines without really believing them?

Jin walked Mina to her door and swooped down to give her a smooch on the lips.

"Hey!"

Jin was already running to the sidewalk. "I'll pick you up at six!" he yelled.

Mina touched her lips and smiled. That was definitely *not* forced.

CHAPTER 18

Making New Memories

Mina went up to her bedroom and added another note to her whiteboard.

Homecoming

Homecoming was the perfect time for something significant to happen. In fact, if she were still in control of the webcomic, she would definitely have timed it that way. It was the "big event climax" trope. Stories always had to have their major battle scenes or romantic fights at concerts or proms or other public events with lots of witnesses. She would have to be prepared.

By six p.m., Mina was a nervous wreck. She understood why girls got ready together or had their mothers help them. While she was able to do everything herself, it had been a lonely experience with no one to tell her she looked beautiful. Bomi whirling about making comforting noises wasn't the same. She wished her mother were there to help her while she got ready for a date with a boy she truly cared about. Her mom would have been so happy. She could envision her mom and Auntie Jackie raving over her dress, showering her with love. Mina had to blink back a tear. She refused to ruin her makeup. It had taken her a long time to get it right. She'd watched YouTube tutorials on creating the perfect cat eyes and practiced for thirty minutes. She'd curled her hair and put on ruby-red lipstick and now was waiting anxiously for Jin to arrive.

When the doorbell rang, Mina smoothed her silver dress and opened the door. The first thing she noticed was how gorgeous Jin looked in his black suit and silver tie. He'd even styled his hair. It was as if he'd stepped out of the pages of a fashion magazine. The second thing she noticed was the stunned expression on his face.

"Hey," she said.

"You look so beautiful," he breathed.

"Thanks. Do you want to come in?"

He nodded, still looking a bit dazed, and tripped over the foyer rug.

"You okay?" Mina asked.

"You look so beautiful."

"Yeah, you said that already." She hid her smile. "Do you want anything to drink?"

"No, I'm okay. Is your dad here? I should greet him."

"He's on a business trip," Mina said with a slight frown. *But it would be nice if he could see us,* she thought wistfully. She could imagine him taking lots of pictures, shaking Jin's hand, giving him the talk that all dads gave to their daughters' dates. As mad as her father made her some-times, she truly missed him at that moment.

"That's all right—I'm sure I'll catch him next time," Jin replied.

Mina sat down to change from her house slippers to her strappy shoes with big block heels.

"Here, let me get that for you." Jin knelt in front of her and tied her shoes. "You even painted your toenails silver! Nice touch."

"I want you to know I went all out for you," she said. "So you should appreciate me more."

"Oh, I do," he said. He looked up at her with his dimpled smile, and Mina's heart thumped so loudly she was sure Jin could hear it.

"Shall we go?" She stood and slung her black leather pack across her body.

"Is that a fanny pack?"

"Yes," she said without elaborating. It didn't match her outfit, but she didn't care. She couldn't risk being without her tablet. Especially if Ms. A was right about something happening at Homecoming.

Jin rose to his feet and frowned. "Do you have a coat? It's a little cold outside."

Mina nodded and put on her black leather jacket.

He shook his head in amazement. "Only you could pull off a fancy dress with a leather jacket and a fanny pack."

She shrugged. "It works for me."

She moved toward the door, but Jin stepped in front of her.

"There's something missing," he said, looking her up

and down. He reached into his pocket and pulled out a small pink box. "You're missing a flower corsage. However, since you're not a fan of them, I got you this instead. You can't eat it, but I hope you like it anyway."

Inside the box, Mina found a beautiful silver bracelet with all sorts of flower charms. Pink peony, red rose, purple lily, yellow sunflower. Mina stared at the sunflower and immediately thought of her mother. She watched as Jin put the bracelet on her wrist.

"It's gorgeous, I love it," Mina said, her voice husky with emotion. "Thank you."

"My mom is a jewelry designer. When I told her you didn't want a corsage, she made me this to give to you."

"It's brilliant. Tell her thank you for me."

Jin nodded, seeming pleased with her reaction. "I don't know who was more excited about me going to Homecoming, my mom or dad. They're such dorks."

"They sound lovely," Mina said.

He smiled. "They want to meet you. You'll have to come over for dinner." Looking at his watch, he grabbed hold of Mina's hand. "Speaking of dinner, we're going to be late for our reservation."

They took a taxi to a cute little Thai restaurant near the harbor that was decorated with flowers and fairy lights. Behind the hostess stand, Mina spied a large bulletin board filled with Polaroid pictures of happy people eating. For a moment, she felt a wave of homesickness.

They were seated at a booth where they ordered spicy drunken noodles and crab fried rice and Thai iced tea served in tall glasses decorated with colorful parasols. Jin pulled Mina close to take a bunch of selfies.

"Would you like me to take your picture?" a server carrying a Polaroid camera asked.

Mina brightened. "Can you take two for us?"

As they waited for the Polaroids to develop, Jin showed her his phone's lock screen.

"We look good," he said proudly. It was a photo of them sitting cheek to cheek.

Mina laughed at a few of the sillier poses they'd made. Seeing that the Polaroids were done, she passed one to Jin.

"Oh, hey! I remember your mom used to always take Polaroids of us," he exclaimed. "She even had ones that were Polaroid stickers, and we would put them on everything."

Mina smiled. "Yeah, Polaroids always remind me of my mom."

Jin leaned over to stare down at the photo in her hands.

"Now, that's a pretty good-looking couple," he said. "They look perfect together."

Mina blushed and silently agreed. She unzipped her fanny pack and put the photo in a secret pocket to keep it safe. It would be her cherished memory. But then she wondered if she'd still be in Jin's pictures when she left this world. The thought was instantly depressing.

The waiter reappeared with generous dishes of noodles, fried rice, and vegetables. The aroma of spices and chilies lifted Mina's spirits again.

"So have you been working on your college applications?" Jin asked.

Mina frowned at her crab fried rice. "Not yet. Have you?"

"I finally settled on the list of schools I'm applying to."

"What are your top three?"

"For now, they're Stanford, NYU, Georgetown. I'm

thinking of going pre-law, and they all have law schools I'd like to apply to. But to be honest, I'll be pretty happy getting into any decent college."

Pre-law was what Mina had written in his bio for the webcomic.

"Have you always wanted to be a lawyer?" she asked.

Jin hesitated, his expression confused.

"No, I wanted to be a doctor," he replied slowly. "I was going to apply to Johns Hopkins because that's where my dad went. I only recently got interested in law. I don't even know why. I enjoy science and math a lot and have always found history and English pretty boring."

Crap! Another thing that's my fault!

"I think you'd make an awesome doctor," she said. "Especially because you want to do it and you don't have Asian tiger parents pushing it on you." Mina grinned and patted Jin's arm. "Besides, you'd hate being a lawyer. Trust me! My dad's one. It's no fun. From what I've seen, all he does is lots of boring paperwork, long phone calls, and tedious client meetings. Plus, he's never home."

Grabbing Mina's hand, Jin smiled, but his eyes were troubled.

"That's what I thought too, but I don't know," he said. "I feel compelled now, which is so weird. I'm not sure it's for me. Even my parents were shocked."

"Don't be a lawyer if you aren't sure," Mina said seriously. "Do what you feel passionate about. Most adults spend their lives working until they die. If you don't like your job, then life would really suck."

Jin nodded. "Good point! I'll have to rethink this whole pre-law thing. What about you? Where do you want to go?"

Mina thought about her art and her father's disapproval. "My mom went to NYU, so I'm pretty sure I'd love it there. But if my dad would let me, my dream school would be RISD."

"Why won't your dad let you?"

"He doesn't really want me to major in art," she answered. "He wants me to have a more stable career path. Work for a big company that has health insurance. That kind of thing."

"You know, this really smart person once told me that I should do what I'm passionate about," Jin said.

Mina grinned at him. "Exactly! Even if art isn't the most stable job, I'd choose doing something I love and enjoy over just making money. I mean, who needs money?" Mina sighed. "Who am I kidding? I can*not* be a starving artist. I love to eat too much."

"Clearly, you need a boyfriend whose mission in life is to make sure you're always well fed, Mochi."

"Hey! First of all, I don't appreciate you calling me a glutton. Secondly, I don't need anyone to take care of me. I can take care of myself, you hear?"

"Absolutely. My deepest apologies." He then served the rest of the crab fried rice onto her plate in a mountainous heap.

"Thanks a lot," Mina said dryly.

"Anytime, Mochi!"

She had to laugh, and he grinned in response. "Isn't RISD near Brown?" he asked. "I may have to rethink my school list and also add some Boston schools. I think it's only an hour away."

Mina's smile faded and she couldn't hold back a wince.

There was no way they could go to school near each other, no matter how much the idea of it thrilled her. She took a big gulp of water to mask her reaction. "Sorry, something was spicy," she said.

She could tell Jin didn't buy it. His expression didn't change, but Mina could see the sadness in his eyes again.

"Or not," he said.

"To be honest, I actually have no idea where I'm going to end up," she said. "I just don't want you to base any of your decisions on what I might do. I want you to go where you would be happy."

Jin kept his eyes on his plate for a minute before looking up at her. "I understand."

But Mina knew that he didn't.

After dinner, they went to the harbor boardwalk. It was crowded with tourists and locals enjoying the cool evening air.

"Don't we have to go to the dance now?" Mina said.

Jin held out his hand. "There's no rush. Let's walk a little."

Just tonight, I can pretend that we have all the time in the world together.

She placed her hand in his and marveled at the tingling sensation that swept through her body. Mina had never been in love before, but she knew without a doubt that she was falling hard for Jin. She realized she'd been fighting against something that she had no control of. This connection. This feeling. It was inevitable from the moment she opened her eyes and first saw him again. Why did people call it falling in love? It wasn't falling. It felt more like floating. It was the sensation that she could soar. He lifted her spirits up and made her feel so alive. Her every breath was sharper and more intense when she was with him.

How am I going to leave him?

They strolled along the boardwalk and stared at the lights flickering across the Potomac River. Then they paused, and Jin stood gazing out over the water for a long time, his eyebrows furrowed in concentration.

"What are you thinking about?" Mina asked, peering up at him.

"I just had this memory of you and me running along this boardwalk," he said slowly. "I fell and hurt myself and cried and cried. And then you made yourself fall right next to me and cried even harder."

Mina's eyes lit up as the memory came to her. "Oh my gosh, I remember that! I wanted to make you feel better, so I screamed louder than you, and you were so shocked you stopped crying and started consoling me." She nudged him gently. "You were always the nice one."

He looked down at her, his eyes confused and anxious. "Mina, why is it that I couldn't remember anything about you until now? It was like a fog. But all my memories are back, and I don't want to lose you again. Promise me you won't leave me."

A few tears slid down Jin's cheeks, and he dashed them away with the back of his hand. "Sorry, I don't remember being this emotional before."

Seeing him cry was too much for Mina. She had to close her eyes to fight the urge to bawl at the unfairness of life. This was the "big misunderstanding" trope that always made her scream in frustration. She would yell at the screen, "Just tell them already!" And yet here she was, trapped in a cliché of her own making.

"Hey, don't cry! You'll mess up your makeup!" Jin let out a shaky laugh. He reached over to wipe away the tears rolling down Mina's face, and she caught him up in a tight embrace.

It felt natural and right to hug him. He was the something that had been missing from her life. She didn't want to part from him again. They stood in a tangle of arms for a long time, warm against the sudden chilly breeze coming from the river.

"I'm sorry, Mina," he whispered above her ear. "I said we wouldn't talk about the past, and here I am breaking my promise."

"It's not your fault," she replied. "I'm the one who's sorry."

"Let's forget it. We found each other now. Nothing else matters."

Mina wished that were true. But there was no future for them. They were the "star-crossed lovers" trope, the worst of the worst. More awful than the love triangle. Doomed to be apart no matter how much they loved each other and how hard they fought to be together. Stupid *Romeo and Juliet* shit.

However, tonight she would pretend that she belonged here in this world with Jin. Tonight she wasn't going anywhere else.

"This is nice," he said. "Maybe we can stay here instead of going to Homecoming."

Mina was tempted. But she remembered Jin's confusion over pre-law and Sophia's crush that became an obsession. She had a responsibility to fix what had gone so terribly wrong.

"No, we should go," she said. "I didn't wear this dress for nothing!"

"I thought you wore that dress for me," Jin whined, his lower lip forming an adorable pout that made Mina want to kiss him. The idea of kissing him sent a rush of hot emotion to her head.

Mina pinched his cheeks. "You know nothing. We dress up to impress other girls, not our dates."

She started walking toward the harbor exit. Jin caught up and casually draped an arm around her shoulders. "Ah, tell me more about the strange ways of the girl creature."

"I don't know if you could handle the truth," Mina teased.

"Which is?"

"We're just smarter."

CHAPTER 19

Homecoming Dance

The school building was ablaze with lights and colorful decorations, and a long queue of students waited to buy tickets for the dance.

"That's a really long line." Mina frowned. "Too bad we didn't buy tickets earlier."

"Who said we didn't?" Jin whipped two tickets from his jacket pocket with a grand flourish.

"Smart boy!" Mina put up a hand for a high five. Instead, Jin intertwined his fingers with hers and pulled her past the line and to the ticket collector.

Several people gushed and catcalled Mina as she walked by. She smiled and waved in response and felt truly beautiful for the first time in her life. Not because of all the people complimenting her. Not because Jin's eyes showed it every time she caught him looking at her. But because she felt confident and sexy and happy.

The gym was split into two rooms by a folding wall,

with a large opening between them. The first room had refreshments and a photo booth and tables and chairs. The second room had a DJ on a stage and a large dance floor. Mina looked around at the crowd and wondered if Saachi and Megan might be here. She then shook her head. They wouldn't be caught dead at Homecoming. It was not their scene.

Lauren screamed when she saw Mina. She was with Tracey, Abby, and Diana, who'd come as a group. They surged toward her and surrounded her, pushing Jin away so they could gush over Mina's dress. They made her take off her jacket and leave it on a chair already piled with their coats.

"Isn't this a designer dress?" Lauren asked.

"Ha, no way, this is a total knockoff," Mina said. Which was true. She'd created it.

"Mina, you look gorgeous, but do you have to wear your fanny pack?" Diana asked.

"Yes," Mina responded simply. They had no idea how essential it was to her.

"Actually, I don't think I've ever seen Mina without it," Tracey remarked. "It must hold something really important or valuable."

"Tampons," Mina replied, deadpan.

All the girls shrieked with laughter and teased Jin, who looked uncomfortable.

Someone asked for a group photo and they all posed for several photos.

As she was talking with her friends, Mina felt a sudden cold, hateful energy. She wasn't surprised to see Sophia, in a cherry-red dress, glaring at her. The other girl would've looked beautiful if it weren't for the ugly expression on her face.

"Uh-oh, it's Sophia again," Abby remarked. "But who's that guy with her? I've never seen him before."

"He's cute," Tracey said.

"Too old." Diana was not impressed. "And he must not be all that because she looks like she's in a bad mood."

Lauren snorted. "She always looks like that. Serious resting bitch face."

"Poor guy. Someone should warn him about her temper," Abby whispered.

Diana shrugged. "Not our problem."

Nobody needs *to warn Sophia's date about anything,* Mina thought. Even though he was dressed in a nice suit and tie, his bearing was more that of a soldier than a student.

Ms. A was expecting something to happen tonight. He's probably part of whatever that is.

An arm snaked around Mina's waist.

"Let's not pay any attention to her," Jin whispered into her ear.

"It's not like I *want* to," Mina groused. "It's because she's always glaring at us!"

"We can ignore her and have a great time."

Mina gnawed on her lower lip. She couldn't ignore Sophia; she had to watch her. Mina couldn't shake the feeling that Sophia would be central to what happened tonight. But for now, she let Jin lead her to where Mark and another guy were standing with Jewel and Kayla. Both girls looked stunning. Jewel was in a beautiful baby-blue evening dress that perfectly complemented her eyes and pale skin. Kayla, in contrast, wore a short sleeveless black dress that was formfitting and incredibly sexy. Mark looked handsome in a black suit with a retro bow tie. But no one seemed happy. Mark kept glancing over at Diana, who turned her back on him after one long hard glare. And Jewel and Kayla were more interested in clinging to each other than their respective dates. Why couldn't they see that they belonged together? Mina sighed, her heart sinking as she thought about her stupid pairings.

As Mark, Jin, and Kayla's date went to get some drinks, Mina caught a tender moment where Kayla and Jewel touched foreheads. Their feelings were almost painfully obvious.

I need to fix this right now.

"You guys make a beautiful couple," she said.

They broke apart immediately.

"What are you talking about? We're not a couple," Kayla responded. At her words, Mina could see the hurt in Jewel's eyes and the answering sadness in Kayla's.

Mina took both their hands. "I'm sorry for whatever is making you feel trapped. But I know you guys are strong, and I can see how much you love each other. I hope you'll follow your heart, and not the weird voice in your head that is telling you to do things you really don't want to do."

Jewel gasped. "Mina, how did you know? I thought there was something wrong with me. I've felt like I was trapped by someone who was controlling me like a puppet."

Kayla looked at Jewel. "What do you mean? What's the voice telling you to do?"

"It told me that I should date Mark because I was in love with him, but I'm not."

By this time, the boys had returned with drinks.

"Mark, I'm sorry you have to hear it like this, but I don't want to date you," Jewel said. "I'm in love with someone else."

Mark let out a relieved breath. "That's totally cool, Jewel. I'm gonna be honest—I really like Diana and wanted to ask her to Homecoming, but I felt I had to ask you. Even though I didn't want to, no offense."

Jewel turned him around and pushed him toward the group where Diana stood. "Go, tell her that."

Kayla caught Jewel by the arm, her expression tense. "Who is it? Who are you really in love with?"

Jewel sighed. "Kayla, you're so dense sometimes. I've been in love with you since ninth grade."

With a slight sob, Kayla launched herself into Jewel's arms. And everyone around them started cheering.

Jin pulled Mina close. "You did good," he whispered.

Mina arched an eyebrow. "How do you know I did anything?"

"I don't know," he replied thoughtfully. "But things have been different since you came. For the better."

Mina smiled and leaned her head against his shoulder. She was relieved to fix one of her mistakes. It was a start.

"What's going on?" Kayla's date asked plaintively, still holding drinks in his hands.

Mina gently steered him away from the happy couple. "What's your name again? Frank? Let me introduce you to some friends of mine."

They all joined Lauren's group, and Mina watched as Frank was consoled by Tracey's sympathetic flirting. Mark was doing his best to win Diana over, and Mina could tell that it was working.

"You look so pleased with yourself, like some little old matchmaker auntie," Jin teased.

Mina shook a finger in mock offense. "That is a grave insult!"

"Why? You can set up a matchmaking service for all your young single friends. Auntie Mina's Marriage Matches. It suits you. You're quite good at it."

"Well, I am," she replied, and stuck her tongue out at him.

His eyes crinkled with laughter. "Come on, let's dance."

They all decided to hit the dance floor together. The music was kicking, and the beat was pulsating and throbbing in their veins.

Out of the shadows, Sophia slid between Mina and Jin and slithered her arms around Jin's neck. Mina was shocked. She could see Sophia's date standing on the side of the dance floor, just staring at them. Jin tried to push Sophia off, but she clung even harder.

Mina stepped back, overwhelmed with pity. It was difficult watching how desperately Sophia held on to someone who despised her. The awkward scene continued, now with more people watching and judging. Turning to her friends, Mina said she needed a drink, and Lauren and Abby left the dance floor with her. As she turned away, she caught a glimpse of Ms. A's face. She was surprised to find a look of alarmed concern. Like Ms. A was worried about Jin.

How odd—why would she be worried if she's the villain? Unless she's not really bad.

Suddenly reminded of her weird dream, Mina wondered

if Ms. A was also fighting the character traits written for her. The real Ms. A would never be a villainous character; she was too nice. Mina had to think about what this meant for the story.

"Abby, Mina, drink this," Lauren said as she passed bottles of water to them.

"That was painful to watch," Abby complained. "What is wrong with that girl?"

"What a bitch!" Lauren fumed. "Mina, I would beat her silly for you if I wasn't terrified of her."

Mina couldn't help but laugh. "Lauren, you are a good and wise friend."

A commotion behind them caught their attention. Jin had broken free of Sophia's embrace and stormed away in disgust. Sophia screamed his name so loud that the DJ stopped the music. Everyone turned to gawk at her, but Jin kept walking. Sophia was now engulfed in blue sparks. Even her eyes glowed an electric blue.

"She's a Gifted!" someone shouted. Dozens of cell phone camera flashes lit up the room.

Frightened by Sophia's erratic behavior, Mina raced toward Jin. From the corner of her eye, she saw Ms. A ordering students off the dance floor as Sophia raised her arms.

Everything happened as if in slow motion. Jin beamed his beautiful smile as Mina got close. Behind him, Sophia shot a tremendous blue surge of electricity at Jin's back.

"Jin!" Mina screamed. She knocked him to the floor and was immediately engulfed in an intense ball of light.

"Mina!"

She opened her eyes to find the world frozen around her, except for Jin, who kept shouting her name in panic.

"You stopped time again," she said.

A look of relief and awe filled his face. "You scared me to death! Are you all right?"

She looked down at herself. The light around her body was dimming, but her skin was glowing as if it was absorbing all the electricity.

"I'm fine, it didn't hurt me."

Jin went to embrace her, but sparks bounced off Mina's body. "Ouch! What's going on?"

"Don't touch me," Mina said. "I feel like I'm going to explode."

The energy pulsated under her skin, seeking release. Mina rushed past motionless bodies, looking for the nearest exit. She dashed outside and unleashed all the electricity into the sky in a brilliant flash of lightning.

"Holy crap! How did you do that?" Jin asked. He stood holding the door open, the unmoving bodies of the students silhouetted behind him.

Dazed from the rush of energy that had surged through her, Mina shook her head.

"It felt like I was a channel," she said. "I absorbed it and then had to release it. I'm just glad I was able to control it."

"That's amazing! But you have to rewind it. We can't let anyone know about your superpowers. It's too dangerous."

Nodding, Mina whipped out her tablet and scrolled to the frame where Sophia stood enveloped in electricity. With only seconds left, Mina tried to erase the blue streaks, but it wasn't working.

"What's going on?" She pressed harder, no longer being careful. The electricity still wasn't erasing. The battery was at 8 percent.

"Damn it! I forgot to charge my tablet!" Desperate, she tried again, using as much force and speed as she could. The tablet was glitching, but the blue streaks began to fade. Mina erased sloppily, furiously, not caring what else she was deleting from the scene.

The next moment, the silence broke as the world came back alive. Mina shoved her tablet and digital pen into her bag.

There was a furious scream, and then gasps and roars of laughter filled the gymnasium. Jin and Mina stepped inside in time to see Sophia dashing through the double doors, her dress a tattered mess. Shocked chaperones and security guards chased after her.

Mina quickly walked to Lauren's side, hoping her friends hadn't noticed that she and Jin had suddenly vanished.

"Did you see what she did to herself?" Lauren was laughing so hard she could barely talk.

"What happened?" Mina asked in bewilderment. She looked at Jin, who was just as clueless.

"Oh lord! Please tell me someone caught that on video! It's priceless!" Abby's tone was more awestruck and amazed.

Tracey rushed over to them with Kayla's old date, Frank; both were buzzing with excited laughter.

"You guys, I got that on my phone!"

They all crowded around to watch the video. Tracey had started filming when Sophia was screaming Jin's name as he walked away from her. They could all see Sophia's hands lit up with sparks and her eyes turning blue.

"She's not even trying to hide it anymore!"

"I didn't know she could do that!"

"That's a cool effect."

On the video, Sophia raised her arms, and what happened next caused everyone to shriek in excitement again. One moment the electricity was there and then it was gone, except for the blue in her eyes, and her hair and dress were in absolute ruins. There were even burn marks on some exposed parts of her skin.

"Whoa, she burned off her own hair and dress!"

"Serves her right. Remember what she did to Jane Powell's hair?"

Nobody noticed that Jin wasn't onscreen anymore; they were all too focused on replaying Sophia's humiliation. Only Jin and Mina knew what actually happened. Mina trembled in alarm. In her attempt to contain Sophia, she could have really hurt her. It was sheer luck that Sophia wasn't badly injured. Mina should have been more careful. If only the erase function hadn't been stuck. She didn't know what happened, but she was overwhelmed with the realization of how dangerous this power was.

It was only when Jin took her hand that Mina began to calm down. She looked up at his face and shivered. Sophia could have killed him. The storyline was dangerous. There had to be a way to grasp control or get rid of all the superpowers before it was too late. Her head was spinning, and all she wanted to do was go home and think.

Mark appeared by Jin's side. "Jin, we need to talk in private."

"Mina comes with us," Jin replied. "She knows everything."

Mark led them out of the gym, down the corridor, and into another hallway, where Kayla and Jewel were waiting.

"Jin, are you okay?" Jewel asked. "That was really scary!"

"I can't believe that girl!" Mark was irate. "Something's not right with her!"

"What do we do?" Kayla asked. "Security and faculty are all on high alert. They've called the police. And too many people shot footage of Sophia for anyone to keep quiet."

"Somebody needs to do something about her," Mark cut in. "She's completely out of control."

"I don't even know who she is anymore." Jewel seemed genuinely shaken.

"She's a monster," Mark said. "If she hadn't shorted herself, she would've killed Jin."

"But if she gets caught, I wouldn't put it past her to betray us. She knows our powers," Kayla warned. "She can be really vindictive."

"What if we out ourselves?" Jin asked. "We've been scared that Merco will use us as lab rats. But if we go to reporters first, tell them what's happening, then they should be able to protect us, right? Maybe we can even help the kids that got taken by Merco."

"We don't have proof that Merco actually took them," Kayla said.

Jin and Mark exchanged a glance. "We know where they are," Jin said.

"What? Why didn't you tell us?" Kayla crossed her arms and glared at the boys. "You thought you were going to play superheroes and save the day?"

"No, that's exactly why we didn't tell you," Mark said. "There's nothing we can do to help them, and all it would do is upset you both."

"That may be true," Jewel said, placing a calming hand on Kayla's arm, "but you still should have told us."

Jin nodded. "You're right and we're sorry. We'll tell you now."

As Jin and Mark told the girls all about what they'd found, Mina felt distant, as if she were watching a scene in a movie. The group was now coming up with a plan to reveal their powers to a trustworthy journalist, but they sounded as if they didn't really believe what they were saying.

Mina knew that there was nothing her friends could do. They were just following a script dictated by the wonky storyline.

From the corner of her eye, Mina spotted a flash of movement. She backed away from the group to get a better look and found herself staring at Sophia's abandoned date. His face remained expressionless before he turned and disappeared.

"Hey, what are you doing there?" Jin asked. "Do you want to go back in?"

Mina shook her head. She looked around at everyone and noticed a drastic shift in their mood. Whatever plan they'd decided on had made them hopeful, despite their fear of Mercer. But that very fact made Mina more anxious. She was not only emotionally drained but once again physically exhausted, and all she wanted to do was go to sleep.

"I think I want to go home," she replied. Seeing Jin's disappointed expression, Mina felt guilty. "I'm sorry. I'm just tired."

"You can't go yet! Let's go to the diner and get late-night breakfast!" Kayla exclaimed.

At that moment, Mina's stomach decided to rumble loudly.

"Okay," Mina said. "I could eat."

Jin grinned. "We can always count on your stomach!"

CHAPTER 20

Secrets and Lies

Mark went off to get Diana and reappeared with Lauren, Abby, Tracey, and Frank. "Let's get waffles!"

They piled into three different cars and drove to the local twenty-four-hour diner. The huge corner booth was available, and they crowded in with a few additional chairs pulled up to the side. Mina quickly chose a chair to avoid being squished, while Jin scooted his seat right next to hers.

They ordered a lot of food and ate ravenously. Mina enjoyed being in the group, listening to the easy banter. It was weird how the wild roller coaster of emotions from the night couldn't stifle the hunger and vibrancy of high school students.

Soon the conversation turned to Sophia, and Tracey pulled up the video from the dance to show everyone again.

"This is the most epic video," Tracey crowed.

"Hold up," Diana said. "Slow down playback."

Diana studied the screen carefully and then turned it around for everyone to see. "Look, guys. I don't think Sophia did this to herself. Because this doesn't make sense. She goes from starting to charge up to looking like her entire body was blown. That's just too weird. It's like someone edited out what really happened."

Mark looked directly at Jin with a question in his eyes. Jin nodded almost imperceptibly, but Mina caught it all.

"Maybe a powerful Gifted intervened to save Jin," Tracey said. "I mean, I would do that. If I had a power, I would use it to save others."

"Me too," Abby said.

"Even if it's dangerous to you and your family?" Kayla asked. "Even if you could be kidnapped or killed?"

Tracey bit her lip. "I . . . I don't know."

"Kids with gifts have gone missing. No one knows where they are. But we've all heard the rumors that they're being experimented on and treated like lab rats because Mercer wants the powers for himself. So having a gift isn't so cool after all, huh?"

"And I know none of you like Sophia, especially you, Jin, but she isn't normally like this," Jewel cut in. "She's a good person who is not handling what's happened to her well. It's changed her. And even though she might have brought this on herself tonight, she still got hurt. There were some pretty bad burns on her arms."

Everyone was quiet for a moment before the conversation moved on to the latest gossip, and the mood switched rapidly once again.

But Mina was badly shaken by Jewel's words. Her chest

hurt, like she'd eaten something that had given her bad heartburn.

She excused herself and went to the bathroom, where she patted water on her face with shaking hands. She was horrified at hurting Sophia and guilty over the danger she'd put her friends in.

Stepping out of the bathroom, she bumped right into Jin.

"Are you okay? What's the matter? Talk to me." He wrapped her in a warm embrace.

She stood stiff, the video of Sophia playing in an endless loop in her mind, the burns on her arms looking worse and worse.

"It's all my fault," Mina whispered. "I did this. I created this horrible story, and now people are in terrible danger, and I just don't know what to do. I should've never written that stupid webcomic. I should've never come into this world. . . ."

"What are you talking about?"

Mina jerked in shock, realizing what she'd just said. "I think I have to go home now."

"Okay, I'll take you."

They paid their part of the check, Mina explaining that she was getting one of her migraines. Outside, Jin ordered car service through his phone, and they rode to her house in silence. Jin held Mina's hand, but his expression was remote and unreadable. Mina was too exhausted to decipher his thoughts.

Outside her house, he stood uncertainly before her.

"Can we talk now?" he asked. "You said some strange things before."

"Okay, but wait here for a minute first," Mina said. She unlocked her door and went inside. Kicking off her shoes, she grabbed Bomi and ordered him to shut down and be quiet. He rolled into a little ball, and Mina put him into the pocket of her jacket.

She reopened the door. "Come in."

"Will your dad be okay with me coming in when he's not home?" Jin asked as he took his shoes off in the foyer.

"Don't worry about it," Mina replied.

She padded barefoot to the kitchen and put water in the kettle.

"I'm making tea if you want some," she said.

Jin shook his head and paced back and forth. He kept staring at Mina as if he didn't know who she was.

Mina knew how badly confused he must be. Just thinking about what she'd said made her wince. She went through the motions of making tea to calm herself. *Boil the water, inhale, steep the tea bag, exhale, add milk and sugar, inhale, stir, exhale.*

She sat down at the table and held the mug in her hands, the heat helping to steady her nerves. This moment was what she'd been afraid of since the beginning.

"You said you shouldn't have come into this world. That you created this terrible story. What did you mean by that?" Jin stood in front of her, his face worried and distressed.

Mina raked her hands through her hair. She didn't want to lie to him anymore. "Jin, the reason you don't see your birth mom anymore is because where I'm from, you died of cancer when you were six years old. Auntie Jackie was devastated. You were her entire world. She loved you so much."

Jin collapsed onto a kitchen chair. He looked dazed. But then he laughed.

"You realize how ridiculous that sounds, right? I'm pretty sure I'm not dead."

Mina clasped her hands in front of her face and breathed slowly through her nose. She needed to explain carefully.

"I'm not from here. I'm from the original timeline. When you died, there was a freak thunderstorm. Auntie Jackie said multiple lightning strikes hit close to your room just as you died. I'm not a quantum physicist, but that anomaly might have caused the timeline to break off. It's why you woke up in the hospital alone and everyone was gone."

He was shaking his head.

"*Stop.* This isn't true."

"It's why you couldn't remember me before. But now you do. Only after meeting me again. You know your mom would never leave you."

"My mom didn't want me and abandoned me. *That's* what happened." Tears dropped from Jin's eyes, and he wiped them furiously. "You've got a wild imagination, Mina."

"Jin, think about everything that happened recently. You suddenly had a gift you never had before. You were going to give up your dream of becoming a medical doctor and were considering pre-law instead. Didn't you think any of that was strange?"

Mina ran her hands through her hair. "I did it. I made that all happen. Before you tell me I'm delusional again, let me just show you."

She removed her tablet from her fanny pack and turned

it on. A low battery notification popped up. Ignoring it, she opened the webcomic to the beginning and handed the tablet to him.

The room was quiet except for their breathing. Mina watched Jin's expression change from confusion to anger.

"You've been documenting us for a webcomic story?" he said.

"No. I created a story that came true."

Jin had scrolled to the episode where they'd met. "Was meeting me just so you could have a romance for your love story? Were you just playing with me?"

Mina shook her head fiercely. "Once I came here, the story continued without any input from me. I haven't been in control of it since I arrived."

He was going back and forth between the scene where Mina stood in front of an exploding tablet and the scene where she was on the floor before him.

"You're saying control of the story changed at this point, right as you entered our world?" he asked.

Mina nodded. "That's when I realized my webcomic story had come alive here."

"And what about me? Where do I fit in to all of this? You think of me as just some character that you made up? Created me to be a love interest for that horrible girl?" His face twisted in agony. "Am I not real to you?"

"You're more real to me than anyone else in my whole world."

"How can I be real when you told me I'm just a character in your story?" he shouted as he jumped to his feet.

"Because you're still Jin." She stood in front of him.

"You're my oldest friend. We share memories and experiences. No one can take that away from us."

"That's our past, but what about now? You wrote me and all these other people into a story that robbed us of our free will. These past few weeks, I felt like someone was forcing me to do things I didn't want to do, feel things I didn't want to believe. As if an unseen force was guiding my every movement. You turned us from people into characters with stories that you predetermined. You were playing with our lives without even knowing it. And you put us in terrible danger."

Every word was true and broke Mina's heart. The pain and guilt ate at her psyche, and she felt weak. She wilted and dropped her face into her hands.

"I'm sorry. I'm so sorry. That's why I have to fix this. I'll solve this problem. I promise."

"How? How will you fix this?"

Mina gazed at him through her tears. His face was one of utter betrayal.

"How are you going to fix my broken heart?"

He turned and headed for the door.

"Jin, please don't go like this," Mina begged. She followed him and grabbed his arm. Jin tried to pull away but he couldn't.

"Let go, Mina," he said. "I need to leave."

She held on tighter. "Jin, please don't go."

He winced. "Ow, Mina, you're hurting me."

Taken aback, Mina immediately released him. Jin massaged his arm with an expression of shock on his face. He slipped his shoes on, opened the door, and stood there, outlined by the darkness of the night. For a long moment, it looked as if he was going to say something, but instead he walked out and slammed the door.

Mina cried herself to sleep. Bomi whirled next to her bed, making soft comforting noises. But nothing helped. She wished her father were here, just so she wouldn't feel so lonely.

This time, sleep brought a horrific nightmare.

She was in the hallway of a prison-like facility. Her steps echoed as she walked down the corridor, passing metal doors with small barred windows. At one window, she saw a hand waving frantically.

"Help me!" a voice from inside shouted.

She peered into the room and saw a boy her age. He was hooked up to a machine that he'd dragged to the door. He was barely able to stand. His face was pale, and his body looked wasted away.

"Please get me out of here," he wailed. "I won't survive another harvesting."

More hands appeared from doors; more people pleaded to be saved.

"I'll save you. I'll save you all somehow!" Mina yelled.

"And how are you going to do that?" a voice boomed. "How can you save them when you can't even save yourself?"

Mina turned around slowly and swallowed her scream of horror. This had to be Rowan Mercer. She'd done a few drawings of him for her webcomic, depicting him as a tall, blond-haired man in his forties. What stood in front of her now was nothing like her drawings. The process of transplanting the harvested powers had changed him drastically. Parts of his face were missing, as if they'd been erased. He was fading from existence.

"But you can help me." His smile was evil. "You can draw me a new face."

Soldiers appeared behind him. And when Mina turned to run, she realized she was surrounded.

"Bring her to me," Mercer ordered.

As the soldiers attacked her, Mina finally screamed.

CHAPTER 21

Finding Help

Saturday, October 22

"It's just a dream," Mina said as Bomi beeped in alarm. The robot was rolled up and lying on her pillow.

Bomi unraveled and their screen bloomed with a heart.

"Is Owner not feeling well?" Bomi asked. "Owner had very disturbed sleeping patterns."

"I'm just so confused," Mina replied. "Can dreams predict the future? I hope not, because that was horrifying."

Bomi tilted their head from side to side, a question mark flashing on their panel.

"Never mind, Bomi. This is my problem to solve," Mina responded, patting the robot on the head. "As brilliant as you are, I really need a human's help right now. I just wish I knew who I could trust."

Jin.

Mina winced to think of him and how much she'd hurt him. He would've been the logical choice, but he was too upset, and Mark was his best friend so she couldn't risk going to him either. Jewel and Kayla were still too loyal to Sophia. What Mina needed was an adult. She wished for her dad's calm presence, his logical thinking, which would usually help her out of whatever bind she'd put herself in. But he wasn't in this world.

Mina thought back to the dance and remembered Ms. A's alarm and concern. How she'd rushed students off the dance floor, away from Sophia. From what Mina had learned so far, her webcomic had forced some people to do what they wouldn't have normally done. If that was true for Ms. A, then she wasn't an actual villain. And she was already investigating the student disappearances.

Could Ms. A help? To be sure, Mina had to find more information. She needed to go back to school and snoop into some student files.

Mina got out of bed, staggering to her feet. She was dizzy and completely depleted of energy. She'd never been so tired before. Looking down, she saw that she had fallen asleep in her Homecoming dress. She walked into the bathroom and was not surprised that her face was a wreck. Her makeup was smudged, and her eyes were a dark swollen mess.

"Ugh, I'm hideous."

But what else could she expect after such a horrible night? She didn't even want to think of Jin. It hurt too much.

Mina took a hot shower and changed into jeans, a white graphic T-shirt that said FEMINIST AF, and a black bomber jacket with the US flag on one sleeve and the South Korean flag on the other. When she went to pack her tablet away, she saw an icon of an almost dead battery flashing.

Mina sighed. "Forgot to charge it again."

She put her tablet in her fanny pack, grabbed a black cap, picked up Bomi, and ran downstairs to the kitchen. As Bomi happily beeped and rolled about her feet, Mina plugged in her tablet and searched for medicine to take for her growing headache. After gulping the pills down with a cold glass of water, she sat and laid her head on the table, overwhelmed by exhaustion.

"I am the battery of life, constantly drained and never fully recharged," Mina griped out loud. "I wonder if this is what getting old feels like."

She heaved a dramatic sigh. "Food. I need food." She dragged herself up and made a peanut butter and jelly sandwich and a cup of coffee.

Fifteen minutes later, Mina felt a lot better. She checked her tablet—the battery was up to 30 percent.

"That should be enough." She swept it into her pack, put on her boots, and left her house with a mission.

The day was overcast and cold. Mina pulled the black cap down over her forehead and walked quickly to school. She used her tablet to unlock a side door, then stepped into a dimly lit corridor that led her to the main hall across from the administrative offices. Mina peered through the large glass windows to see if anyone was there.

"What are you doing here? How did you get in?"

Mina jumped in fear and spun around to face Ms. A, who looked just as surprised to see her.

"You're the new transfer student, Mina Lee, correct?" Ms. A asked.

Mina nodded as she wondered what she should say.

"So why are you here?" Ms. A asked again.

"I need your help," Mina said.

"I'm sorry, but you have to come back on Monday during school hours," Ms. A responded sharply.

"I'm not here about school. I'm here to ask you about anomalies."

Ms. A's eyes focused intently on her. "What are you talking about?"

"The changes that have happened recently have no reasonable explanation. I know you are looking into them," Mina said. "I'm hoping you can help me."

The assistant principal just continued to gaze at Mina with suspicion. Then, abruptly, she walked away.

"Come with me," she said over her shoulder.

Mina followed her to her office. Ms. A pulled a file from a pile of documents on her desk.

"There were some unusual items on your record that I wanted to talk to you about. Specifically, why you have a transcript from Bellington High School, Washington, DC, to transfer to Bellington High School, Washington, DC. I thought for sure that it was a typographical error, but it doesn't seem to be, and I find myself at a loss to explain it. The strangest thing being that no one else has noticed the issue, as you are here and attending this school now."

From the corner of her eye, Mina spied a huge pile of physics books.

"May I ask you how long you've been assistant principal?"

"Why do you ask?"

"Because if it hasn't been for more than forty days or so, then you probably have a lot of questions for me."

Ms. A stood very still, but her eyes and flaring nostrils gave away her surprise. She gestured for Mina to sit at the conference table with her.

"What can I do for you?"

"I need advice," Mina said. "But I'm not even sure how to explain everything."

"I find it always helps to start at the beginning," Ms. A said dryly.

"Okay, this is going to sound unbelievable, but please keep an open mind." Mina told her about creating the webcomic and being pulled into the world.

When she was done, Ms. A laughed. "And you expect me to believe you?"

Mina took out her tablet, scrolled to the most recent scene, and passed it to Ms. A to read.

Her eyes grew wide with shock. The last frame of the webcomic showed Ms. A asking Mina the same thing.

"I'm not sure that's supposed to prove anything," Ms. A replied.

Mina bit her lip, then noticed a coffee mug on the desk. She threw it on the floor, where it broke in a large puddle.

"What do you think you're doing?" Ms. A jumped to her feet.

Ignoring her, Mina focused on erasing the broken mug that had just appeared on her tablet. Like the night before, it didn't erase at first, as if the tablet was malfunctioning. But by pressing down harder and scrubbing faster, Mina was finally able to erase all vestiges of the spill.

She heard Ms. A gasp as the mess vanished and the full coffee mug reappeared on her desk.

"It's not a gift," Mina explained. "It's because I'm the creator of the whole superhero story."

"Interesting. You can erase something that happens in a scene," Ms. A mused. "Can you erase entire scenes that already happened?"

"I'm limited to what happened within sixty seconds."

"Is it always such an effort to do that?"

"No, sometimes it's easy, but I think my tablet might be malfunctioning. It was hard to erase last night also. It's why Sophia ended up getting burned. That was my fault."

Ms. A sat down and folded her hands on the table.

"So it was *you* who stopped Sophia," she marveled.

Mina nodded.

"I remember she was going to attack Jin Young Kanter. I saw you running toward him, and the next thing I remember is her screaming and running out of the gym. And you and Jin came in from outside. Can you tell me what happened?"

Mina took a deep breath and explained how she had absorbed the electricity and released it into the air.

"I don't think I can get hurt in this world," she said. "But I do get really tired."

"That makes sense," Ms. A replied. "If you aren't from this world, then nothing here should be able to harm you."

"But it was weird. I didn't deflect the electricity. I absorbed it and then felt like I was going to explode."

"Interesting. Your body couldn't retain all that energy. It had to be released. Thank goodness you thought to go outside. Otherwise a lot of people would've gotten hurt, not just Sophia."

They sat silently for a moment, Mina anxiously watching Ms. A, who was staring off into space.

"So what do you need my help for?" Ms. A asked finally.

"I need to put everything back the way it was," Mina said. "But I don't know how."

Ms. A pulled out a large memo pad and started to write down notes.

"Mina, give me a list of the most important similarities and differences between our two worlds. Like your school and this school are the same. You said your house is the same, but there's no sign of your dad in this world."

Mina nodded. "The neighborhood and the city, so far as I can see, are all the same. The differences are the changes I made. Like the gifts and people's relationships and actions."

"How are the people different?"

"Well, you're a physics teacher at my old school."

Ms. A smiled. "I'm actually a physics teacher here also. I was extremely confused when I suddenly became an administrator. I much prefer teaching."

"I'm really sorry about that," Mina said.

"I'm more offended that you made me a villain," Ms. A replied. "But the beautiful thing about free will is that it allows you to be who you are, no matter how hard the situation might be. Luckily, the worst I was doing was collecting data on the Gifted and asking students I trust to help me. It wasn't hard for me to resist passing that information on to Merco because I don't trust billionaire playboy types who send henchmen with bags of money and zero personality. They scream of evil conglomerate scum stereotype straight out of a cheesy superhero movie."

Mina winced. "That bad, huh?"

Ms. A raised her eyebrow. "You read a lot of comic books, I take it?"

"Yeah," she replied sheepishly. "Guilty pleasure."

"Well, perhaps it was a good thing to do," Ms. A said. "It allowed me to gather as much information as I could and try to understand what was happening."

Mina had a strange moment of deja vu before she realized she'd heard Ms. A say the same thing before.

"Although the last thing I would have ever guessed is that some teenager was playing God with our lives," Ms. A continued.

Mina cringed, but before she could say anything, Ms. A held up a hand. "Don't apologize again. I know it's not your fault. There was no way to know that our worlds would link up in this manner. But what is that link?"

She tapped on her list with the end of her pen.

Mina leaned forward and circled "Jin."

Ms. A gazed at her keenly. "Explain."

"Jin was my best friend from childhood who died when he was six years old," Mina said. "But in this world he's alive."

Ms. A's eyes lit up in surprise and also a strange delight.

"Then we are in the alternate timeline," she said. "Tell me where you think it branched off."

"It must've been when he died," Mina whispered. It hurt her heart to talk about Jin. "My auntie Jackie always said it was a thunderstorm that took her Jin away. When he died, multiple lightning strikes took out the hospital power."

"What about Jin? What's his earliest memory?"

"He thinks his mom abandoned him," Mina said. She

then explained how Jin's memories of his past, which had been repressed, had suddenly returned after meeting her.

"I made the mistake of telling him all this yesterday, and he is really upset," she whispered. "I don't know what to do."

"Well, I'm not sure what you can say to Jin to help him process this information. It probably has upended his world," Ms. A replied straightforwardly. "But what I do know is that what's going on here has gone too far. The danger is very real, and we have to do something about it."

Mina nodded. "That's why I came to see you. I was hoping you could help me."

"If you hadn't drawn Jin into your webcomic, it would probably not have affected our world at all."

"Yes, but I don't understand why."

Ms. A wrote some more notes and then sat tapping her pen on her pad for a minute.

"I don't think we're supposed to understand it. Life is mysterious. One interesting thing is that you and Jin share an amazing bond, and that might be where the answer lies." Ms. A gave Mina a sympathetic smile. "I saw you two at Homecoming. Talk about chemistry!"

Mina flushed.

Ms. A rapped her fist on the table. "But the more pressing issue is what to do about the storyline run amok."

"I don't know how to fix this."

"Mina, I think the answer is something you have to come to realize on your own. I can only guide you. Think about everything that's happened. What have you tried so far?"

"I tried to delete all the episodes with my mini tablet,

but it won't let me, maybe because it is all on my main tablet at home. I can only delete a scene within sixty seconds of it happening. I tried to draw my way out of here. But that didn't work. I think the answer is to get rid of all the gifts. But I can't do that from here."

"What about changing the storyline?"

"I can't. Believe me, I tried! I think it's because I'm in the story and can't see all that is happening." Mina sighed. "Stopping Merco doesn't get rid of the dangers for the Gifted because I have no idea how wide the story has spread, who's involved, what plans are in the making. I can stop one thing and not know what else is happening or what direction the plot will take."

"You're right," Ms. A said. "There's no choice. You have to nip it at the root. You must return to the source material. So the priority is to get you home. That's the only way we can resolve the Mercer problem. You've unintentionally created a monster. He has to be stopped."

"Gah! I know," Mina griped. She put her head down on the table with a thump, which sent Ms. A's memo pad and pen flying. "Oh, I'm so sorry!"

"Mina, did you give yourself gifts?"

"No, I didn't give myself any!"

Ms. A stood up and went to the recycle bin. She pulled out a thick manual and handed it to Mina. "See if you can rip this in half."

Mina was confused. "Huh? Why?"

"I'm testing out a theory."

"Okay, but there's no way I—" Mina stopped in amazement. "What the heck?" She'd ripped the manual as easily as if it had been one piece of paper.

Ms. A nodded again, picked up her pad and pen, and wrote something down. "So what do we know are the rules of your tablet?"

Still in shock over what she'd just done, it took a minute for Mina to compose herself. "I can erase what happened sixty seconds earlier. I can create almost anything as long as it isn't a living creature. I can't be hurt in this world, but I do get really tired. Like I'm completely drained of all my energy."

"And how long have you been here?"

"Twelve days."

Ms. A was lost in thought for a moment.

"I was thinking of the impossibility of having the creator of the story within the world they made," she said. "It's a paradox. How can you create within your creation? The paradox has to adapt to the world or everything will collapse."

"I don't understand," Mina said.

"You created a story that has overpowered this world. But when you came here, you lost control, and you've been trying to wrest it back. The story is fighting you, trying to neutralize your power. So I believe that the longer you stay in this world, the more you will become a part of it," she answered. "And then you will lose your creator powers. At which point you will no longer be immune, and you could die in this world."

CHAPTER 22

Ms. A Takes Charge

"Oh my gosh," Mina whispered. "I think it has already started to happen."

"What do you mean?"

"Since I came into this world, I've become the main character of my own webcomic."

"Hmmmm." Ms. A stared at Mina in utter fascination. "The creator is now the hero on a journey to save the world from . . . the creator."

Frowning in confusion, Mina asked what she meant.

"You are both the problem and the solution."

"And you think I can fix this?"

Before Ms. A could respond, there was a knock on the door. A little girl with messy gold curls and a chocolate-covered face and a middle-aged man holding a toddler walked inside. "Mommy! We're here!"

Ms. A's reserved expression changed to a radiant smile as she went to hug her daughter.

"Mina, this is my husband, and these are my daughters, Marnie and Lily," Ms. A said. Turning to her husband, she asked, "What brings you here?"

"You forgot your lunch," he replied as he handed over a lunch bag and thermos.

While the parents chatted, the older girl, Marnie, came close to Mina and stared up at her. "You look like a space princess!"

"What's a space princess?" Mina asked in surprise.

"She's a princess from space, silly. She's not like a poufy-dress princess 'cause space is very dangerous. So instead of wearing fancy dresses, she wears clothes good for fighting. Like you."

Mina laughed. "She sounds really cool. I think I'd like being a space princess."

Marnie stepped closer to Mina. "I like your hair. Will you babysit me?"

Ms. A laughed and scooped Marnie into her arms. "Sweetie, you can't just ask anybody you meet to babysit you. Now say goodbye, you have to go home with Daddy."

Watching Ms. A's glowing expression, Mina was struck by a sharp pang of grief as she was reminded of her own mother.

"Bye-bye, space princess! Don't forget to come back and babysit me!" Marnie shouted.

"I'm going to walk them to the car," Ms. A said to Mina. "I'll be right back."

Mina waved goodbye and sat down again. She stared at the torn manual and remembered all the times Jin had appeared in pain after she'd hit him lightly. She snatched a metal letter opener from the desk and bent it in half using only one hand. As she marveled at it, Ms. A returned.

"How did you know I had super strength?" Mina asked.

"I didn't," Ms. A replied. "I surmised that you could do anything you put your mind to in this world as the creator. At least for now."

"Wait, so what does that mean? I'm not strong but I can act strong?"

Ms. A took out a large piece of paper and pencil and said, "Let me show you."

She drew a Venn diagram and labeled one side "Mina's real world (no powers)" and the other "Alternate timeline world (no powers)." Where the circles intersected, she drew a stick figure and labeled it "Mina's story (powers)."

"As creator, you have godlike powers only here." Ms. A pointed to the intersection. Then, within the intersection, she erased parts of the "Alternate timeline world" circle, turning the solid line into a broken one. "My theory is, once you, the creator, entered this world, the superheroes plot could no longer be contained in your story. That's why you can't control it."

Ms. A put down her marker and faced Mina. "It's not safe for you to be here," she said. "But I'm also concerned about what it means for this world."

"I know, the story . . ."

Ms. A waved off the suggestion. "No, I'm worried about the repercussions of a paradox disrupting the timeline. If it is true that the timeline broke off when Jin died in your world, then this is a world where everyone from Jin's previous life is not here. You, your dad, Jin's mom. In this timeline, you are all supposed to be missing. I don't know what will happen when someone from the original timeline enters this one. It could be absolute chaos. It could potentially collapse this timeline."

Mina's heart froze. "What does that mean?"

"Well, it means the alternate timeline would merge back into the original one, but since Jin is only alive here ..."

Mina gasped in horror.

"No, I won't let that happen! But if I return to my world, everything should go back to the way it was, right?" Mina asked.

"I'm not sure," Ms. A replied. "I believe it should alleviate the immediate threat at least."

She glanced at her wristwatch and sighed. "I have to leave soon to join my Science Olympiad team practice."

"Science Olympiad?" Mina was confused.

"I may be an administrator now, but I'm still their coach." Ms. A smiled.

Mina tensed up. They hadn't come to any resolution of her problem. "But what do I do?" she asked.

"I have an idea. In order to get you home, we may need to re-create the exact circumstances that got you here."

"A lightning storm?" Mina asked incredulously.

Ms. A nodded. "In fact, my science team might just be able to help!"

Mina was shaking her head. "This sounds impossible and also really dangerous."

Ignoring her, Ms. A went to her pile of boxes and started searching for something.

"Ms. A! I don't want anyone else to get hurt!"

Pausing her search, Ms. A looked at Mina sympathetically.

"It's already dangerous for everyone involved. The safest thing for all of us is to get you home."

Still worried, Mina watched as Ms. A continued to rummage through her boxes until she pulled out a textbook. She leafed through it and tabbed several pages before handing it to Mina. "While you still have your creator powers, why don't you re-create these machines in the school gymnasium today?"

"You want me to make all of this?"

"Yes, and I'm also going to need several other things," Ms. A said. "If we're going into battle, I want us to be completely fortified for the siege."

"Battle? What do you mean?"

Ms. A patted Mina's hand. "You're the main character now. That means Mercer is definitely going to be coming after you. That much is obvious in this storyline. And since he's such an over-the-top villain, we have to be prepared for the worst."

Mina felt both reassured by Ms. A's help and alarmed at her words. It was good to talk to an adult, but frightening to think of what was coming next.

"When are you planning to send me back?"

Ms. A tapped her fingers on her desk. "We need reinforcements and time to gather everything up. The earliest we can do this is tomorrow night. But let's not make any mistakes. You can stay here and work while I'm at practice."

If Ms. A's plan worked, then Mina would have only one more day in this world. And she'd never see Jin again.

"Ms. A, are you sure it will work?" she asked.

"I'm not sure of anything," Ms. A responded. "But we have to try."

CHAPTER 23

Love and Forgiveness

It was midafternoon by the time Mina was done drawing all the equipment and machines for Ms. A, who then told her to go home to rest and charge up her tablet.

"I think your tablet malfunctioning and your exhaustion are related."

"How's that?"

"It's the source of your power, am I right?"

Mina thought back to every moment she'd had a migraine or felt completely exhausted. Her tablet battery had been low.

"But how can that be?"

Ms. A shrugged. "You had it plugged in the whole time you were working, and yet the battery is now lower than when you first came to see me. Which to me means that when you use it, you deplete it and your own energy. So charge it fully and tell me how you feel."

Ms. A could be right. The battery was now at 20 percent,

and once again Mina was exhausted. Her hands were cramped and achy, her head was pounding, but she felt hopeful for the first time since arriving in the webcomic world. Being on her own without any adult supervision was both freeing and terrifying. She welcomed Ms. A's guidance. But there was this niggling concern in the pit of her stomach. A worry that, as smart as Ms. A was, she might be wrong and this big plan was all for nothing.

Arriving home, Mina nearly tripped at the sight of Jin sitting on her front step.

"Where've you been?" he asked.

Her throat welled up and she found it hard to speak. She'd just convinced herself to get used to the idea of not seeing him again. That he hated her, so there was no point in staying. But here he was, and she was an emotional wreck all over again. She shook her head and walked past him to open the door. He followed her inside.

Slowly, Mina poured herself a glass of water and popped some medicine for her throbbing headache. She removed her tablet from her fanny pack and plugged it in.

"Why haven't you been answering your phone?" Jin asked. "I've been trying to call you all day!"

"I'm sorry," she whispered.

She shuffled past him, lay down on the sofa, and closed her eyes.

"Mina, what's the matter?"

"So tired," she mumbled. She fell asleep as he called her name.

She was running. Someone was holding her hand and pulling her along. It was Jin.

"Hurry, Mina!"

They were in a wide hallway. It looked like school. Mina could hear the pounding of footsteps behind them. But before their pursuers could get too close, Jin would freeze time, getting them a minute ahead.

"Don't use your power too much, Jin," Mina said. "It'll wipe you out."

"We're almost there," he said. They rounded a corner only to run right into a squad of soldiers. Jin instantly froze them, and Mina erased them from the scene. But now Jin was stumbling, and blood was trickling out of his nostrils.

Mina hauled Jin up and wrapped her arm around his waist, urging him to run.

"Don't you dare give up, Jin!" she screamed.

"Leave me, Mina!"

"Never! Come on! Come on!"

They had to get to the gym. She'd spent all day making the room completely impenetrable. Once they were in, they'd be safe.

They reached the gym hallway. The one door they could enter was less than a hundred feet away. From the other end of the corridor, Sophia appeared, electricity crackling from every part of her body.

Jin tried to stop time, but his power was spent. Sophia was racing forward, her hands blazing as she shot electricity at them. Mina pushed Jin to the floor and faced the blast and—

She opened her eyes and saw Jin staring down at her.

"What are you doing?" she asked.

"Watching you sleep," he answered. He pushed a stray lock of hair away from her face. "You were having a nightmare."

Mina realized she was lying in his lap. She sat up and

leaned away. Looking at the time, she saw she'd been asleep for an hour.

"Why are you here? I thought you'd hate me."

"I could never hate you," Jin replied. "You're my oldest friend. You're the one I love the most in the world. I spent the night realizing that it didn't matter what you did—I don't care. To be honest, I would forgive you for anything. I'm just so glad you're in my life again."

Mina buried her face in her hands, surprised that she still had tears to shed.

"I don't want you to cry anymore, Mina," he said softly. "I will always love you, no matter what happens."

Pulling her hands away, he touched his lips to her forehead. They were firm but oh so soft. He slid them down her cheek until they rested on her mouth. Mina shivered as he pulled her closer, one hand cupping the nape of her neck while the other wrapped around her waist as he deepened the kiss. What little of Mina's mind was functioning turned off as the kiss lengthened and intensified, and her only thoughts were of how right it all felt. She smiled as he rained kisses all over her face, then in the sensitive hollow of her collarbone, until he found her lips again, and the magic continued.

This is what it feels like to be truly, deeply, madly in love. This is what it means to be alive.

Mina pressed her body away and exhaled a shaky breath.

"You must have a lot of questions for me," she said, trying to organize her thoughts.

"Your robot buddy answered most of them already," he replied. "Although I admit it scared me to death rolling up on me like that."

"Bomi?"

A series of happy chirps and beeps signaled his appearance at her side.

"I can't believe you made it," Jin said in wonderment.

"Out of all the things you've heard, Bomi is what you can't believe?" she teased.

"Come on, Bomi's pretty awesome!"

The little robot beeped and whirled around in thanks.

"Tell me more about my mom," Jin said.

"She's the coolest person in the world," Mina said before launching into all the ways Aunt Jackie had been there for her. "I wish she could see you. She would be so proud of you."

"Me too. I'd love to see your dad again. I remember him giving me shoulder rides."

"He's different now," Mina said. "My mom's death really changed him."

"He still loves you," Jin replied. "Even if you don't agree with him, you know that won't ever change."

"He just doesn't understand me and how I feel about my art."

"So you have to change his mind."

"You don't understand, it's hard," she whined.

"Mina, you created a story that altered an entire world. I think you can change your father's mind."

She laughed, but thinking of her father reminded her of Ms. A's plan and of going home. It meant leaving Jin. She pushed the thought away and hugged him close, wanting to cherish the moment as long as possible.

They whispered endearments to each other and laughed at how silly they got. The kisses moved from face to neck to collarbone and back. Hands traveled the length of their bodies and left them both reeling. And the talking. Hours of catching up on the spaces of their lives they'd missed. They would've kept talking if Mina's stomach hadn't decided to remind them it was dinnertime. Mina made some spicy ramen with egg and watched Jin eat it up with gusto.

Checking her phone, Mina saw that Ms. A had sent her more things to create. As much as she didn't want to, she had to get back to work.

"I wish you could stay all night, but I'm really exhausted and I think I need to sleep," Mina said.

"Stay all night? Whatever were you thinking?" Jin asked with a raised eyebrow.

She cupped his face and gazed into eyes that sang directly to her soul. "I wish you could stay forever," she whispered.

This time he kissed her with a hunger and urgency that felt as if he was imprinting himself into the very fabric of her DNA. His hands hot against her back, pulling her ever closer as they lay down on the sofa, their bodies fitting together like two puzzle pieces. Mina could no longer think; she was pure raw emotion. Love. Desire. Joy.

After several long minutes, they broke for air but stayed wrapped in each other's arms.

"I'd better go now," he whispered.

Mina nodded into his chest.

"I'll come first thing in the morning," he said. "I make really good pancakes for breakfast."

Smiling, Mina followed him through the door. She wrapped her arms around his waist and closed her eyes.

This is what Jin feels like.

He kissed the top of her head and gently pushed her inside.

"Go on in," he said. "I can't leave until you lock up."

She nodded. "Good night."

"Good night, Mina," he said. "I love you."

"I love you too," she replied as he pulled the door shut. Mina locked the door and watched through the window. Waving goodbye, Jin walked to the sidewalk and disappeared from view.

Mina sat at the kitchen table, too giddy to even think of sleeping. She'd never felt such intense emotions before. Her skin tingled with the memory of his touch. She'd been on dates, but they'd never left her feeling breathless and excited. If anything, kisses had been a wet slobbery affair that she had not been interested in. But kissing Jin was an entirely different experience. It was almost not fair to compare her prior kisses. In fact, it was virtually impossible to compare them.

"I am the moth trapped by his hot sexy flame of lust." Mina giggled.

Just thinking of Jin's kisses made her flushed and bothered and filled with longing. She suddenly remembered the webcomic. Mina rushed to check her tablet and nearly died of embarrassment to see their kisses highlighted in the frame. Mina groaned but couldn't stop smiling at Jin's handsome face. She wished she'd taken more photos with him.

The thought was sobering. This time tomorrow, she should be back home in the real world. And she'd never see Jin again.

Mina slumped in her chair. Ms. A's plan was the one thing she hadn't told Jin about. She didn't know how to. And now it was going to be harder than ever to leave him.

The house seemed colder and emptier with Jin gone. Mina shivered from the sudden drop in temperature. It felt ominous, as if it were a sign of something bad to come. Checking her tablet, she saw it was fully charged.

"I guess Ms. A was right," Mina marveled. "Charging the battery charges me also. Weird."

She slid her tablet into her pack, slung it over her body, and prepared to go upstairs. As she was turning off the living room lights, she caught movement outside the window. Someone was spying on her.

Immediately on alert, Mina looked around for a weapon, determined to go out and catch the person herself. She spotted the metal poker next to the fireplace, grabbed it, and put on her jacket and zipped it closed.

Suddenly, the front door burst open. Soldiers with rifles poured in, shouting.

"Drop your weapon and get down on the ground!"

Startled, Mina released the poker and watched as the soldiers began tearing the house apart. From the corner of her eye, she saw Bomi roll up into a ball and scoot under the sofa next to her. Mina knelt and quickly snuck him into her pocket.

This must be Merco, she thought as a soldier approached her with a large needle. He shoved her facedown on the floor. She felt a slight pressure as he jabbed her in the shoulder, but nothing happened.

"What are you doing?" Mina asked sharply. The soldier had his knee on her back and was trying to pull her arms behind her. "Get off of me!"

She yanked her arms free and pushed herself up, sending the soldier flying.

"She's unusually strong, sir!" he shouted.

"Hold her down!"

Now three soldiers were trying to restrain her. Mina wasn't even fighting them, and yet they were struggling to keep her from rising.

"Give her another dose!"

"Sir, that could be lethal!"

"These kids aren't normal, just do it!"

Kids? Did they kidnap the others?

Mina felt another shot, and this time she closed her eyes and pretended to be unconscious. If they had Jin, then she needed to go with them.

"Tase her to make sure she's really out."

Something hot struck her on the shoulder. It pulsed but caused no pain.

"Is she dead?"

"She's breathing."

"Tie her up and let's go."

Mina curled herself into a fetal position and made herself heavy and stiff as a board.

The soldiers zip-tied her hands and feet and carried her out to a truck. Inside, she could make out the unconscious bodies of Jewel and Kayla. After a long ride, the truck finally came to a stop. Mina carefully peered through her lashes and watched as men in lab coats pushing gurneys grabbed the girls.

Because Mina had frozen like a statue, the soldiers could do nothing more than place her sideways on a gurney. Under her lashes, she could see they were in a large industrial compound. They wheeled her into a room and locked the door. She opened her eyes to find herself in what looked like a windowless hospital room.

Sitting up, Mina pulled her hands and feet apart, snapping the zip ties as if they were merely thread. She was relieved that her creator powers were still strong. Whatever knockout drug they'd tried to use on her had no effect. The taser hadn't worked either. The soldiers couldn't hold her down. She knew she could break out of the room, but instead she decided to wait for them to come to her. Surprise could be a great advantage to find out what was going on.

CHAPTER 24

Becoming a Superhero

Sunday, October 23

She was in a dark corridor with metal doors surrounding her. Her body wasn't there, just her subconscious, or at least that was how it felt. Someone was screaming. She moved toward the sound into a large room with bright lights shining down on a patient strapped to an operating bed. Three thick needles were protruding from the chest and pelvis. The patient wailed horribly. As Mina approached, she recognized the patient. It was Jin.

Mina heard the door opening. She must have dozed off. Through her lashes she watched as three men in medical garb entered. One was pushing a small cart with needles, an IV bag, and an array of tiny bottles of drugs.

"Subject is Mina Lee. Not much information on her. However, she apparently has abnormal strength. It took double the dosage of sedative to put her out."

An orderly was setting up an IV stand next to Mina as the other two spoke. He took Mina's arm and swabbed it down.

"Wait a minute. Why isn't the subject restrained?" one of the doctors asked in alarm.

At his words, Mina's eyes popped open and she sat up. The orderly immediately tried to hold her down, but she shoved him away, sending him crashing into the wall.

I didn't even push him that hard, Mina thought.

She jumped off the gurney and grabbed the sleeves of both doctors before they could escape.

"Where are my friends?" she asked.

One doctor began fumbling for a syringe and a vial while the other grabbed the metal tray off the cart and bashed her on the head. Instead of hurting her, the tray ricocheted and slammed into the doctor's face. He crumpled like a rag doll.

The other doctor froze in fear.

"Where's Jin? Where are my friends?"

"I don't know—you're the first I've seen today," the doctor whimpered.

"What about the other Gifted who were kidnapped earlier? Where are they?"

"I have no idea! Please don't hurt me!"

Frustrated, Mina put out her hand. "Give me the keys."

The doctor reached into his pocket and pulled out a white pass card on a lanyard. As Mina moved to take it, he stabbed her with a needle and pushed down the plunger, leaving it sticking out of her chest.

"Crap!" It didn't hurt, it just irritated her. Mina pulled

the needle out, striking the doctor in the face in the process and sending him careening. He collapsed on the floor, unconscious.

Mina checked all their pockets, confiscated the pass cards, and used one to escape her room. In the hallway, she saw a bunch of closed metal doors with no windows. The number on her door read B-7. Using the pass card, she entered several rooms but found them all empty. A nurse pushing a medicine cart came around the corner.

"Excuse me, where are the other high school students?" Mina asked.

"What are you doing out of your room?" the nurse demanded. She grabbed a syringe off the cart and quickly began filling it with a small vial of medication.

Mina stepped close enough to grab the nurse's arm.

"I don't need any more shots," she said.

As the nurse struggled hard to free herself, Mina simply released her hold and watched in fascination as the woman hit the wall and fell.

"I just want to make clear that I didn't hurt you," Mina said to her. "You hurt yourself."

Mina opened an empty cell, dragged the nurse inside, and pushed the cart in after her, then waved goodbye and locked the door. Turning the corner of the hallway, she came to an office area. Surprised to find it empty, she walked in and found a wall of video screens showing numerous students in small rooms like the one she'd been locked in. Some were pacing, some were lying in bed, and all were hooked up to monitors. These were the Gifted who had been kidnapped. Looking closely, she could see numbers in the top right corners of the monitors. Room numbers—C-2 to C-10. She scanned all the screens but couldn't find her friends. As she was checking a third time, she heard a noise behind her.

"What the hell are you doing here?"

Mina looked up to see a security guard reach for a taser and shoot it at her. The two prongs hit her, one on her chest and the other on her thigh. She could feel heat and pulsing. Irritated by the "attack first, question after" mentality of the bad guys, Mina ripped the prongs off her body and yanked the taser out of his hands. With a loud yell, the guard charged toward her. Curious to see what would happen, Mina shot her arms straight out, catching him in the chest and sending him soaring through the air and crashing into a file cabinet on the other side of the room.

"Cool!" Mina said out loud. "But if there are a whole lot of bad guys, I'll need weapons."

Her fanny pack was still nestled securely across her body under her jacket. The soldiers never found it because they'd been unable to pry her out of her fetal position and had given up. Congratulating herself on her cleverness, she pulled out her tablet and sat down at a desk. When she turned the tablet on, she realized there was no wireless service.

"Crap, I can't do anything without wireless," she muttered.

A beeping sound came from close by.

"Bomi?"

The beeping got louder. Mina pulled Bomi out of the front pocket of her jacket.

"Bomi! I'm so glad to see you!"

The little robot beeped happily.

"Access Wi-Fi for Owner?" Bomi chirped.

"Yes!" Mina clapped her hands.

Bomi rolled to the wall, plugged into an outlet, and let out a confirmation beep. When Mina checked her tablet, the Wi-Fi signal was strong. She pulled up the webcomic to see what had happened.

Since coming to this world, Mina had noticed that the webcomic highlighted only the scenes she was involved in. The last panels included one kiss out of many with Jin, the soldiers breaking in, Mina seeing her friends in the truck, waking up while the scientists were jibber-jabbering, locking in the nurse, sending the guard flying, and finding Bomi. She winced again, but she was grateful for the editing.

"Thank you, third-person limited omniscient!"

Mina took stock of her situation. She had no socks or shoes on and was hungry but otherwise felt completely fine.

"Okay, cartoon villains. Time to do some superhero business. Bomi, let's have some fun!"

Bomi chirped, a smiley face showing on their screen.

"What I need are weapons," she muttered. "Some serious ass-kicking ultimate superhero-type weapons!"

Staring blankly at her tablet, Mina wondered what to draw. Sledgehammer, sword, bow and arrows? None of those seemed right. Definitely not a gun. She hated guns. But what about those Star Trek phasers that could be set to stun? Mina couldn't remember what they looked like, and she didn't want to risk losing them.

"Wait, I can make them look however I want, so why not gloves!"

Mina drew a pair of malleable metal gloves in dark pewter gray.

"If they can stun, then they can also make a force field for protection!" She grinned and finished drawing the specs for the gloves. Closed fist for stun, open palm for force field. As soon as she was done, the gloves appeared next to her.

"But how do I get everyone out of here?" Mina wondered out loud. "Bomi, where are we? Can you show me a satellite map of our location?"

Bomi's panel lit up and projected a 3D picture on the nearest wall. It showed a large wooded area with several buildings spread out among the compound.

"Zoom in on our exact location, Bomi."

The map widened to show one building with a side lot where several large black vans were parked.

"Got it." Mina quickly sketched out the building and lot and then added two more identical black vans parked right next to the building entrance. She then drew the desk she was sitting at and placed two sets of car keys on it.

That should cover it all!

The minute she put her pen down, the vans appeared on Bomi's wall projection, and the keys materialized on the desk. With a satisfied smile, she pocketed the keys, stood up, and promptly stubbed her toe. While it didn't hurt, it reminded Mina that she had no shoes on and her feet were getting dirty. She sat down again and drew big black combat boots with reinforced steel toes for maximum damage. Zippers, no laces. And a pair of thick black socks. The screen started glitching.

"What is it? Aw, come on! Now you stop working?"

Mina shook her tablet. It began to malfunction even harder, and then it turned off.

"You've got to be kidding me!"

Bomi beeped sympathetically and said, "Tablet reboot."

"Bad timing," Mina groused as she shoved her tablet and pen into her fanny pack and stuck Bomi into her pocket. She then put on the socks, boots, and gloves and stepped out of the office area into another corridor. She was checking the numbers on the doors when she found herself face-to-face with a unit of soldiers.

"Don't move or we'll shoot!"

"Oh good, I can test out my gloves," Mina said. She opened her left hand just as they started firing. Immediately, a shimmering force field appeared around her. "Sheesh, aren't you guys supposed to give another warning before firing?"

She pumped her right fist and stunned the whole unit. Lowering her arms, Mina was stepping over the incapacitated men and women when two soldiers attacked her from behind. One grabbed her right arm and the other tackled her around the waist, only to find she was immovable. She elbowed the one at her waist in the back of the head and punched the other soldier in the face, knocking them both out cold. Three new soldiers stood in a line in front of her, gaping. Mina pointed her fist at them, and they collapsed like marionettes whose strings were sliced.

"This is fun!" Mina exclaimed as she stunned a new squad of men that appeared.

She walked to the nearest door—C-2—and swiped a pass card to unlock it. In the room, she saw the boy from her dream, the one who'd cried for help. He struggled to sit up and asked who she was.

"I'm here to help," Mina said. She removed all the wires and tubes attached to him, then checked the next few rooms and found more teenagers, many in the same condition.

"I'm gonna get you all out of here," she said. "How many of you are there?"

"Nine," said a boy with black hair, glasses, and a swarthy complexion. Unlike the others, he was in his regular clothing and wasn't attached to any wires.

"Who are you?" Mina asked.

"I'm Ryan," he said. "I'm a healer. They don't harvest my gift in order to make sure I keep all of my powers."

"The others are in bad shape. Can you heal them?"

"Yes, but get Christy—she's the other healer." He pointed toward the end of the hall. "I'll need help."

Mina was running down the corridor, opening all the doors, when a new group of soldiers arrived. She knocked them down like bowling pins. From the last cell, a blue-eyed brunette with very fair skin pushed past Mina, calling Ryan's name.

"Christy!" Ryan shouted. They hugged each other hard.

"Enough of that," Mina cut in. "We don't have much time. Heal them quickly." Some of the Gifted had walked out into the hallway; others were too weak to leave their beds. The two healers immediately got to work.

"How are they?" Mina asked after ten minutes.

Ryan and Christy turned to her, their faces gray from effort. "We healed them as much as we could, but they are all in pretty bad shape," Ryan said.

"Where are the doctors that did this?"

"There's a lab at the end of the next corridor." Ryan pointed. "They're probably all in there."

"Okay, stay here, I'll be right back." Mina used her gloves to cover the entire area with a force field. She ran to the next corridor and immediately saw the lab; there were several people inside. More guards appeared, deploying their tasers. Over twenty electrical charges punctured her body, making her hot and angry. This would have killed any normal human being. She pulled all the wires off and formed force fields around her gloves by opening and shutting her hands several times. Shimmering light encircled her fists. As the guards continued to shoot at her, she advanced, knocking them out with blow after blow, until the floor was littered with bodies. Mina turned back to the lab, where she could see the horrified faces of the scientists. She broke down the locked door with one punch.

Stepping inside, she asked, "Who's in charge?"

Four of them all pointed to a pale older man with a deep receding hairline and frightened expression.

"Come with me," Mina said.

"I'm not going anywhere," he replied.

At her approach, he shrank back in fear.

"Don't touch me!" he shrieked. He reached for a large beaker and slammed it on Mina's head. The shower of glass surprised her. She threw her hands up reflexively, catching the scientist under his chin. His eyes rolled back as he crashed to the ground.

"Crap." Mina looked at the other scientists, who were

now cowering on the floor. "One of you come with me or . . ." She made a fist.

The youngest-looking scientist stood up with his hands raised. His name tag read DR. TAHIR.

"Okay, doc, come with me."

The doctor followed Mina into the hallway.

"Where are we going?" he asked.

Mina didn't answer; she just led him back to where she'd left the Gifted.

"Why are they like this?" she asked, her tone fierce and angry. It was hard to see all these kids, her age and younger, looking like walking skeletons.

"They had their bone marrow and blood harvested for stem cells and plasma," Dr. Tahir replied. "Some of them up to fifty percent. They really need to go to the hospital."

"This is evil! How could you do such a thing?" Mina demanded.

"Believe me, I have no idea why I'm even here," the doctor said. "I'm supposed to be an ER doctor. And then suddenly I'm working in this supersecret evil laboratory, and I don't even know how it happened. One day I was at the hospital, and the next day I'm here against my will. I really just want to go back to my old job."

Mina bit her lip. *Stupid storyline.*

"Well, here's your chance!" she exclaimed. "Help me get these kids out of here. But first, tell me, do you know where my friends are? The ones that came last night?"

"They're in the other building, being prepared for harvesting," he said. "The chief doctor is trying some kind of radical procedure. Since the serum of stem cells has not been lasting long, they plan on inserting the stem cells directly into Mercer's spine with the help of a healer."

"There's another healer?" She turned to Ryan and Christy. "Did you guys know about another healer?"

They both shook their heads. But then Christy gasped.

"There was a soldier dude!" she exclaimed. "He had more than one gift. He could heal, but it was more a side effect of his real talent."

"Which was?"

"Killing people. He can make them have heart attacks without touching them."

Mina's mouth gaped. She'd never created a character who could do that.

She turned back to Dr. Tahir. "Can you lead us to the exit?"

The doctor nodded.

"Let's go."

Mina organized the Gifted into two groups, those who could walk and those who couldn't. She placed the most critically ill kids on three gurneys, then pulled one behind her while Ryan and Dr. Tahir pushed the other two. Christy helped guide the rest of the kids. Outside the building exit stood a large faction of Merco mercenaries.

"Everyone, wait here," Mina ordered.

As soon as she appeared, the soldiers screamed "fire" and began shooting. She immediately formed a force field to protect herself and everyone in the building behind her. Bullets ricocheted off the shimmering shield, sending up a cloud of smoke so thick that it obscured her body. The soldiers stopped shooting and watched in stunned amazement as Mina strode through the dissipating smoke. After setting her gloves to stun, she rapid-fire blasted the mercenaries, leaving no one standing.

Turning around, Mina gestured for the group to come out.

Ryan, Christy, and the doctor were shocked as they took in the chaotic scene.

"How the heck did she do that?" Ryan asked as he began helping the injured kids into the closest van.

Dr. Tahir just shook his head. "To be honest, I don't want to know. I just want to get out of here."

Ignoring them, Mina turned to Christy. "Can you drive?"

The girl nodded numbly.

"Good, you're gonna have to take them to the hospital. Doc and Ryan, I need you both to come with me. I'll need a healer for my friends."

Ryan nodded. "Of course."

Christy whimpered. "But, Ryan . . ."

"It's okay, you'll be fine! Look how awesome you've done so far." Ryan hugged Christy before Mina rushed them apart once again.

"You can PDA after this is all done! Right now we've got to get everyone to the hospital."

Once all the injured kids were in the van, Christy got into the driver's seat.

"Christy, I'll clear the way for you." Mina turned to Ryan and Dr. Tahir. "Let's get in the other van. Doc, take us to the exit."

Dr. Tahir drove them down the road to the front gate of the compound. There, Mina stunned the guards on duty and blasted the metal fencing.

Catching Christy's worried expression, Mina smiled and waved her through.

"Don't worry, I'll take good care of Ryan," she said.

They watched as Christy drove off, a few of the kids waving goodbye as their van disappeared around the wooded bend.

Facing the doctor, Mina asked, "Which building are the others in?"

Dr. Tahir pointed to a large building in the farthest part of the compound.

Mina took a deep breath. "Let's free my friends."

CHAPTER 25

Regaining the Narrative

Dr. Tahir parked in front of the building. The windows were dark, and the doors were locked but surprisingly un-guarded. Mina bashed them in.

"Down that hallway," Dr. Tahir exclaimed. "First operating room!"

"Thanks, doc, we can take it from here. You should go before it gets bad."

He looked worried. "But I should help."

"It would be best if you went to the hospital to check on the kids and speak to the authorities about what happened," Mina replied. "And you really don't have to worry about me."

Dr. Tahir nodded in relief. "Good luck!"

He handed Ryan the keys to the van and left the building.

"Let's go!" Mina said to Ryan grimly.

Not waiting for him to respond, she primed her gloves and stormed toward the operating room.

She burst through the doors and took in the situation. Two people lay in the middle of the room, their upper bodies naked, surrounded by doctors and nurses. One was Mercer; the other was Jin. Oxygen masks covered their faces, and tubes and wires ran from both of them into complicated-looking machines. Three large needles were protruding from Jin's body, one in his sternum and two on either side of his pelvis. Blood was being extracted from Jin and flowing into a machine. Clear fluid was coursing from other tubes into Mercer.

There was a young man seated by Mercer's side. Mina recognized him instantly. He was Sophia's date from Homecoming and a Merco spy. This was probably the soldier dude Christy had mentioned—the healer who could kill people.

He made a fist and pointed it at her, seemingly trying to wield his power. But nothing happened. He used both hands. Still nothing. Mina smirked at him. At that moment, Ryan appeared at the doors behind her. The soldier turned his attention to Ryan, who clutched his chest, his face turning red. Mina grabbed the closest item, a metal pot, and sent it flying at the soldier, smashing him hard on the head and knocking him unconscious.

Ryan coughed but said he was all right. "Nice one, you took him out with a bedpan."

"Too bad it wasn't full," Mina replied.

The nurses and doctors had backed away and were now cowering in the corner. Mina signaled to them as she ran to Jin. "Take these tubes out of him *now*."

Ryan placed his hand on Jin's shoulder and concentrated on healing him.

"How much did you extract from him?" Mina demanded of the nurses who were bandaging Jin up. They shrank back in fright at her tone.

"We don't know," one of them said. He turned and looked at the head surgeon. "Ask her."

Mina stepped toward the surgeon, who arrogantly held her ground.

"How much did you take from him?"

The surgeon gave an elaborate sigh and peered at the numbers on the machine. "We'd just started the procedure when you barged in. Only about ten percent of his plasma and bone marrow were harvested."

White-hot rage coursed through Mina's body. Needing an outlet, she smashed her gloved fists down on the machines monitoring Mercer. He began to twitch uncontrollably on the operating table.

The surgeon rushed over to check his vitals. "Without the healer, his body is rejecting the bone marrow and plasma," the surgeon said.

"So?" Mina replied. She had already turned away, concentrating only on Jin.

"He could die!" the surgeon exclaimed.

Mina glared at her. "Good."

Jin was now free of all the tubes and needles and had been bandaged up. But he was still unconscious.

"The anesthesia will take some time to wear off," one of the nurses said.

"Where's his clothing?" Mina demanded.

The nurse ran to a cabinet and grabbed a plastic bag. Mina snatched the bag and several blankets from the shelves. She wrapped Jin's body with the blankets, lifted him carefully into a nearby wheelchair, and placed the bag of clothing on his lap.

"Come on, Ryan, let's go."

They rolled Jin out of the operating room.

"Kayla, Jewel, Mark, where are you?" Mina yelled. "Can you hear me?"

She ran down the corridor, looking into rooms, shouting their names. Ryan pushed Jin after her. They went around a corner, and this time there was a response.

"Mina! Over here!"

Mina could hear pounding. She followed the sound to a cell, smashed the lock, and pushed the door open.

Kayla stared at her. "How'd you do that?"

Ignoring the question, Mina asked, "Where are the others?"

"I think they're in cells nearby."

Mina destroyed several more doors before finding Jewel. They found Mark unconscious in the last room.

"What happened to him?"

"They drugged him so he couldn't use his power," Jewel said.

"Kayla, what about you?"

"They threatened to kill Jewel if I did anything," Kayla whispered. "I couldn't risk it."

Mina hugged her. "Of course not. We gotta go."

She pulled the bed into the hallway.

"How did you find us?" Jewel asked.

"No time to explain."

She led them to the building entrance, where the head surgeon appeared with a huge number of soldiers.

"There she is! Get her!"

Mina spewed a string of nasty curse words and an expletive-filled list of horrifying things she would do to the surgeon as she raised her fists and blasted them all unconscious.

"Mina! You're a superhero!" Kayla shouted in glee.

Mina ignored her outburst and directed everyone to the van. "Kayla, can you drive this thing?" she asked.

"Hell yeah, baby!"

Mina picked up Jin and then Mark and placed them carefully into the van.

"Now that's just showing off," Kayla groused.

Ryan got in next to Jin, while Jewel sat with Mark.

"Hold on, guys." Kayla drove the van out of the now deserted parking lot and down a long wooded road. "Where am I driving to, Mina?"

"To school," she responded. "Don't be alarmed when you see Ms. A. She's actually not bad. And she's been helping me a lot."

"I'll believe anything you say," Kayla quipped.

Mina switched on the overhead light, took off her gloves, and shoved them into her pocket. She reached over to hold Jin's hand.

"How is he?" she asked Ryan.

The healer smiled. "I think he's finally getting better. I can always sense when they're too sick, like the other kids. But he wasn't as bad off as they were. At this point, it's just the anesthetic."

As if he heard them talking about him, Jin moaned and opened his eyes.

"Mina, are you okay?"

The tears of worry she'd been holding back finally released. Bawling, Mina pushed past Ryan and launched herself into Jin's arms. Her crying fit lasted only a minute, and she sniffled as Jin lightly caressed her hair.

Ryan laughed. "I didn't know superheroes cried so much!"

"Hey, crying is not a weakness," Jewel snapped. "Crying is a cathartic release that actually is proven to make a person feel better, especially when they are under a lot of stress."

Ryan threw his hands up. "My bad, sorry, Mina!"

Mina wasn't listening; she was happy to be snuggled up against Jin's chest.

"I'm sorry to interrupt, but do you happen to know where my clothes are?" Jin asked.

Mina laughed and released him as Ryan handed over the plastic bag.

Jin dressed quickly and scooped Mina back into his arms. "I was so worried about you," he said.

Mina shook her head. "You were the one on an operating table having your stem cells and blood plasma harvested." She shuddered. "That was the most horrible thing I had to see."

"I'm sorry!" He slid his mouth down the side of her face and homed in on her lips, kissing her hard.

"Knock it off, you two!" Kayla said. "I can see you in my rearview, and it's distracting me from driving!"

Jin smiled and gave Mina one last long kiss.

"Hey, Jin." Jewel popped her head over the seat to gawk at them. "You missed a lot. Your girlfriend is a badass superhero."

Mina rolled her eyes and introduced Jin to Ryan. "He's the one who's been healing you."

A sudden bump sent Mark flying out of his seat and woke him up.

"Where am I? What's going on?"

At their laughter, Mark glared at everyone in surprise. "Wait a minute, how'd you guys get here? I'm so confused and my head hurts."

"I can help with that," Ryan said. "I'm Ryan. I'm a healer."

Mark let out a thankful breath as Ryan worked his magic.

"Mina, why are we going to school?" Jewel asked.

Mina worried about how much she should tell them. "Ms. A has a plan to stop Merco once and for all."

"Ms. A?" Mark looked shocked. "Isn't she a Merco spy?"

"Trust me, she's not," Mina replied. "How much longer, Kayla?"

"We're close. About ten minutes away."

"What's going on?" Jewel asked. Her perceptive eyes rested on Mina in concern. "Is there something you need to tell us?"

This was the hardest part. Mina had to tell them the truth. She looked at her new friends and felt a rush of affection and sadness, knowing she would lose them soon.

"I have to ask you all a question. If you could go back to the time when you had no gifts, would you?"

"Hmm, well, I like my gift," Kayla said. "But I don't like the changes that came with it."

The others nodded.

"When you say no gifts, you mean no Merco, no danger, no hiding?" Mark asked.

"No Sophia hurting people?" Jewel asked.

Mina nodded. "Yeah, if you could go back to that time, would you be willing to give up your gifts?"

Ryan was the first to respond. "Yes, absolutely. I was locked up in that facility for weeks. I saw what they did to the Gifted. It's not a gift, it's a curse. I don't want it."

"Those people are psychopaths!" Kayla exclaimed. "Our lives meant nothing to them. I don't need this gift if it means people I love have to be scared all the time. That's no way to live."

Jewel reached for Kayla and hugged her from behind. Mark was nodding.

"Agreed," Jewel said. "I'd give up the gifts if it meant we were all safer."

"Why are you asking, Mina? You got the superpower to wind back time or something?" Mark asked.

She was quiet for a long moment. And then she told them most of the truth about their worlds being connected through the webcomic. The only part she didn't share with them was the alternate timeline. Ms. A had suggested keeping that fact to herself, knowing it would be too hard for them to believe. But it still wasn't easy.

They were all quiet as Mina explained Ms. A's plan. She could sense their palpable shock.

"I don't understand—you're from another world?" Jewel asked. She turned to Jin. "Did you know about this?"

Jin nodded.

"Dude, you believe her?" Mark asked in surprise.

"I know what it sounds like, but she's telling the truth,"

Jin replied, his tone low. Mina could hear the sadness in his voice.

"So Ms. A is going to create a lightning strike like in *Back to the Future* to send you back to your world?" Mark said. "That sounds really dangerous. There's absolutely no guarantee that you'll do anything other than die from electrocution."

"I'll be fine," Mina replied. "Remember, that's how I came to this world in the first place. The worst that will happen is it won't work."

At that moment, Kayla turned in to Bellington High School's parking lot.

"Kayla, drive to the back of the building where the gym is."

Once she parked, the van went silent.

"So we're really doing this, Mina?" Mark asked.

"Yes, we have to," she replied firmly. "That way you all can go back to living normal, safe lives."

Everyone got out of the van to head inside, but Jin stayed put, holding Mina's hand.

"There's gotta be another way," he said. "We haven't thought everything through yet, right? Let's take some time, come up with alternatives."

There was fear and worry in Jin's eyes, and Mina knew exactly what he was feeling because she was feeling it too.

"Let's go inside."

"No, Mina, I can't let you go."

She looked at his familiar face, trying to memorize it.

"I have to do this."

Jin shook his head and grabbed her other hand. "No, you're not leaving me. I won't let you."

261

"Hey, what are you doing? Aren't you coming in?" Mark called to them.

"We're coming," Mina said.

Jin locked his legs and wouldn't budge. "If that's what Ms. A wants, we're not going in there."

"Jin . . ."

He was shaking his head. "Please listen to me," he begged. "We can work something else out."

Mina leaned up and kissed him. Once. Then twice. Then a third time, extra long. Extra loving. Extra full of what might have been.

She smiled. "It'll be all right." And then she jumped out of the van and entered the school.

CHAPTER 26

Fighting Terrible Tropes

Just inside the doors, Ms. A stood waiting.

"You were extremely busy yesterday, Mina!" she said. "You couldn't have fortified the gym more if it was Fort Knox." She turned to look at the rest of the group. "I got a call from the police that all of our missing students are at Holy Cross hospital and that they are doing fine. They are also on their way to the Merco facility to investigate the kidnappings."

Ryan smiled in relief. "Can I go see Christy now?"

"No, not yet," Ms. A replied. "Merco is probably on the way here and could arrive any minute. Everyone into the gym. It'll be the safest place for us."

"Why is Merco coming here?" Mark asked.

"My dear students, you just broke out of a Merco facility after they kidnapped and imprisoned you. Do you think they'll just let you free like that?"

"But Mina is powerful enough to stop all of them," Kayla said. "We saw her."

"Mina is one person," Ms. A said. "I'm sure by now she's told you why this happened. It's our job to help her."

A wave of gratitude eased Mina's stress. Ms. A was the adult she needed right now. It was as if the webcomic was providing her with the wise mentor archetype. Her Obi-Wan Kenobi.

Usually the mentor character dies. Mina shook the terrible thought out of her head. *No, not gonna happen in my story.*

She and Ms. A rushed the group into the safety of the gym. They bolted all the doors, and Mina's friends looked around in amazement. The walls had been fortified with steel beams and the doors reinforced with steel walls that pulled down and deadbolted to the floor. In the middle of the gymnasium stood the generators. Several students in lab coats and protective goggles were tinkering with machines. Mina had drawn all the pieces but didn't know what any of it was. On the other side of the gym was a glass-walled safe room with computers and more students.

"Who are all these kids, Ms. A?" Kayla asked.

"My Science Olympiad team," Ms. A replied. "They're the smartest scientists you'll find willing to help us."

One of the students in the safe room waved and came out. "Mina!"

"Diana! I can't believe you're here!"

Diana hugged Mina hard. "When Ms. A told us about all of this, I didn't believe it until I saw a high-voltage Marx impulse and high-current generators in the gymnasium! This is absolute genius! These generators are capable of producing up to 2.4 million volts and two hundred thousand amperes of current! It's unbelievable!"

Mark approached Diana from behind and tapped her shoulder. "Babe, you're so cute when you geek talk!"

Leaving the happy couple to themselves, Mina turned back to Ms. A.

"We're almost ready for you," Ms. A said. "We are running one last test."

"Thanks, Ms. A," Mina said. "Thank you for believing in me and helping me."

"Of course. I'm pretty sure that's my role. And much better suited for me than being the villain." She smiled and headed to the safe room.

Mina stood staring after her, still trapped by her previous thought.

What's this nagging feeling I'm having? It feels like impending doom. Like the webcomic is going to throw me a curveball. Is the dreaded "plans go horribly wrong" trope about to happen?

"What's the matter?" Jin asked.

Mina shook her head. "I'm just worrying about all this. Wondering what can go wrong next."

"Then don't do it," he said. "We're rushing full speed ahead with this one plan and not thinking about what else we could do."

"Jin, if you were me, and because of a mistake you made, your world was in danger, would you stay?" she asked. "Wouldn't you do everything in your power to fix it?"

"Then let me go with you! Let me go into your world." Jin's eyes were full of unshed tears.

She shook her head violently. "I don't know what would

happen to you. Ms. A said it would kill any normal person. I can't risk that."

"Let me try!"

"No! I won't let you die again," Mina cried.

They stared at each other, full of grief. Mina had so much more she wanted to say to Jin, but the words were stuck and there wasn't enough time.

"Mina," Ms. A called out from near the generators. "We're almost ready. Everyone, go into the safe room."

From outside the gym came a loud thumping sound, and then voices yelling.

"Hurry, Mina, they're going to throw everything at the doors to try to open them. We don't have much time."

After one last hug, Mina pushed Jin toward the safe room and put on her gloves. She was about to walk over to Ms. A when an explosion went off right behind her. It ripped through the steel reinforcements, sending rubble flying through the gym. Then a cloud of smoke filled the room. Mina immediately formed a force field around herself and everyone else. A stream of uniformed soldiers with flashlights entered the gym. Mina stunned as many as she could, but the thick smoke made it impossible to see what was going on.

"Jin!" she screamed, desperately searching for him.

When the smoke cleared, Mina finally found Jin. He was lying on the floor, clutching his chest and gasping in pain. Mark and Jewel were by his side, Jewel trying to comfort him. A terrible realization struck Mina. She'd seen this before.

She looked up to find Mercer standing in front of her,

right outside her force field. Next to him was the healer soldier, his fist pointing at Jin, a sadistic smile playing on his face.

"Don't worry, I promise he won't kill him if you and I can come to some sort of arrangement," Mercer drawled.

The sight of Jin suffering froze Mina in place.

"Good girl," Mercer said approvingly. "First, why don't you take off those gloves and toss them over here."

Mina didn't hesitate; she stripped off the gloves and threw them on the floor, causing the force field to instantly dissipate. One of the soldiers picked them up and handed them to Mercer.

"I see you're very smart," he said as he examined the gloves. "You must be to have created these with . . . what did my scientists call it? Oh yes, a magic tablet. I wouldn't have believed it if I hadn't seen the video footage myself. Imagine that. A tablet that can give you powers and create anything you want. I could've saved myself a lot of trouble."

He then began to laugh uproariously, the soldiers chuckling along with him. Mina was fascinated to see that the holes in Mercer's face had gotten bigger, so she could clearly see the soldiers who stood behind him.

"Now, since you are a smart kid, let's make this really easy," he said as he pocketed Mina's gloves. "The tablet for your boyfriend's life."

This was the "I have your wife" trope. It dawned on Mina that the webcomic was probably entering its final climax.

"How can I trust you?" she asked.

"Honestly, you can't," Mercer responded. "But what choice do you have? Your boyfriend is dying as we speak."

"Mina, if you go back home, you can save Jin," Ms. A whispered. "But if you give Mercer the tablet, you can't do anything."

I know, but I still can't bear to let Jin suffer such terrible pain!

"Mina," Ms. A warned.

Tuning her out, Mina saw Jin turn his head slightly to look at her. She could see he was trying to get enough strength to use his powers. She needed to help him.

Making steady eye contact with the healer soldier, Mina shouted, "Yo, dumbass! He's not my boyfriend." She pointed to Ryan. "He is."

Surprised, the healer's eyes shifted to Ryan. Right at that moment, Jin snapped his fingers, and everything froze.

"Jin! Are you all right?" Mina asked. Her voice trembled with the rawness of her fear.

He was breathing easier but finding it hard to talk.

In a fury, Mina grabbed her tablet, turned it on, and opened a new panel. She couldn't just erase them because they would reappear again. She drew an island in the middle of water, then copied, cut, and pasted Mercer and his men from the previous frame onto the island. She then erased the killer healer from the last scene to remove the immediate threat.

Time moved again, and the gym was filled with screams and gasps of horror as the soldiers pixelated and vanished.

The last thing she saw was Mercer's eyes bulging with rage before he disappeared completely.

"What did you do to them?" Mark asked.

"Sent them somewhere they can't bother us," Mina responded.

She knelt by Jin's side and held his hand. Ryan was already healing him, but Jin was still weak.

"I hope that's the last of the climax," Mina said.

Jin smiled. "Me too."

More screams filled the air behind her. They all turned to see Sophia, who had a bluish-white electric force field spiraling around her.

"Crap! I spoke too soon."

Everyone backed away from Sophia, who was generating enough electrical power to explode the whole gym.

"Oh, come on!" Mina shouted. "This is not fair! This is everything *and* the kitchen sink!"

Sophia looked dazed and unwell, as if she were under a spell. She had eyes only for Jin.

"Jin! Why can't you be mine?" she screeched.

"If she says 'If I can't have you,' I'm going to murder her!"

Mina stood in front of Jin, who had risen unsteadily to his feet.

At the sight of Mina, Sophia turned red with fury. "If I can't have you, she can't either!"

"Would you stop with the cheesy dialogue already?" Mina fumed. "This storyline is going to be the death of me!"

Kayla tried to direct a wind tunnel at Sophia, but it just bounced off the electric force field and sent Kayla careening into the wall.

"Kayla!" Jewel stumbled over to her side.

"I can't get anything by her electric shield," Mark said. "Jin, can you stop her?"

Jin shook his head. "I've been trying, but my power isn't working!"

Sophia shot several bolts of electricity, forming a fire near them.

"Mina!" Ms. A shouted. "If she hits the generators, they will explode the entire building!"

Electricity bounced like crazy all around Sophia. She hurled a pulse of it upward, sending a steel beam of lights crashing down on the teacher.

"Ms. A!" Mina dashed to the fallen woman's side and lifted the lights as if they were made of nothing but cardboard. Furious, Mina threw them at Sophia. They exploded against her force field, sending a shower of electricity everywhere and knocking her off her feet.

Mina went to check on Ms. A and was horrified: she had burns all over her face and body.

"You have to stop her!" Ms. A gasped.

Mina's hands shook as she unzipped her bag to get her tablet out.

"No, Mina, there's no time!"

"Shhh, don't talk, please." Mina fumbled with the tablet, trying to erase the last few panels, but the screen was glitching. She didn't know what was wrong with it until she saw that, once again, the battery had drained low. "Oh god, don't die, Ms. A, please!"

She could see how much pain the teacher was in. Her breathing was tortured.

"Ryan! Help me!" Mina screamed his name over and over, but he was nowhere to be seen.

"Mina, we have to get out of here!" Jin had crawled to her side and was trying to pull her away.

"Where's Ryan?"

Jin shook his head. "I can't find him."

She couldn't move. She couldn't leave Ms. A. It was chaos in the gymnasium. Fires were erupting everywhere. Sophia was back on her feet, and students were fleeing and getting randomly electrocuted. Mark was using his telekinesis to throw objects at Sophia even as he held up a metal door, shielding other kids.

But Ms. A was dying in front of Mina.

"I can't save her," she cried in anguish. "What do I do?"

Mina and Jin frantically examined her tablet, trying desperately to get it to work. But the scene remained stuck.

"What happened to it?" Jin asked. "Is it broken?"

"No, it can't be," Mina said. She shook it hard and the page went haywire, shimmering with diagonal lines. Mina froze. She'd seen this happen before.

"Wait a minute, lightning, electricity!" Wasn't this the re-creation of events that Ms. A said Mina needed to return home?

With nothing to lose, she held the tablet and started walking toward Sophia.

"Hey, you ugly bitch! Look at me!" Mina yelled.

Sophia's eyes flashed blue as she put her electric hands together and pointed them at Mina, sending a streak of lightning directly at her. The bolt struck Mina's tablet and was absorbed into it. Mina kept walking straight at the other girl until she stood right in front of her. Electricity poured out of Sophia for several minutes, the tablet soaking up her powers.

Sophia fell to her knees, completely spent. Mina stared at her tablet, waiting for it to do something—to open up a portal and send her back home. The last feeble trickle of electricity sizzled on the tablet before vanishing, but still Mina remained. The tablet glitched one final time and went black.

"Ryan," Jin called out. "Ms. A's badly hurt!"

From the corner of her eye, Mina saw Ryan limping over to Jin's side. The healer shook his head sadly. She could hear students sobbing loudly. The members of the Science Olympiad team converged on their teacher.

Mina struggled to swallow the lump in her throat as she stared down at Sophia.

"She had two little girls. Their names are Marnie and Lily," Mina said quietly. "Their mom is dead now."

For a moment, she could see the utter despair and horror on Sophia's face before it was gone.

"It's not my fault, it was an accident!" Sophia jumped to her feet. "It's not my fault! It's not my fault!" Screaming it over and over, she ran away.

Mina stood next to Jin and Ryan outside the circle of students gathered around Ms. A's still form. Jin put a comforting arm around Mina, but she barely felt it—she was numb. Diana knelt at Ms. A's side, weeping. Mark, Jewel, and Kayla surrounded her, clinging to each other.

Mina watched as if at a distance. It was too hard to accept. She thought of Ms. A's daughter Marnie asking her to babysit. This was not how the story should end.

Mina's heart tightened painfully, and the voice in her head screamed that this was wrong, so wrong. It drowned out every other thought until something within her snapped. And her mind completely cleared.

She blinked back her tears. She wasn't going to cry for Ms. A's family; she was going to save them. Because she realized why all of Ms. A's planning had failed. Mina now knew what she had to do.

"I'm so sorry, Ms. A. We did a lot of work for nothing. You were right in the first place. The answer was always in me. I just didn't see it. Because from the moment I opened my eyes in this world and saw Jin again, I didn't want to leave. I still don't. I want to stay with him." Mina looked at Jin, who grabbed both her hands as if he knew exactly what she was going to say. "But I know now that I could have gone home at any time. I just needed to really *want* to go. And now I have a reason. I'm not going to let Marnie and Lily lose their mom. Take it from me and Jin—it really sucks."

Mina felt the change in her gut, and she knew she was ready.

"I have to go now, Jin," she said. "I have to make sure that two little girls will still have their mom."

"What are you going to do?" Jin asked in alarm.

"I have to fix it all," Mina replied. "I have to delete it."

"But what about us?"

Mina swallowed the huge lump of tears in her throat. "You'll forget about me, Jin. It will all go back to the way things were."

Jin pulled her into his embrace and held her as close as possible.

"I can't do that," he whispered. "I can't forget you. Please don't go, Mina. I need you."

Mina couldn't stop the answering tears that now coursed down her face.

Star-crossed lovers. The last miserable trope. I hate you, web-comic world.

She wrapped her arms around him, trying to imprint the feel of his body, the smell of his essence. How could she survive in a world without him?

"It's not fair!" Jin said. "For the first time since I lost Mom and you, I'm happy. But now I have to lose you again."

His words were identical to the emotions in her heart.

She shook her head. "You'll forget me," she repeated.

"No, I won't," he said. "I can't."

Mina gently cupped his face with her hands and kissed him. She put her heart and soul and every fiber of her being into that kiss. All her years of loneliness, all the heartache of loss, and every ounce of happiness she'd had from being with him were caught up in her kiss.

"I love you, Jin! I will always love you." Mina felt herself disappearing. She kissed him one last time, her lips fading.

CHAPTER 27

Life Without Jin

Mina fell with a bang on the hard floor. She opened her eyes—it was dark. Blinking, she could see the contours of her bedroom. She jumped up to find her beloved Wacom Cintiq tablet on the desk. It was off. Frantically, she hit the power button, but nothing happened. She unplugged it and noticed that the light on her surge protector was off too. Mina tried turning on the desk lamp and then the overhead light and realized that the power in her whole room was out. When the lightning struck, it must have blown a fuse.

She ran downstairs to the kitchen where the circuit breakers were and switched them all on. The house lit up around her, warm and welcoming. But all she could think of was the world she'd left behind. She ran back to her room, turned on her tablet, and waited for it to boot up. When she opened *The School of Secrets*, the last episode was almost too much to take. She read Ms. A's last words to

275

her; she could see all the destruction. She hadn't even noticed that Kayla had been injured. The last panel was of Jin sitting on the floor in tears.

"You think I can forget you that easy, Mina?" he was saying. "I won't. I can't." He looked directly out of the frame, as if he were staring into her eyes. "Mina, whatever you do, I promise, I'll remember you. Always."

The pain in her chest was like nothing she'd experienced before. It was intense in its grief and loss. No matter what he said, once Mina deleted the webcomic, there was no way he could remember her. It would be a hard reset. His world would return to normal, and he'd have no memory of her time there. It would be as if she'd never gone to his world. She felt a twinge of anger at the thought that it would be so much harder for her. Because she would never forget him. She would know that he was alive somewhere, but she could never see him again. This was the end.

She was never going to get over him.

Mina opened up her settings page and clicked on the deletion tab. It read, *Are you sure you want to delete your webcomic? This action cannot be undone.*

Her hand paused for a long moment. An intense longing for Jin caused her to squeeze her eyes shut. But the thought of all the pain and chaos her actions had imposed made her take a deep steadying breath. She opened her eyes and clicked the delete button firmly. The web page for *The School of Secrets* was gone.

Mina turned off her tablet and slid to the floor.

It was over.

One lone tear streaked down her face.

CHAPTER 28

Life Goes On

Sunday, September 11

In the early hours of the morning, Mina woke up with eyes puffy from crying. A sudden urge to look for memories of Jin got her out of bed. She began to search through old boxes for items from when she was little. She found albums of her and Jin and spent hours poring over every picture, trying to recall the story that each one told. There were mementos and shared treasures, all lovingly packed away by Mina's mother. In one last box, she discovered their old picture book, *The Adventures of Horse and Cookie*. Memorialized on the pages were her mother's illustrations of Jin and Mina as little kids.

She hugged the book to her chest and cried herself to sleep once again. She dreamed of Jin and her mother and sunflowers.

Later, there was a knock on the door. Mina didn't answer.

After a minute, her father stepped into the room.

"Mina, it's almost noon. Come down and have breakfast," he said. "I'll make you eggs and bacon."

Ignoring him, she pulled her covers over her head. She felt her mattress shift as he sat down next to her.

"It's okay if you aren't hungry now, but we need to talk about why you missed your SAT class."

She remained unresponsive.

"Mina, I expect you to take this seriously," he said. "This is your future."

Her future was one without Jin. The thought made her so angry. She'd had no choice but to leave Jin behind, but the future she had to live would be hers and not what her father wanted. Otherwise, it was no different than Jin going to law school instead of med school because a story had stolen his free will. She'd left Jin's world so that he and the others would be allowed to go back to their normal lives. Now she had to work on what would be normal for her.

"You know, this really smart person once told me that I should do what I'm passionate about," Jin said.

Mina sat up to face her father. She'd lost a lot when she'd lost Jin. She would at least take back the direction of her life.

"I'm quitting the SAT class," she said loudly. "My score is high enough for RISD, which is where I really want to go. And besides, most of the art programs and art schools I want to apply to don't even need an SAT score."

"Mina, I thought we agreed on this," her dad said carefully.

She shook her head. "I've been so worried about telling you how I really feel because I didn't want to disappoint you. But, Dad, you have to let me make these difficult decisions. Even if I make a mistake, let me learn from it. Don't coddle me. Let me grow up into the person I think I'm supposed to be."

"You're still so young. You need guidance...."

"No, Dad, you made a judgment call without my consent," Mina responded firmly. "You decided that art isn't a good enough career for me. You decided that I should find a different career path. While you're at it, do you want to live the rest of my life for me also?"

"Mina!"

"I know you're still heartbroken about losing Mom, and that's why you hide away all of her beautiful artwork. But you never look at it anymore. Never remembering how much you loved her!"

Her dad closed his eyes in pain.

"Dad, I love you, I really do. But you don't know me at all. And if you don't try to get to know me now, you're going to have a very lonely life. Because unlike Mom's paintings, you can't lock me away in this house."

She jumped out of bed and went to the bathroom, slamming the door. When she finally came out, he was gone.

The fight with her dad reminded her of Jin, and suddenly she felt guilty. As much as her dad was in the wrong, she still loved him. He was her only parent. And while stuck in the webcomic world, she'd really missed him. She thought of Auntie Jackie and felt a strong urge to call her, but what would she say? After all, Mina couldn't talk about the one person she desperately wanted to tell her auntie about. In fact, she couldn't talk about Jin with anyone, which made it so much worse. Her heart was permanently scarred.

A few hours later, her dad called her down to dinner.

"It's been a long time since we had lobster tails," he said. "I thought it would be a nice change of pace. I went to Shelley's and also picked up some corn on the cob, baked potatoes, hush puppies, and coleslaw. You hungry?"

Shocked, Mina sat down as her father served her. Last time they'd had lobster was when her mother was alive. It was her mom's favorite dinner. Mina liked the sides better, but it felt so good to get to eat it again. As if Mom were at the table with them.

"Mina, I want you to know that I have never stopped loving your mom. It's true I put away her art. I did it because her paintings were too painful for me. And when I saw them hanging all around the house, I couldn't escape from my pain. What I didn't realize was that by hiding away Mom's art, I was forgetting about all of our happy times. There were more joyful memories than painful ones. But I was wallowing in self-pity."

Her dad let out a deep breath. "I think it's time to celebrate Mom's paintings again. That way we can always keep her here, as part of the family."

At her father's words, Mina teared up. He got up and wrapped her in a warm embrace.

"It's okay to be sad," he said. "It's okay to miss her. But

I almost forgot that it's most important to remember her, to celebrate her life. That way, she is always with us."

This was what Mina had wanted. This was the way she had hoped her father would be.

"Thank you, Dad. Thank you for not hiding Mom away anymore."

"Thank you, for reminding me how much I loved your mother."

After a long moment, her dad wiped his eyes and blew his nose.

"So RISD, huh? I'm okay with that, but CalArts is out of the question!"

"Why?" Mina asked.

"It's too far!"

She smiled. "Okay, Dad. I promise I'll stick to East Coast schools."

"You'd better," he growled.

As her father was dishing out ice cream and berries for dessert, the doorbell rang. Mina went to the door to see Saachi and Megan waiting for her. Her heart sank as she realized they were probably there to yell at her about deleting her webcomic. She opened the door and braced herself.

"Woman! What is wrong with you? How dare you not answer your phone!" Saachi yelled.

Megan was shaking her head in wide-eyed disbelief. "What kind of evil no-good rotten friend are you to do what you did and then turn off your stinking phone?"

Before Mina could respond, her father appeared and invited the girls in for dessert.

"Hi, Mr. Lee," they said as they barged by Mina and went into the dining room.

"So, what's going on?" Mina's father asked.

Saachi and Megan sat across from Mina and eagerly accepted their bowls of ice cream.

"Well, your daughter had the absolute nerve to create the best webcomic in the world and then did us absolutely dirty," Saachi answered.

"Completely destroyed us," Megan agreed.

"A webcomic?" Mina's dad arched an eyebrow. "What's it about?"

"It's no big deal," Mina cut in.

"NO BIG DEAL?" Saachi and Megan shrieked in tandem. "It's in the top ten best new webcomics!"

"Really?" Mina was surprised, but then shrugged. "Well, it doesn't matter since it's gone now...."

"Of course it matters!" Saachi said. "Honestly, you put other creators to shame! They post once a week and drag a story out for years. Meanwhile, you've posted your entire webcomic in the space of a week! Your fans absolutely adore you!"

Mina was puzzled. "Wait, aren't they mad I deleted the webcomic?"

"Of course they are," Saachi replied. "That was the cruelest thing you could have possibly done."

"But you have to admit, it was brilliant," Megan interrupted.

"Brilliant but cruel," Saachi agreed. "Also, the way you had both Jin and the Mina character in the same pose at the end just killed me."

"You are the worst," Megan said. "I cried all night."

"Me too!" Saachi wailed. "And then to ignore us all day was too mean. What are you, a sadist?"

"She's the worst, I tell you!" Megan slammed her fist on the table. At Mina's dad's raised eyebrow, she apologized quickly.

"But we are your best friends, and you owe it to us to tell us what happens next," Saachi demanded.

Megan was making a pleading gesture with her hands while Saachi batted her eyelashes.

Mina was completely baffled. What were they talking about?

"So let me get this straight," Mina's dad said as he leaned his elbows on the table and stared in fascination. "Mina created a webcomic that is so good you guys couldn't wait until tomorrow to ask her what happens next."

"Yes!" they both shouted, their eyes still glued on Mina.

"Can I see it?"

To Mina's great surprise, Megan took out her phone and pulled up *The School of Secrets*.

"Wait, it's still up?" Mina asked in shock.

"Of course it's still up! It's the most recent episode that you uploaded last night!" Megan passed her phone to Mina's dad. "Here you go, Mr. Lee. Just scroll up to read."

Mina's mouth fell open. Without a word, she ran upstairs to her room and turned on her tablet. Her webcomic was where it always was. On the episode page, the latest addition was listed as FINAL.

"How is this even possible?" Mina whispered.

With a shaking hand, she scrolled to the very end. There were several new panels after Jin's promise to remember her.

There was her bedroom, empty. In the next frame, Mina materialized, a shimmering figure. The comic didn't show her going to the fuse box; it skipped straight to her standing over the tablet. The next panel focused on the *Are you sure you want to delete your webcomic?* message as her pen hovered over the delete button. Then the Mina character slipped to the floor, head cradled in her hands. The next panel showed the tablet again, with the message *The School of Secrets has been deleted* across the screen. And the very last panel was a side-by-side scene of Mina and Jin sitting in identical poses of despair, separated by a line that was both thin and unbreachable. As she kept scrolling, the words *The End* appeared.

Mina sat back in disbelief. She'd deleted the webcomic—why was it still up? And even more shocking, why were her actions in the real world on the webcomic after she'd deleted it?

There was a loud rapping on her door, and her friends burst in and swarmed around her.

"Mina, this can't be the end, right?" Megan said. "You can't be that cruel!"

They were now kneeling on both sides of Mina, giving her their best puppy eyes.

"I mean, even if you end it like this for everyone else, we are your best friends," Saachi whined. "You'll tell us what happens to them."

"Maybe this is just season one," Megan said brightly. "And she's planning season two in her head. Am I right, Mina? You will get them together again, right?"

The words were like hot oil on her tender skin. Searing

pain and a throbbing ache that seemed like it would never heal.

"There's no sequel," Mina replied sharply. "They never get back together. That's the end."

Standing, she pulled her friends to their feet and shooed them out of her room.

"I'm really tired, guys. I need to sleep."

After closing the door on their protests, Mina sat in front of her tablet and scrolled up to look at Jin.

Gently tracing her finger across his face, she whispered, "I miss you."

CHAPTER 29

The Epilogue

Over a month passed, and Mina fell into a new pattern. Her father had changed his schedule so that he would be home for dinner more often and travel much less.

"I told my office that I can travel again once you're in college, but for now I'm going to spend as much time as I can at home," he told Mina.

He'd even taken Mina on a four-city college tour, visiting seven different schools in Baltimore, New York, Philadelphia, and Boston. Mina had agreed to apply to liberal arts schools if she could major in art, and her dad had allowed her to apply to art schools. She'd really liked all the New York schools, which delighted Auntie Jackie, who had already begun talking about internships for Mina and all the restaurants they'd go to every week.

It was both lovely and painful to see Auntie Jackie. Mina longed to tell her that Jin was alive and well. That he missed her and wished he could see her again. But these were words Mina could never relay. Instead, she vowed to be the best honorary daughter her auntie could ever wish for.

The house had also gotten a new look. Not only were her mother's art pieces on full display, so were several of Mina's. New and old photographs of the family covered the mantel and every flat surface her father could find. Mina's favorite sunflower painting was back in the living room, where it belonged. But the piece her father was proudest of was something Mina didn't actually make herself. The little robot Bomi sat in a glass display case in a place of honor.

Mina had found Bomi in her jacket pocket, rolled up in a ball. When she'd pushed on Bomi, they had opened up and then hardened into a metallic sculpture. Bomi's cute face was smiling, and a heart showed on the front panel. When her father had seen Bomi, he had marveled at the detail and insisted on putting them in the display case. She was glad to have the keepsake, but at the same time, Bomi was a reminder of what she'd lost. Better that they weren't in her room.

• • •

It was late October and the weather had turned chilly. Bright orange leaves were piled high on the curb. Mina stepped out of her house to head to school. She put in her earbuds and turned on her K-pop channel to listen to as she walked. Halfway to school, a new song began to play. Mina jerked violently in reaction.

You're the only, my one and only
Without you, I'd be so lonely
Baby, don't leave me

Standing completely still, she listened to the Sabotage song she had heard back in Jin's world. "You're the Only" had recently been released and was already a chart topper. The worlds had somehow connected again through a song.

It gutted her.

Going to school was sometimes too hard for her. Mina had become a minor celebrity, as everyone knew her as the creator of *The School of Secrets.* Reactions were mixed. She had as many antis as she had fans. But the one who hated her the most, Bailey, also stayed far away. She had clearly not liked being portrayed as the bully in Mina's webcomic.

Almost every day, she'd see someone who resembled one of her webcomic characters. A boy who looked just like Mark passed her daily. She was positive she'd seen Kayla's distinctive hair in the hallway a couple of times. And she'd definitely passed Lauren in the stairwell just the other morning. The one person Mina didn't mind seeing was Ms. Allen, who seemed to have no idea that she'd been memorialized in a webcomic. She even got to see Marnie again when Ms. Allen brought her kids into the office one day.

But Mina never felt the urge to talk to any of them. Her heart was too sore. Because the one person she wanted to see more than anyone else would never show up in front of her again.

In the first few weeks of art class, everyone had teased

Mina about her webcomic, including Ms. Ellis. But now the seniors were focused on their portfolios for college applications, and the teasing had died down.

"Mina, are you applying early anywhere?" Christina asked.

Mina shook her head. "I've decided to just do regular decision and hope for the best. I'm sort of confused about where I really want to go. Besides, it'll give me more time to work on my portfolio."

Christina laughed. "You could do your whole webcomic as your portfolio and get in, Mina. It's so brilliant."

With a shrug, Mina changed the topic. Nobody knew that she wasn't including her webcomic in her college art portfolios. She had no intention of mentioning it at all. All she wanted to do was forget about it, but it was near impossible.

• • •

"Mina, don't kill me, but you have to check your webcomic page!" Saachi said.

"I don't want to," Mina replied.

They were sitting on the decorative stairs along the wide corridor of the music department since it was too cold to eat outside. And also because Mina couldn't bear having lunch where memories of Jin were the strongest.

"Have you been checking your webcomic email?" Megan asked.

"No, I've been too busy trying to finish my art portfolio for college apps." She took a big bite of her sandwich and chewed aggressively to avoid saying more.

"Mina, you don't get it! Your webcomic is number one in fantasy!" Megan said.

This got Mina's attention.

"Huh?" She choked so hard on her sandwich that Megan had to pound her back. After drinking some water, Mina asked, "How's that?"

"You have a quarter million subscribers and over a million likes and counting! *School of Secrets* is a hit!"

"Are you serious?" Mina blinked, glancing from one rapturous countenance to the other. She couldn't believe it.

"It's probably good that your notifications have been off because you must have a thousand comments on your last episode. Now, granted, most of them are the 'How dare you end like this' and 'I have to know what happens next' types of comments, but still! Your webcomic is wicked popular!"

"Here, let me pull it up," Saachi said.

"No, that's okay." Mina got up. "I'm going to go to the art studio to meet up with Christina and keep working on my portfolio pieces." She didn't want to cry in front of them.

As she walked away, she could hear them whispering.

"She's so depressed lately," Megan said. "Do you think it's because the webcomic ended?"

"Maybe," Saachi responded. "It's as if she has a broken heart."

"You're right, Saachi," Mina whispered to herself. "I'm broken."

Several weeks passed into a cold and rainy January morning. Not wanting to go to her next class or talk to

290

anyone, Mina slipped out into the empty courtyard where Jin had first introduced himself. Standing under the covered entranceway, she stared up at the pouring rain and wondered what Jin was doing at that moment. Suddenly, she noticed someone standing in the middle of the courtyard, getting drenched.

"Jin?"

Mina blinked, and he was gone. He looked so real, but it was just her imagination. If only she could imagine him into reality. That night Mina was finally emptying out her fanny pack. She hadn't touched it since she'd left Jin's world. There wasn't much in it—she'd left her broken tablet behind. As she shook the pack, a Polaroid fell out.

Mina covered her mouth to hold back a sob. She'd thought the photo would disappear once she came home, but there it was. A real memory of their dinner date at the Thai restaurant on Homecoming night. They looked so happy.

"Hey, that's a pretty good-looking couple. They look perfect together."

She missed him so much.

Seeing Jin's face pierced through the numbness that Mina had been living under. The photograph was the sole evidence that he existed. A picture of the real him instead of a comic character.

She smiled through her tears. She was so happy to remember him. Real and alive. Not imaginary or a dream. Mina wanted to get to the point where she could think of him and not be grief-stricken.

They were happy tears, she lied to herself.

She framed the Polaroid and placed it next to a picture of her mom. Someday she would remember Jin without crying. But not today.

Winter turned into spring and college admission season. The applicant pools had been more competitive than ever before, and many kids were disappointed by the results. After all the visits to NYU with Auntie Jackie, Mina had mixed feelings about her results when she was rejected by NYU Steinhardt. But her acceptances to several prestigious art schools, including RISD, more than made up for it.

The results were bittersweet for the trio of friends. Saachi was headed to UC Berkeley, while Megan was attending the University of Miami.

"Could we be any farther from each other?" Megan griped.

"Well, at least you're both in places I'll want to go visit," Mina said. "But I doubt either of you will come to Baltimore."

"Hmm, let me think. Baltimore, Maryland, or Miami Beach?" Megan teased.

Saachi shoved her and gave Mina a hug. "Of course we'll come! We're so proud of you, Mina. But I still don't get why you chose MICA over RISD. I thought RISD was your dream."

Mina had accepted her offer to attend Maryland Institute College of Art over RISD, which had disappointed Christina, who had gotten into the RISD/Brown program as Mina had predicted.

"First, they gave me a very nice merit scholarship, which made me feel special and wanted," Mina said as she ticked off the reasons on her hand. "Second, my dad and I've been bonding a lot and I wanted to stay near him and maybe finally convince him to get a dog. Third, Dad told me he'd bring me a week's worth of Mrs. Song's food every weekend if I stayed close."

Saachi arched an eyebrow. "So it was food. That was the reason."

"Of course!"

Megan bear-hugged them both. "Doesn't matter where you are, we'll come hang with you."

• • •

Group chat texts woke Mina up on Saturday morning.

> **Saachi:** Mina! I can't believe it! You finally posted another update! All these months later . . . Does that mean you're willing to talk about it? Mina? Mina?

> **Megan:** Thank you Mina, it was really satisfying, until the end. That part was just flat out mean. MEAN! If I didn't love you, I would hate you . . .

Update? Mina dashed out of bed, turned on her laptop, and clicked on her webcomic page. There was a new episode titled "Epilogue." Mina trembled as her hand hovered over the trackpad. She couldn't understand why there was an update. The story was done. She'd been the one to end it. Or so she'd thought.

Maybe that wasn't technically correct. The webcomic had shown Mina in her real-world bedroom, as if to say she'd never been in control, even up to the final scene. To add an epilogue seemed cruel. And yet she couldn't stop herself from looking. Scrolling down, she once again immersed herself in the webcomic world.

It started with Mark, who was holding up his MIT acceptance package. He celebrated with Diana, who waved a Harvard banner. They were clearly a happy couple now. In the next scene, Lauren, Abby, and Tracey were all wearing their college shirts to show off school pride: Vassar, Tulane, and Wellesley. Mina sniffed. She missed all of them.

The next frame showed Jewel and Kayla at prom together. They were still happily dating and planned to attend the University of Maryland. There was even a panel of them with a drastically changed Sophia. She looked completely different—reserved but with a lovely smile as she shared her joy in being accepted to the San Francisco Conservatory of Music.

Mina was relieved to see Sophia's return to a normal life. She would never have to know that she'd almost destroyed a family. Which reminded Mina of Ms. A. And there she was in the next frame, at dinner with her husband, Marnie, and Lily. Mina could still hear Marnie's little voice asking her to babysit. It was so good to see all of them again.

She hesitated. The last panels had to be of Jin. Mina could feel her heartbeat racing. Even though she dreamed about him all the time, she wasn't ready.

She scrolled down and saw Jin's beautiful face. The frame showed him at school, accepting an award. He'd gotten into several great colleges and had decided to go to Johns Hopkins University in Baltimore for pre-med.

"Baltimore?" Mina whispered. "The same city and yet so far away."

In the next panel, Jin explained that he was taking a gap year. When asked what he was going to do, he replied, "I'm searching for someone I lost."

The last scene of the webcomic was of Jin's full face, his eyes sad and serious, but his dimple showed in a slight half smile. Across the bottom of the panel it said, "I miss you, Mina."

Mina gasped.

He remembered.

ACKNOWLEDGMENTS

In which I thank a whole lot of people who made this book possible and kept me from the pits of authorial despair.

Phoebe Yeh, my brilliant editor, who I have now been working with for over a decade! Daniela Cortes, her genius editorial assistant. The incredible Barbara Marcus, president of Random House Children's, Mallory Loehr, EVP & Publisher of Random House Books for Young Readers, and the wonderful team at Penguin Random House: Angela Carlino, Liz Dresner, Ken Crossland, Melinda Ackell, Tisha Paul, and Nathan Kinney.

My awesome agent, Marietta Zacker.

My fabulous writer friends who read and cheer me on: Axie Oh, Kat Cho, Hena Khan, Minh Lê, Christina Soontornvat, and Soman Chainani.

My family, who is always so supportive of me, but most specifically my oldest, Summer, who helped me the most with this book and actually read it several times unlike the other members of my family who did not. So only Summer will receive a share of royalties. The rest of you will have my undying love.

ABOUT THE AUTHOR

ELLEN OH is a founding member of We Need Diverse Books and an award-winning author of numerous middle-grade novels and the YA Prophecy trilogy. She has edited and contributed to *You Are Here: Connecting Flights, Flying Lessons and Other Stories,* and *A Thousand Beginnings and Endings.* Ellen is a former lawyer who loves K-pop, K-dramas, and cooking shows, but her favorite thing to do is to try new places to eat good food.

A Gen Xer who grew up with MTV, Ellen credits A-ha's iconic "Take on Me" video as the inspiration for *The Colliding Worlds of Mina Lee.* Originally from New York City, Ellen lives in Rockville, Maryland, with her husband, three human children, and two dog children, and has yet to satisfy her quest for a decent bagel. You can visit her online at ellenoh.com, on Instagram at @elloecho, on TikTok at @theellenoh, and on Twitter at @elloellenoh.